KHAKI = KILLER

By

Connie Corcoran Wilson

Published by Quad Cities' Press

Original cover art by Vincent Chong

eBook and Cover design by eBook76.com

Chapter One:
December 31, 2004, Friday

No New Year's Eve Party This Year

It was early on New Year's Eve day, a Friday, when they disconnected the heart-lung machine that was keeping Melody Harris Carpenter alive. A fierce internal struggle broke out between and among the Harris and Carpenter families.

Some family members were in denial. Sean, Melody's husband of less than two weeks, and Harold and Ruth Harris, her parents, insisted that everything would be fine.

"She's gonna' be fine," Sean, the new husband, repeated to anyone within earshot. "She just needs time. She'll wake up and be as good as new." His words were brave, but his voice cracked as he spoke.

"You're right, Sean," Harold Harris echoed. Harold's liver-spotted hands shook slightly. He was sweaty. Unshaven. The happy tuxedo-clad father who had given Melody away at the Methodist Church thirteen days before was gone. That happy man had vanished. In his place was this sad, broken creature. Harold kept patting his wife Ruth's arm. Ruth looked distraught. Drawn. Weary.

Harold spoke. A husky almost-whisper. Intensive care in a hospital was foreign to him. The antithesis of everything normal and happy. Every hour on the hour another gravely ill patient entered, hoping to be "saved." Praying for help.

One young African-American patient entered with a police escort, screaming obscenities. He was handcuffed to a gurney. Harold had seen a lot of medical shows on television, but he had never set foot in a hospital, himself. Almost fifty years old, of solid Swedish stock, Harold was born on the family farm. He had never been in a hospital's intensive care unit, even to visit.

Until now.

Harold Harris hoped he'd live and die in the same family farmhouse that had been in the Harris family for six generations, one hundred and fifty years. He loved his wife and only child with an abiding passion. His heart was breaking. Harold would not let the idea that Melody might die enter his mind.

Melody will be all right, he thought. *She just took a bad fall. She just got a bad bump on the head. She'll come out of it. So will the baby.*

It was as though the bottom had dropped out of Harold and Ruth's lives. Their little girl lay there: a small, fragile doll, fighting for her life amidst the antiseptic smells and clinical atmosphere of Cedar Falls Memorial Hospital.

Before Melody was born, Ruth Harris suffered three miscarriages, each one more heart breaking than the last. "Maybe I'm not meant to be a mother," Ruth said to Harold after the second. "God must not want me to have children."

Harold's heart broke at Ruth's words, too. "Nonsense, Ruth. It will all work out," Harold had reassured her. "You'll be a wonderful mother!" Harold was right. Soon, Ruth was a wonderful mother.

Premature at birth, Melody was so small that the doctors thought she might not make it. She weighed only three pounds. But Melody did survive. At only four feet eight inches today, she was a small ray of perpetual sunshine in Harold and Ruth Harrises' lives.

Tiny Melody, the four-foot-eight-inch dynamo who fell from atop the human pyramid at the UNI Dome game December 28th lay motionless in the hospital bed. Her long brown hair spilled across the white hospital pillow, a chocolate brown contrast to the stark whiteness of the hospital linen. Unconscious. Tubes and masks and the heart-lung ventilator making noises that set Harold's already rattled nerves on edge.

Everybody liked Melody. She was petite, dark-haired and endearing in the way that an enthusiastic puppy or kitten tugged at your heartstrings. Any time there was a trophy for Miss Congeniality, Melody won it. A wonderful gymnast and all-around athlete, despite or because of her small size, her plans after high school: marry Sean Carpenter. She had been Sean Carpenter's girlfriend since sixth grade.

Sean imagined the same future. Neither Sean nor Melody would be class Valedictorian. The academic side of school had never been easy for either of them. In fact, Melody was struggling to pass her accounting class. She was taking it to prepare for a position in the family business, Carpenters' Corners Paint and Paper. Melody was also having difficulty in Mrs. Anderson's English class. She needed to pass with at least a "C." She needed to keep her grades up to be eligible for sports and extra-curricular activities, like cheerleading.

Doctors appeared and disappeared. They explained the probability that Melody was brain dead. Sean wasn't ready to hear it. Harold Harris wasn't receptive, either. Ruth Harris appeared incapable of hearing anyone or anything. She was lost in a fog of maternal concern.

Mr. and Mrs. Carpenter stood by, saying little. They looked grim. Their silence spoke volumes. The Carpenters were not as blind to reality as the Harrises. Paul and Linda Carpenter were salt-of-the-earth Iowans. They were grounded in reality. The Carpenters understood the risks if Melody delivered the baby too early. The longer the baby boy could survive in utero, the better the little guy's chances.

Each time Sean would say something dismissive about the severity of Melody's injuries, Linda Carpenter would shoot "the glance" at Sean's father, Paul. They knew. They wanted to believe in miracles. But they knew. They were not naive trusting souls.

When Melody told her parents and Sean's parents that she was pregnant, both families would have preferred that the couple completed high school first, but they were happy about the baby. This baby would be the Harrises' first grandchild. The Carpenters, who had three older sons (Brian, Blake and Kenneth), had five grandkids already. That did not diminish their joy at welcoming Melody and Sean's baby into the family. Melody was the daughter the Carpenters never had.

Neurosurgeons and specialists were nearly unanimous in their opinion: Melody would never wake up. She was a young, healthy girl, but she was a dead girl in all the ways that mattered. The baby inside her was only six months along.

Doctors were fighting to save Melody's unborn child. The reality was, Melody was being kept alive so that her baby could be given a fighting chance at life. Harsh as it sounded, Melody was reduced to little more than a human incubator.

"She looks like she's just sleeping," Ruth said to Harold. There was a tremor in Ruth's voice. She darted a quick, hopeful look at her husband.

"I know, Honey. I know." Harold again patted Ruth's arm.

"How can the doctors be right that she's gone? How can that be right?" Ruth was distraught.

As she asked this question of her worried husband, Ruth's voice rose in a plaintive wail. Her voice reflected disbelief, confusion.

Part of the reason Sean could not or would not accept the bad news from the medical team was his life-long conditioning at his father's knee.

"Don't always trust what you think you are seeing," Paul Carpenter sometimes told his youngest son. Sean's father, a savvy businessman after years spent running Carpenters' Corners, often cautioned Sean, "Trust no one."

"If it seems too good to be true, it probably is," Paul told Sean. "Trust your instincts. Don't let people lead you down the garden path."

Sean was not present when Melody tumbled from atop the human pyramid at the UNI Dome game. He asked, again and again, "What happened?" There was a *Sublime* song lyric from the nineties: "Got to find a reason things went wrong." That was Sean's response to the tragedy.

Sean had been minding the store at Carpenters' Corners when the accident happened. Again and again, Janice Kramer described Melody's fall from atop the human pyramid at the UNI Dome for Sean. It did no good. Sean wasn't listening objectively. He married the girl of his dreams—his girlfriend since sixth grade. He was over-the-moon anticipating the birth of their first child together. Everything was falling into place in Sean Carpenter's life.

Until it wasn't.

Sean couldn't or wouldn't believe that his wife and unborn child were in peril. *Melody can't die. She can't! We've only just begun our lives together. The baby isn't even due for three more months! What kind of God would let Melody die? What kind of heartless Supreme Being would kill my baby?*

Sean shook his head to clear it of even the possibility of such random cruelty to two innocent beings. He felt helpless. Powerless. It was as though he were caught in a strong current, being swept toward a precipice. He would surely die if he drifted over the edge. But the current was too strong. Despite fighting back, he was being pulled closer and closer to the edge.

Nonetheless, Sean tried to project complete confidence. Melody would wake up at any moment.

"She'll be her old self in no time. You'll see. You can't keep Melody down. You all know what she's like. She'll shake this off. She'll be as good as new!" Sean's voice broke when he uttered the last line.

He left the room abruptly to get a Coke from the machine at the end of the hall.

Sean clung to hope by refusing to accept reality. He might as well have put his fingers in his ears like a two-year-old and made noises to drown out the experts' opinions. He didn't want to hear the truth. He couldn't handle the truth. He didn't want to anticipate the truth. Because the truth hurts. The truth can even kill. What doesn't kill you doesn't make you stronger: it leaves you broken.

Sean's parents, after hearing the doctors explain Melody's injury and seeing the EEG's (electro encephalogram's) flat brain waves, felt resignation. The Carpenters prayed that Sean would come to grips with the situation. They hoped that the Harrises, too, would eventually come to their senses. Accept what was happening. Accept what had *already* happened.

"They have to know," Linda Carpenter said to her husband. She looked deep into Paul's eyes. "They have to know that she's gone."

"No, they don't," Paul responded. "They don't want to face it. It's too awful to admit. They want what was. Nobody can make things the way they were. It's too late for that. You can't turn back time. All we can hope for now is that the doctors can save the baby." They hugged each other in support of the awful reality of what was.

"How terrible! My heart hurts. I just feel sick," said Linda. She sank down into a leather hospital chair. "Sean loves her so much. He always has."

Linda glanced over at her tall, blonde son. Sean was a good-looking young man, six feet tall with cornflower blue eyes and a ready smile. But there was no smile left in Sean now. He was a shell person, a husk person exuding inauthentic confidence. Telling everyone not to give up hope, even though hope had given up on him.

There'd be no return from the oblivion that a persistent vegetative state represented

In the hallway during a much-needed break, Paul Carpenter told his wife Linda, under his breath, "The Harrises should know better than anybody the risks of a baby that's born too soon. after all they went through having Melody. Losing those three babies." Paul shook his head, contemplating the tragedy of three infants Ruth had miscarried or had delivered dead on arrival. Paul was praying that his unborn grandchild wasn't going to be the fourth.

When the heart-lung machine was disconnected, would Melody breathe on her own? The machine was disconnected at one p.m. on New Year's Eve Day. Melody's heart kept beating. Her first breath was ragged. Reedy. But she was breathing on her own. Melody had been an eighteen-year-old girl in excellent health. Her final gift to her unborn son—simply inhaling and exhaling, heart pumping blood to her organs— would buy the unborn child time. Despite Melody's comatose state, it was almost as though she understood that her labored respiration, achieved without a machine's assistance, would help her child survive.

Linda and Paul Carpenter were adults. Sean was a husband of only fourteen days. Eighteen years old. He wouldn't listen to voices of gloom and doom. If he ignored the dire warnings, things would improve. Things would get better. Sean pinned all his hopes, dreams and prayers on recovery.

Sean thought, *How will I live without Melody? Can Adam make it on his own, if he's born this early? And if he lives, but Melody dies, how will I care for a child all by myself?*

Four days had passed since the December 28th game at the UNI Dome. Melody's family shared the news of her pregnancy with the doctors on her way to the hospital in the ambulance. Tests were run on the unborn child. Melody was about 200 days along. She might have conceived little Adam—the name she and Sean had chosen—while celebrating the last day of summer school: June 14th.

Sean remembered the day well.

June 14, 2003. Melody Harris' house. 5:00 P.M.

"I'm through with school work forever, Sean! Hip hip hooray!" Melody threw discarded versions of her English paper in the air, laughing and waving her final American Literature theme. She wrote the paper for the final credit in English she needed to graduate. Melody was happy to put aside the academic demands of high school forever.

"Aw, baby! I'm glad you finished your paper," Sean said. "What was it on?" The rough draft pages drifted to the floor of the den where Melody was working. Melody hadn't done well on either midterms or finals in English class. Her accounting class also needed work. Mrs. Anderson had agreed to let Melody hand in an extra-credit paper to raise her English grade. She had already retaken the accounting final exam, with improved results.

Melody wrote a paper on *Julius Caesar*.

To show off for Sean, she recited, "For let the gods so speed me, as I love the name of honor more than I fear death." She turned and cast a coquettish glance at Sean, batted her eyelashes, and added, "Act one, scene two."

"Wow! Well done, Mel! Can you translate that into plain English for me?" Sean laughed as he asked.

"Well, they're trying to warn Julie—that's Julius Caesar, to you— not to go to the Senate because there might be a hit out on him. But he says he's not afraid of death. I think that's stupid. *Everybody's* afraid of death. I know I am! But Julius Caesar says he 'values honor' more than dying. I don't understand most of it, either," said Melody, with a puzzled shrug. "But I do like the line, 'Yon Cassius hath a lean and hungry look' because I've seen a lot of politicians coming through Iowa during this primary season who had that same look."

Iowa had been receiving national attention as the first-in-the-nation caucus state. The 2004 presidential election was looming in November. Howard Dean's "Sleepless Summer" campaign in Iowa was just past, orchestrated by political strategist Joe Trippi. *Time* magazine featured the candidate on its cover as the front-runner, dubbing his time in the state the Sleepless Summer campaign.

Melody had driven to Muscatine to hear him give a speech in a grassy backyard lawn on a hot summer night. (Sean stayed in the car to listen to the Cubs baseball game on the radio.) Governor Dean had the crowd enthralled, especially when he answered all the tough questions, including some on abortion and gun control.

"I was a doctor for thirteen years before I was a politician," the candidate answered that night, in response to a question on his position on abortion. "There was never a late-term abortion in the state of Vermont in all those years," he said. "We don't do third trimester abortions. We do everything we can to deliver healthy babies to loving parents." His instant command of such facts impressed Melody.

"Like, who, that you saw, did you like?" Sean asked. Sean wasn't very political, but Melody always turned out to see "the cute ones." Her history teacher, Miss Nicholson, gave members of the class extra credit points if they could prove they had been present at a rally by any presidential contender, Democrat, Republican or Independent. It was all part of encouraging the students to become informed citizens.

"Well, I thought Howard Dean was kind of cute," Melody said.

"Howard Dean? Are you kidding me? That short little guy with the gray hair? The one who shouted the Scream Heard 'Round the World? The former Governor of New Hampshire?"

Here, Sean did his best Howard Dean imitation. "And then we're going to North Dakota! YAAAH! And South Dakota! YAAAH! And Oregon! YAAH! And Michigan! YAAAH! And then we're going to Washington, D.C., to take back the White House!" Sean punctuated each state's mention with a maniacal cackle and fist thrusting meant to imitate the former Vermont governor whose campaign self-destructed at the Val-Air Ballroom in West Des Moines, Iowa on primary night. The Scream had played on the airwaves repeatedly since that night.

Melody just gave Sean a sour look. "It wasn't *THAT bad*, Sean. And it wasn't very fair, either. The Kerry campaign double-miked him. I was in the room. Inside the ValAir Ballroom, you could barely hear him. Besides, he was just rallying the troops. What's wrong with that?"

Sean responded with another "YAAAH!" Then he said, "It was like he was on crack or laughing gas or something." Sean had a funny look of wonderment on his face while speaking.

The tone of Sean's voice made Melody giggle in spite of herself and in spite of really liking Governor Howard Dean.

She corrected Sean. "He wasn't the governor of New Hampshire, either, Sean. He was the governor of Vermont."

"Whatever. Same difference. He's the governor of nothing now. And the president of nothing, as well." Sean was disinterested in politics at all levels.

"Well, Sean—he *IS* a doctor, you know. And so is his wife. And now he's the Chairman of the Democratic National Committee."

"Good for him. Can we give all these politicians the old heave-ho and start having some fun around here? Let's celebrate!" As he said this, Sean drew Melody close, put his arm around her waist, and kissed her.

"Sure thing, Sweetheart. Just don't make fun of my paper *OR* my politics," cautioned Melody.

"Your politics, maybe. Your paper? Never!" Sean laughed.

He pulled Melody down onto the couch for a serious make-out session.

Melody's last class, June 14th, inspired a celebration that lasted into the night. That night, their baby was conceived. Adam—that was the name she and Sean had selected for a boy. If the baby was a girl, her name would be Eve.

Chapter Two:
December 31, 2004, Friday

New Year's Eve

It was New Year's Eve, but Janice Kramer was not celebrating. Far from it. She was bedside at Cedar Falls Memorial Hospital, standing by her friend and fellow cheerleader Melody Harris Carpenter. Janice and Melody had bonded because of their pregnancies.

Janice was rattled. Upset. She felt guilty.

If I were to lose Jeremy's child, she thought to herself, *it would not be a disaster. But it will be if Melody loses Sean's baby.*

She remembered how happy Melody had been at the thought of becoming a mother. Melody's attitude was the polar opposite of Janice's. Yin versus yang. Yet it was Janice who sat here and— although not quite as far along as Melody (Janice was in her fifth month) — felt gratitude that her own child was safe.

If it were me, and I went into labor, I wonder if my baby could survive? she thought.

Janice realized that, for the first time, she had referred to the life growing inside her as "my baby."

Sean Carpenter was en route to the hospital from Carpenters' Corners as soon as he heard the news of Melody's fall. He was waiting for the ambulance when it arrived. Inside the hospital, tensions ratcheted to a fever pitch. Doctors asked permission of Sean, the father and new husband, to deliver Melody's premature infant by emergency C-section, if she were pronounced.

"What do you mean—pronounced?" Sean asked.

Sean wasn't ready to hear the word "dead." He was as frightened of that concept as Melody was when she talked with him in June about her Julius Caesar paper.

No one answered Sean's question about the meaning of the term "pronounced." He plunged on with another question.

"The baby's only six months along," Sean replied. "Is that enough? Will Adam survive if you take him now? Is Melody going to make it?" In Sean's mind, Adam was already a real person, his firstborn son.

The doctor was brusque and to the point.

"If she goes into cardiac arrest again (*Melody had arrested in the ambulance on the way to the hospital*), we'll take the baby right away. If she breathes on her own and we can stabilize her, we'll try to keep them both alive. Give the fetus more time."

Other six-month fetuses had survived an early entry into the world. It would be best for everyone, however, if the baby could continue to mature. Doctors offered little hope that Melody would regain consciousness, but as long as she was able to breathe on her own, she could be fed intravenously while the baby matured.

"If she delivers now," one doctor said, in response to Sean's question, "the baby will need special neo-natal care. We have a preemie unit second to none in the state. But we'll have to deliver the child immediately if her heart stops again. We might not be able to resuscitate her a second time. We won't have any other choice but to take the child, if Melody doesn't breathe on her own."

That was Dr. Klein speaking, head OB/GYN doctor at Cedar Falls Memorial Hospital. He was the surgeon slated to perform the emergency C-section, if necessary. Dr. Klein did not bring up the lack of any detectable brain wave activity in the mother.

Better to get into all that after we've safely delivered the child, Dr. Klein thought.

Arguments broke out amongst family members. Melody's parents did not accept the advice of the doctors that the machines be disconnected. They were apprehensive. Melody was so young. She had never spoken about death—except that June night when Adam was conceived.

Melody's thoughts, expressed only to Sean, could best be summed up this way. Death was a long way off. Death was something that happened to other people. Death was for the old and sick. Death happened to grandparents. And, sometimes, tragically, to your own parents. It didn't happen to YOU. It didn't happen to your young friends.

Until it did.

"But how do you know she's brain dead?" Harold Harris insisted, when presented with the EEG evidence that a fall had turned a healthy young woman into a vegetable.

"I don't trust their diagnosis," Sean told his father. "I think they're wrong."

Sean's dad put his arm sympathetically on the shoulder of his grief-stricken son. He shook his gray head, nodding assent.

"We'll get the opinion of a specialist, son. We'll get somebody here from Iowa City. Or else we'll take her there. Miracles do happen," he added hopefully.

The University of Iowa Hospitals and Clinics were the best in the state. They were among the best in the nation. The place was huge. It was located adjacent to Kinnick Stadium, the Hawkeye football field. Normally, the University of Iowa and Northern Iowa University were rivals in all things. But in health matters, both families agreed, Iowa City was the best. A specialist, a neurosurgeon from Iowa City, was contacted and drove from Iowa City to Cedar Falls. He confirmed Dr. Klein's diagnosis.

"I'm sorry, said Dr. Karachi, the specialist from Iowa City who examined Melody. "I'm afraid that what you've been told is correct. There's no brain wave activity." The doctor was looking at charts and graphs as he spoke.

He turned towards Sean, "We'll keep the child in utero as long as possible. But don't condemn your wife to a vegetative existence like Terri Schiavo's. That poor girl in Florida has been in a coma since 1990. Almost fifteen years. You don't want Melody just kept alive by machines. The Melody you knew and loved may be gone forever."

Terri Schiavo cardiac arrested in St. Petersburg in 1990. She was twenty-seven. Now, she was forty-two and her husband and her parents were at odds about what was the best course of action for the brain-dead patient. Terri hadn't really known anyone or anything around her for fifteen years.

Dr. Karachi continued, "You'll all have to make some difficult decisions. Hopefully, your family will do the right thing. If she can't be brought back, let her go."

Dr. Karachi gathered up his briefcase and strode from the room.

"No!" Sean screamed. Harold and Ruth Harris rushed to their son-in-law's side. The three hugged each other. Ruth sobbed quietly. The Carpenters, Paul and Linda, stood by uncomfortably.

It was hard for any of them to wrap their minds around the idea that Melody had been fine one moment. Happy. Energetic. Healthy. Full of life.

And then, in an instant, she wasn't.

Night fell.

Chapter Three:
January 15, 2005, Saturday

Thin Ice

"Girls! Get off the ice! It won't hold your weight! Heather! Come here!"

Uncle Declan ("Dec") Hunter was yelling at his niece, Heather Crompton. Heather was his sister Nora's child, the beautiful daughter who had already cheated death. Heather had been with Jeremy Gustaffsson on Lovers' Lane when serial killer Pogo came calling, looking for Tad McGreevy. Heather was still emotionally fragile from the experience. She'd never lost a moment's sleep over a knife fight over her at school between the Jimenez cousins last year, but being in the middle of fatal violence on a lonely deserted road was a different story. That night, Heather was absolutely certain that she was going to die.

Jeremy's murder was a case of mistaken identity: Pogo meant to kill Tad McGreevy, but mis-identified his victim. The sights and sounds she experienced that night would forever haunt Heather Crompton. She remembered jumping over the side of Jeremy's '57 blue ragtop T-bird convertible. She remembered running through knee-high woods into the forest. Burrs and branches grabbing at her ankles and legs. Breath ragged. Heartbeat as erratic as a bird trapped against a glass window, trying to escape.

Heather Crompton now displayed the same hyperaware vigilant symptoms that Uncle Declan suffered as a result of his Vietnam experiences.

But Heather's came, not from wartime PTSD (post-traumatic stress disorder), but from the after-effects of the attack last August 29th. Since then, Heather often over-reacted to perceived danger. She had been next on Michael Clay's "to kill" list. That wasn't something a girl forgot easily. Or soon.

Four months later, Heather was still traumatized. Any strange noise or foreign event raised her senses to a hyper-alert stage. Perhaps only her Uncle Declan Hunter could really empathize with Heather's feelings—if the two had ever shared their emotions, that is.

Declan Hunter came home from two tours of duty in Vietnam with the same PTSD that Heather was experiencing. Hyperawareness. Hyper vigilance. Adrenaline-sharp quick scanning for danger. Super stimuli-sensitivity. All these symptoms and more developed after Dec's second tour in 'Nam.

Declan had enlisted in 1965, at age eighteen. Forty years later, the fifty-eight-year-old Declan still carried psychological scars. Lately, the voices in his head had become louder. Declan had difficulty maintaining relationships. He had difficulty holding a job. He was prone to erratic outbursts. He'd been diagnosed with borderline personality disorder at the VA Hospital in Iowa City.

Over time, Dec learned to control or mask most of his symptoms. Declan Hunter's concern over the girls' skating on the ice of the Cedar River seemed normal to Heather, who knew Uncle Dec only slightly. It seemed normal to Kelly Carter (also, sometimes, known as Kelly Jamison because of her stepfather, Joe Jamison), who barely knew Declan Hunter. Friend and fellow cheerleader Kelly was just killing time on a Saturday afternoon with her friend Heather. Kelly wasn't particularly keen on ice skating. She went partly to steer clear of her stepfather, Joe Jamison.

Kelly wasn't much of a worrier. She tried hard not to take anything too seriously. That was why Kelly wasn't very helpful during the search for Stevie Scranton. She always felt that things would work out the way they were supposed to work out. Laissez faire. *Que sera, sera.* Fate. When Tad McGreevy asked her to spend her Saturday handing out flyers with Stevie Scranton's picture on them at the Farmers' Market in town, Kelly said, "Sure," just to get Tad off her back. She promptly discarded the flyers in the nearest trashcan.

If Stevie is alive anywhere in the country, he doesn't need me wasting my Saturday passing out his picture. He'll come back, if it's meant to be.

It was January 15, 2005, Saturday. School had just resumed after Christmas break. Four months post Pogo. Heather was like an antenna tuned to any strange sound. The cracking sound of the ice spooked her. It sounded dangerous. When she glanced at the ice's black, glassy surface, she imagined Jeremy's bloody body trapped beneath the ice of the Cedar River, head bludgeoned by the crowbar's blow. She had violent flashbacks. Heather shook her head to clear it of the images. The flashbacks happened with increasing frequency ever since August 29th. A tree branch sweeping against a windowpane could cause Heather to rise from her chair with a startled involuntary cry.

Heather's mother Nora suggested therapy. Nora sought psychotropic drugs for Heather. She wanted them to help Heather sleep. Nora had called Dr. Abraham Eisenstadt in October, two months after the attack, asking him to provide something to help with Heather's insomnia. Dr. Eisenstadt declined.

"I can't prescribe for Heather without seeing her," Dr. Abe said, at the time. Nora took Melody in to the local psychiatrist. Dr. Eisenstadt prescribed a light muscle relaxant for Heather, Clonazepan, 5 mg.

"Do you want a stronger anti-depressant?" he asked Nora. "I have to warn you, Mrs. Crompton. There can be serious side effects to MOA inhibitors used for depression. Some young people become suicidal. If Xanax is mixed with alcohol, it can even be fatal. If Heather's problems are confined to nightmares—an understandable after-effect of her experience—maybe she'd be better off starting out with just the sleep aid? See how that works?" The two talked about Heather coming in for additional sessions.

Dr. Eisenstadt had a questioning tone when he asked Nora about her wishes. Nora reluctantly agreed and gave up on securing Xanax for Heather. She thought, *I can always bring Heather back to Dr. Eisenstadt for stronger drugs.*

But that was the last day of Abraham Eisenstadt's life: October 28th, 2004. The autopsy on October 29th showed that Abe died of a massive coronary, a widow-maker.

Nora thought talk therapy might be good for her troubled daughter. She planned to bring Heather in for some sessions. Nora even mentioned something about Heather's anxiety attacks to her brother Declan, knowing that Dec had similar issues. Nora suggested that Heather invite a good girlfriend over. Heather invited Jenny SanGiovanni, Jeremy Gustaffsson's old girlfriend.

Nora thought Heather's invitation to Jenny SanGiovanni for a weeknight sleepover was strange, but since she was genuinely concerned about Heather, she agreed. Heather had always been so upbeat. So carefree. Sometimes, Heather could seem insensitive. Boy crazy. Shallow. "All the emotional depth of a puddle," as one classmate described her. But Heather had never seemed troubled.

Until now.

Now, Heather was apprehensive. Perpetually upset. Anxious.

Despite it all, Heather was a pretty little thing. In Nora's mind, Heather was the prettiest girl in her class. Nora loved her daughter unconditionally. She would do anything she could to help Heather recover from the trauma experienced that night on Lovers' Lane. No one knew better than Declan Hunter's sister that getting over death could take a long time.

Sometimes, you never got over it. You just got through it, as best you could.

Chapter Four:
January 15, 2005, Saturday

Declan Hunter

When Declan Hunter enlisted at age eighteen, he was sent directly to Vietnam. He was involved in the fighting nearly non-stop throughout two tours of duty. When the war finally ended, Declan Hunter returned to society a broken man.

Dec craved companionship and someone to talk to, but he wasn't able to sustain a lasting relationship. After several romances crashed and burned because of his emotional instability, Dec developed a fear of abandonment. Sooner or later, one after another, each woman grew weary of Declan's hyper vigilance. The exhausting distress. The fury that flash incinerated with little provocation.

Declan craved wilderness. The solitude of sparsely populated regions. His loner nature and inability to deal with crowds made him a natural for states like Alaska or North Dakota or Montana, all places where he tried to begin a new life before returning to Cedar Falls, where he had lived for the past ten years. When the position as Scoutmaster and Superintendent of Camp Wapsie "W" opened up, Nora told Declan about the job.

At the time, he was living in Fargo, North Dakota, next door to Moorhead, Minnesota, the flattest and coldest place Nora ever visited. Nora could never tell when she crossed from Fargo to Moorhead. It seemed to be one long, flat concrete strip of snow and cold joining two similar, frigid cities. In the winter, the best you could hope for was a cozy place inside, near a roaring fireplace.

"Dec, the old guy who was running Camp Wapsie 'W' died. They need someone with a background in scouting (*Dec had been active as a Scoutmaster for years.*) Someone with a love of the wilderness and the ability to teach wilderness skills to young people. The campground needs him now. Like yesterday. You'd be a natural! Come home!"

Nora sounded enthusiastic. She was eager to help her battle-scarred older brother. She had no idea if Dec would consider a move back to Cedar Falls, Iowa. She hoped he would, because she had never really gotten to know her big brother that well before he left for the war.

Up until now, Dec had mainly worked construction, including living in a large mining camp. If you enlist at eighteen, you have no higher education. Your chance at a job that requires a college degree is nonexistent. In 2005, a college degree was the equivalent of a high school diploma. Delan Hunter's chance of finding the perfect position? Slim to none. North Dakota had not been good to him, nor had life.

Nora's husband, Chris Crompton, was important in Cedar Falls. He was an engineer with his own firm, Crompton Engineering. Chris had his finger in almost every pie in town, whether construction or engineering. The Cromptons had money. Old money. Through Hunter/Crompton Construction, another family owned business Chris ran with his father-in-law, the company built half the newer homes in town.

It didn't take much to convince the town fathers that the poorly paid job of keeping watch over an isolated campground far from town should go to Chris Crompton's brother-in-law. Declan Hunter' job would be readying the twenty cabins for the spring, summer and fall occupants. Devoting his life to what most would consider a dead-end job. It would be a perfect fit for a single war veteran with "issues."

Nora Hunter Crompton didn't know the extent of Declan Hunter's "issues." There were lots of things Nora did not know about her older brother. What Nora Hunter Crompton didn't know actually *would* hurt her. And in the worst way imaginable.

When Declan Hunter was Scoutmaster of Stevie Scranton's Boy Scout Troop, when Stevie was in third through fifth grade, it was not a happy time for Stevie. It started with Declan's desire to have someone he could turn to for comfort. Stevie seemed gentle. Weak. Sensitive. Compassionate. One thing led to another.

The twisted psyche that Declan Hunter developed in Vietnam, coupled with the drug habit he picked up during the war, led to abuse of the pudgy eight-year-old outcast. "Interfering with" Stevie, as the British call it, emerged as a pattern without conscious thought or premeditation. Some of the other communities where Dec Hunter had spent time during the past forty years since his return from Vietnam were also touched by Declan Hunter's problems.

Declan Hunter left behind a trail of children—young, vulnerable, sensitive boys and girls—young people Declan hoped would never leave him, as all his significant adult others had. Declan Hunter was not homosexual. He was just twisted. The kids would say that Declan Hunter was "screwed up."

Declan also suffered residual pain in his back from bullets still in place in his body. Some were war wounds. Some were bullets fired by Earl Scranton at last year's Homecoming game. No one thought there was a reason for Earl to target Declan Hunter. After all, Earl shot four other people that day, some of them students. It appeared that Earl simply went berserk and opened fire randomly on the crowd at last year's Homecoming game. Declan Hunter was luckier than Principal Peter Puck and Daniel Malone, dead at Earl Scranton's hands. Hunter was still alive. And still troubled.

When Uncle Dec told Heather Crompton and Kelly Carter that the ice on the Cedar River was unsafe, they believed him. She trusted her uncle's judgment more than her own.

What other reason would Uncle Dec have for telling us to take our skates off and get in his van? He's just trying to protect us, Heather thought.

Heather drew the sleeve of her parka across her runny nose. "Do you know of some safer place for us to skate, Uncle Dec—maybe where the ice is thicker?" Heather asked. "We can't be out too long, anyway. We're supposed to be home for dinner."

Innocent unquestioning acceptance of this man, her mother's older brother.

"Come with me, girls. We have a man-made rink at the camp. Nobody's using it. Climb in the van. Take off your skates. Tie the shoestrings together and leave them there on the riverbank. I'll throw them in the back. I'll give you girls a ride out to Camp Wapsie 'W' and still have you back home in time for dinner!"

Dec said all this in a faked hearty tone. Declan Hunter smiled what he hoped was a reassuring smile at the two pretty teen-aged girls.

The girls were willing to hop into the heat of Uncle Dec's warm van. They put on their Ugg boots, leaving their ice skates under the tree.

That is where the searchers found the skates, hours later— shoestrings still carefully tied together.

No sign of Heather or Kelly.

Trust no one.

Chapter Five:
January 15, 2005, Saturday

Winter Formal

It was that time of year—after New Year's Eve and prior to the Superbowl—when social calendars become bleak. The weather is cold. The days are long and dark. The temperatures are frigid. Often below zero. It was the beginning of the long, slow slog towards spring and better weather. Except for the SnowBirds—old, retired people who went south every year like migrating birds—the natives were restless.

Thus, it became a Sky High tradition to hold a Winter Formal on the third Saturday in January. The Winter Formal tradition was relatively new. It originated from a club formed by one of Sky High's more famous graduates, young actress Annabeth Gish.

Annabeth graduated from Sky High and then went on to star alongside fellow newcomer Julia Roberts in the film "Mystic Pizza" in 1988. The daughter of professors at UNI, Annabeth traveled with them to Europe, specifically Germany. So, the odd German name of a girls club at Sky High—Madchens— was attributed to Annabeth Gish, whether the story was true or not.

Tad McGreevy—who had cared for Jenny SanGiovanni ever since meeting her at the movies with Stevie Scranton in the summer of 2004— at Stevie's urging finally worked up the courage to ask Jenny to the Winter Formal.

"Come on, Tad. You know you want to," Stevie said to Tad on the phone. Stevie was right. Tad did have feelings for Jenny—feelings that were not reciprocated. Emboldened by Stevie's urging (*"Come on! I'm taking Janice! We can double date! It'll be fun!"*), Tad finally thought, *My bad case of unrequited love might as well take another bashing now as later.* Playing football had made Tad tougher. More assertive. And more attractive to the other females at Sky High, who frequently commented on Tad to Jenny in private. Always favorably.

Tad waited till after school. He paced back and forth nervously. Jenny had Mr. Kellogg's chemistry class last hour of the day. Tad waited in the hallway outside Kellogg's lower level classroom. When he saw Jenny walking towards him, fumbling with her book bag, Tad took a deep breath. He walked towards her.

"Jenny? Are you doing anything on January 22nd? Do you want to go to the Winter Formal with me? We can double date with Stevie and Janice." (Everyone was now aware that Janice and Stevie were going steady). Tad waited nervously for Jenny's response. *If she turns me down again*, he thought, *I'm going home and play that Bonnie Raitt song with the lyric 'I can't make her love me if she don't.'*

It was difficult for Jenny to think of Tad as more than a helpful longtime friend. They'd known each other for so long. *But,* she thought, *Lord knows, I've had little luck with dating!* She thought back to the doomed Jeremy Gustaffsson, her first boyfriend. She remembered the indifferent and sometimes actively cruel young men of Central High in Boulder. Jenny SanGiovanni had been meeting with Sky High Counselor William Randall ever since she returned to Cedar Falls because of problems that began when she was at her dad's house in Boulder. Her bouts of self-mutilation, experienced after she returned to Sky High, finally had stopped. Here in Cedar Falls, Jenny had friends. She felt accepted. She wasn't dealing with a jealous older female in the house, as she had been when living under the same roof with Tammy Tolliver SanGiovanni, her stepmother. As Jenny's self-esteem soared, and she sought counseling, her general malaise abated.

Jenny regarded the handsome young man standing in front of her. He looked apprehensive, nervous, kind.

She said, "Sure, Tad. It'll be fun!" Jenny gave Tad a shy smile to reassure him as she accepted his invitation.

Tad felt so happy. He hoped he didn't look like an idiot. He could not help but return her smile with a beaming smile of his own.

The two walked off down the corridor together, talking of other things.

Tad McGreevy had asked Jenny SanGiovanni to a formal dance and Jenny, for the first time, had accepted. Stevie, when he heard the news, slapped Tad on the back and said, "Way to go, guy!"

Tad was happy. He had had no bad dreams for a long time and Jenny had not turned him down, as she had when he invited her to Homecoming in the fall.

God was in His heaven. All was right in Tad's world.

***

This year's Winter Formal theme was *Snowflakes are Singular.* No one knew exactly what the theme meant. It was Angie Yancy who had lobbied long and hard for it at Madchens, the official girls' auxiliary social club. All the cool girls belonged to Madchens. The group helped plan and execute all dances and social gatherings sponsored by Sky High.

When objections were raised regarding the theme, Angie Yancy said, "You guys know what it means. It means that no two snowflakes are alike. They're all unique, all different."

"Yeah? So?"

That remark from Kelly Carter, Vice President of the Madchens Girls' Auxiliary Club (MGAC, for short). Madchens was supposed to mean "women" or "girls." Something feminine in German, but German was not taught at Sky High, and nobody could remember how this name change had occurred. How did an obscure German word come to represent corn-fed Iowa coeds in Cedar Falls, Iowa? It was a mystery.

In the absence of a better, more creative idea, the Winter Formal theme "Snowflakes Are Singular" stuck. At the meeting, a heated discussion centered on whether the name made sense.

"Snowflakes is a plural word," said one MGAC member. "How can a plural thing be singular?"

One member of Madchens lobbied for "Snowflakes are Sensational." One member suggested "Snowflakes 'R Us." Ultimately, the entire club was pretty sick of discussing snow and snowflakes.

"Snowflakes are Singular" carried the day. Some of the more contentious members argued that it was a dumb name to use when talking about snowflakes. Angie Yancy finally settled the argument in the same short to-the-point manner she handled everything. She said, "Yeah? Well, this entire club has a dumb name, so the theme should fit right in."

Nobody could argue with that.

Chapter Six:
January 17, 2005, Monday

Unhinged

After Sunday came and went with no sign of Heather and Kelly, the already-worried parents began to become unhinged. It was noon on Monday, January 17th.

"Where did the girls say they were going when they left here?" Cedar Falls Police Officer Nels Peterson asked the hassled Cromptons for the hundredth time.

"We told you. Heather and Kelly walked to the river to go ice-skating. We live close enough. They walked down the hill. Your cops found their skates. You know where they were." Nora Crompton was growing testy. She'd been asked this same question at least twenty times.

Nels Peterson remembered questioning the SanGiovanni family when Gregory Tuttle disappeared, only to be found later, dismembered by serial killer Michael Clay at Ike Isham's cabin. That had been an intense, angst-filled scene. This scene was potentially just as disturbing.

Two teen-aged girls had disappeared within sight of one girl's house. Heather lived just atop the hill, with a panoramic view of the Cedar River and a vast lawn leading to the river below. Nobody had heard from them since they left to go skating at noon Saturday. All day Sunday, the distraught parents made phone calls. It was now noon on Monday, two full days and nights later.

At first, Nora said, "Maybe they just lost track of time? Maybe they stopped over at Jenny's house? Or Angie's house? Or maybe they went to the hospital to visit Melody. Maybe they decided to spend the night at the Carters." Wishful thinking.

"Honey—Heather would call. Kelly would call." Chris Crompton stated the obvious.

Kelly Carter's mother, Megan, and her stepfather Joe Jamison were contacted. They were just as distraught as the Cromptons. They had not heard from their daughter, either. That was not like either girl. Repeated phone calls to the girls' cell phones rolled over to voice mail. After a while, even leaving a message did not work. The calls did not connect and a tinny message informed the callers, "This caller is unavailable." A day later, the girls' cell phones would be found in a downtown dumpster.

All theories were checked. None were correct.

Nobody had seen either girl for days now. They were last seen walking towards the river, skates slung over their shoulders. Since then, nothing.

"Can't you put out an All Points Bulletin or something?" Christopher Crompton asked.

"Yes, Sir. We can and we have. Nobody has seen your daughter. Nobody has seen Kelly Carter, either. Nobody has heard from either of them since before they left to go skating on Saturday." Nels wiped his eyeglasses with a handkerchief from his back pocket. He was old-fashioned in using a cloth, monogrammed handkerchief in the Kleenex age.

Nels hated thinking the worst about a situation, but being gone from noon on Saturday and overnight for two nights did not look good. The girls didn't have a car. They were on foot when last seen by Nora Compton heading towards the river. Theories about running away were advanced and discarded. They would be checked out, nonetheless. Dire theories about falling through the ice didn't seem logical, since the girls' ice skates were found at the scene and there were no holes visible in the frozen surface of the river.

All of the friends of the two girls were contacted. Officers questioned students at school. Nobody had heard from either girl in over forty-eight hours.

January 17, 2005, Monday, Cedar Falls Memorial Hospital, 5:00 P.M.

It was five o'clock on Monday. Janice Kramer left the hospital, where she'd visited the still-comatose Melody Carpenter. Janice phoned Stevie Scranton as she headed home.

"Is there any word on Heather and Kelly?"

"No. The cops have been asking questions about them at school. Nobody has heard from them or seen them or knows anything."

"That's crazy! They can't have just disappeared! Nobody just drops off the face of the Earth like that." Janice zipped up her parka while holding her cell phone against her chin.

"I know. It's crazy, but that seems to be what's happened," said Stevie. "I have a plan—sort of—that I want to run by you when I see you. Everybody worked so hard to help bring me home. I want to help find Heather and Kelly."

"Okay," Janice said. "I want to talk to you, too. I have something I want you to do for me, if you will."

Stevie said, "Sure, Janice. Anything. Just ask."

"With the Winter Formal coming up at the end of this week, I have to tell my parents that I'm pregnant. I'm scared to tell them alone. Once, you said you'd go with me when I told my parents. Did you mean it?"

"Of course I meant it. I love you, Janice. If you want me there, I'm there."

"Well, I want you there. And I want to tell them tonight. After dinner. If I'm still alive after that, I want to get a new dress that will expand with me through the weekend and beyond. *(Janice laughed, but it was a nervous laugh, not a convincing laugh.)* Nothing I have now fits. I haven't been able to wear most of my jeans for a while.

I'm running out of sweatpants, sweatshirts and skirts. I'm really beginning to show, so I *HAVE* to tell them, and soon."

"What time do you want me to come over?" Stevie asked.

"It's five o'clock now. We usually eat at six o'clock. Come over at seven thirty, okay?"

"I'll be there, Janice," Stevie said. "And, Janice, don't worry. It will be all right. We'll make it all right. I'm there for you, no matter what."

Janice hung up the phone and burst into tears. She was overwhelmed. Riding an emotional roller coaster. Her best friend was lying comatose in intensive care. Two other close friends were inexplicably missing. There was the looming duty of telling her strict Catholic parents about Jeremy's child. Pregnancy hormones were kicking in.

Janice felt that she, too, was growing slightly unhinged.

Chapter Seven:
January 17, 2005, Monday Night

The Revelation

The Kramers bowed their heads at the dinner table, as they did every night before the evening meal.

"Bless us, oh Lord, for these thy gifts, which we are about to receive. From thy bounty, through Christ, our Lord. Amen." Each family member made the sign of the cross. Janice's mother added a personal blessing, a homily, as she did each night: "And thank you, Lord, for our family and for all your blessings upon us. Help Janice do well in school, and help us all to do what is right. Amen."

Every night it was something different—something meant to make the standard Catholic Grace more personal.

Spaghetti was passed around the table. Garlic bread accompanied the pasta, the garlic-y aroma filling the air. A lettuce salad with vinaigrette dressing sat at each place. John and Gina Kramer looked over at Janice. Darting glances.

Janice wasn't eating. She was pushing spaghetti noodles around her plate, but she was not putting any in her mouth.

"What's the matter, Janice? You're so quiet. And you're not eating. Trying to lose weight before the big dance this weekend?" Gina Kramer asked in a pleasant tone.

Gina smiled at her daughter, but as soon as she made the remark about losing weight, she wished she could take it back.

It's true that Janice has a more voluptuous figure than at the beginning of the school year, but cheerleading is over, thought Janice's mom. *Cheerleading burned up a lot of calories. Now that the girls don't practice or perform—well, it's understandable that Janice might gain a few pounds after the season ended*, Gina rationalized.

To Gina Kramer, Janice would always be the most beautiful girl in school. Possibly the most beautiful girl in the world. Janice was certainly the light of her mother's life. Gina Kramer would never intentionally say something to hurt her daughter's feelings. She just had not been thinking when she spoke.

John Kramer, a man of few words, didn't say anything. He had put in a long day that began at four o'clock in the morning at the family bakery. He'd eat dinner, watch one program on television, and be off to bed so he could start all over the next day.

The family's calico cat, Fraidy, wandered into the kitchen and began meowing piteously. Fraidy had become a terrible beggar lately. The Kramer family was blaming it on a new cat in house, Lola, who still had her claws. (Fraidy did not).

Lola seemed to be eating both Fraidy's food AND her own food. Therefore, Lola was getting fatter every day. Lola's form showed her increased intake, as she now weighed seventeen pounds. A hefty weight for a cat. When Lola jumped in your lap, it was as though someone had dropped a twenty-pound bag of potatoes there unexpectedly. And these potatoes had sharp claws and teeth!

In an effort to make small talk, Gina said, "Look at poor Fraidy cat. Lola has eaten all her food. Fraidy's getting thin as a rail, while Lola is getting fatter and fatter every day."

When Gina said this, John—never a man to mince words or observe social niceties—said, "Like some other girls in this house. I think it's good you're cutting back on the pasta, Janice. You don't want to lose your figure. You'll never get a husband if you let yourself get fat." John Kramer was much less sensitive in his remarks than Gina. Her thoughtless remark was unintentional, while John was always tough on his children.

Gina gave John a dirty look. She wanted to sink beneath the table and disappear.

Janice burst into tears just as the doorbell rang.

Gina Kramer rose from the table, saying, "I wonder who that could be? Right at the dinner hour like this?" She was secretly relieved that there was a distraction. Her husband's insensitive contribution to the conversation had obviously upset Janice.

It was 7:30 p.m., right on the dot. Stevie Scranton stood outside on the porch.

Gina flipped on the porch light and opened the door, saying, "Stevie! Come in. We didn't expect company. We're just finishing up dinner." She smiled at Stevie pleasantly.

Janice had been going out with Stevie for a while now. Both of Janice's parents were aware that Stevie had asked Janice to the Winter Formal and she had accepted the invitation.

Janice trailed in from the kitchen, already upset, eyes red, wiping tears from her cheeks. Her father, looking stern, followed. Stevie, not knowing what had happened so far, thought, *Janice must have told them already. Her mom doesn't seem to be taking it too badly. Her father ALWAYS looks mad. Janice sure looks upset, though.*

Stevie took all this in at a glance.

"Sit down, Stevie. How can we help you?" Gina asked. The obvious question. A polite way of asking, "Why are you here?" Stevie thought, *Janice's mom seems okay. Maybe this won't be so bad.*

Janice interrupted. "Stevie's here because I asked him to come. There's something I need to tell you both." She took a deep breath and blurted it out: "I'm pregnant."

John Kramer almost lunged for Stevie. Janice quickly added, "It's not Stevie's."

"WHAT? Whose is it?" asked John Kramer. He looked ashen. Eyebrows knit together over his glowering countenance.

"Jeremy Gustaffsson's."

Gina Kramer looked stricken.

"Oh, Janice! How could you! I never thought something like this would happen to you! And now you're pregnant with a dead man's child?" Janice's mother looked as though someone had sucker punched her. Her face was an off-white color that mimicked the spaghetti noodles, but John Kramer's face was more the color of the spaghetti sauce.

"Why are you here, Stevie?" John Kramer asked. He did not sound happy.

"I'm here to support Janice. I know she's been really afraid to tell you about the baby. I also want you to know that I love Janice. I want to marry her. I'll get a job. I'll raise this child as though it were my own. Really, Mr. Kramer—I'd marry Janice tomorrow, if she'd have me. I'd marry her tonight! I love her." Stevie's eyes misted up as he professed his love for Janice so publicly and under such difficult circumstances. He really meant it.

"I'm sure you would like to marry my daughter, Stevie. She's a good girl, but she has shown some bad judgment. She should have known better than to get herself pregnant without benefit of the sacred sacrament of matrimony. But she's not eighteen until May third. She isn't going to be getting married before then. And probably not after then, either. Not to you and not to anybody else. But *especially* not to you!"

John Kramer's fists clenched and unclenched as he spoke. His face was distorted in anger. He looked like he might blow a gasket any minute. He was holding himself in check, but he was very upset.

"Why, Daddy? Why are you saying such awful things to Stevie? He's been wonderful to me. I love him!"

This was the first time Janice had ever said those words aloud. Stevie felt his heart dance within his chest. At the same time, he was keeping a wary eye on Mr. Kramer, who seemed close to losing it. Stevie had taken his fair share of playground beatings over the years, but John Kramer was a big guy. Six foot five. Italian. Volatile.

John Kramer turned the full wrath of his emotions on Janice, then, and said, "You, little girl, will finish high school. You graduate in June. How far along are you?"

Janice blinked and looked down. "I'm five months along. My due date is May 28th."

"Great God in heaven!" exclaimed John Kramer. "That was my sainted mother's birth date! It's sacrilegious to think that you might have this bastard child on my dead mother's birthday! And you're *NOT* going to marry a boy whose father killed two people and wounded four others! How quickly people forget! In fact, I don't want you having anything to do with him after tonight. This boy's father was a monster. His mother is a nitwit. My youngest child is not getting mixed up with the likes of Stevie Scranton!"

John turned the full force of his wrath on Stevie then. "Get out of my house. You're no longer welcome here. And stay away from my daughter! She's made enough mistakes and she'll pay for them. But not by being yoked for life to a murderer's son. She'll have the child and give it up for adoption, like unwed pregnant girls have always done. We don't want your kind in our family."

Stevie was backing up the entire time, but still standing his ground.

John Kramer stood at the base of the staircase as he delivered his ultimatum. He turned and stomped upstairs. His face was the red of a bad sunburn.

He did not look back at his sobbing daughter. But he did make sure he heard his front door slam.

Chapter Eight:
Nine Weeks Earlier, Friday, November 12, 2004

Before the Fall

Earl Scranton carefully sealed the black-and-white composition notebook within the mailing envelope. He added extra tape, to make sure the contents arrived at the Cedar Falls Police Department intact.

I'm going to make sure that everybody in this town knows what's been going on. Principal Peter Puck. Scoutmaster Declan Hunter. The both of them pedophiles. It's sickening! These people were in positions of power. They abused their positions. They abused my son. And who knows how many others? They pass themselves off as paragons of virtue when they're anything but. You can't trust anybody any more! They'll pay for what they've done. If I don't get them tonight at the Homecoming game, at least there'll be this evidence— Stevie's journal—in the hands of the cops. They'll pay for their crimes! What they did isn't right.

Earl went back to polishing and loading his guns, preparing for that night's Homecoming game. His mouth worked soundlessly with repressed rage, like the mouth of an old person trying to chew with new dentures. He was muttering to himself.

I'm gonna' dish out a little payback—some old-fashioned revenge—to some of those snot-nosed kids who made fun of Stevie for years. Rodney Black. Stewie Truitt. Zack Porfino. They treated Stevie like a dog. Stevie's not a dog. He's a good kid. He's MY kid. From now on, I'm going to make it right for him. If I can't get the job done tonight, well, then, I know who can.

Earl regretted that high school classmate Charlie Chandler had retired from the force. After the SanGiovanni standoff with Pogo, there had been a lot of publicity about the female sharpshooter in the department, Rita Cernetisch. Earl thought a woman cop who made the Olympic team would have the necessary dedication to do the right thing for his son.

I'll address it to Rita, since Charlie has retired, Earl thought.

Stevie's composition notebook was the very one Stevie had left in the refrigerator on top of his father's six-pack of beer, hoping his father would read it on the momentous night Stevie decided to end his own life. That notebook had been retrieved from Stevie's room by the increasingly disturbed Earl Scranton. Earl didn't know if he would be successful in his quest to punish the evildoers on Homecoming night. He didn't know if he'd live or die after Homecoming night. He didn't much care.

Earl thought, *If I fail, the cops can take over where I left off.*

Earl had visited the post office earlier in the week with the notebook in a manila mailing envelope. He asked Sherry Green, who worked there, wife of funeral director Gary Green, to weigh the slim manila envelope. Fortunately, it wasn't a big package. Since 9/11 of 2001 you couldn't simply drop a large package in a mailbox; you'd have to make a special trip to the post office to mail something large. But this was not a large package, although the contents would have big consequences.

This was the last thing that Earl Scranton would do: make sure his boy was avenged. Make sure that Stevie got justice. Earl mailed the package before departing for the Homecoming game.

Then, speaking to himself again, Earl mumbled, *If I should die, before I wake, I pray the Lord my soul to take.*

Chapter Nine:
January 15, 2005, Saturday

Mike Parker: A Lean, Mean Killing Machine

Michael Clay (aka Pogo) —or Mike Parker as he was known in Jesup, Iowa—had been working at the Kalafut Diner for five months. After the August 29th attack on Jeremy Gustaffsson and Heather Crompton on Lovers' Lane in Cedar Falls, Pogo left the Waterloo/Cedar Falls area. He planned to return for the November 12th Homecoming game to finish what he started. He'd kill Tad McGreevy to shut him up. The original plan collapsed with the interference of Iowa Highway Patrol Officer Joseph Hafner, who pulled Pogo over for speeding.

Pogo returned to Jesup after murdering Officer Hafner along winding, twisting old Highway 218. He buried the young officer's body in a shallow grave. He was very careful not to leave any incriminating circumstantial evidence at the scene. So far, even though Joe Hafner's body *was* found two days later, there were no suspects in his death.

Pogo drew a paycheck as a fry cook all of September, October, November and December. When he wasn't putting in long shifts at the diner, he exercised faithfully. Mike gradually dropped almost fifteen pounds each and every month, for a current total of sixty-five pounds. But Michael Clay wanted to lose more. Much more.

I'll become a lean, mean killing machine. I'll be stronger and better than ever before!

Pogo's lips curled in an evil grimace. *I can't wait to get my hands on that McGreevy kid. He's been nothing but trouble. He needs to be taken down a peg or two. And I know just the guy to do it.*

Pogo replaced the barbells on the stand in his home gym. He'd been using heavier and heavier weights, building up his upper and lower body strength and changing his appearance dramatically. His brown eyes were now blue, courtesy of contact lenses. His head was currently shaved, although he was thinking of purchasing a wig. As he looked in the mirror at the "new, improved" Pogo, he thought, *Maybe I'll grow back my own hair and dye it black. That could work. I want to look as different from before as possible. I'll be a new man!* He grinned approvingly at his thinner self reflected in the mirror.

Michael Clay had been in prison a long time before he escaped and killed Charlie Chandler's wife, Cassie, and Gregory Tuttle at Ike Isham's cabin. He was at least one hundred pounds overweight then. He admitted to himself that he did not work out as faithfully as he should have when he was behind bars. Although Clay was still an imposing physical presence at six foot three and two hundred and eighty pounds, losing sixty-five pounds was a good start.

Even now, regular customers at the diner would comment to him or to his boss about the fry cook's changed physique.

"Damn, Mike! I barely recognized you. You've dropped a ton of weight? How much have you lost?" This was regular customer Sammy Swanson. Sammy came in every morning and ordered the same breakfast: hash browns, scrambled eggs, black coffee and bacon.

"I've lost about sixty-five pounds—so far," Mike answered, through the cook's window, as Sammy sat at the Formica counter, perched on an uncomfortable silver bar stool with red Naugahyde upholstery.

"Damn! You're lookin' good, buddy! Keep up the hard work!"

Sammy got up, paid for his breakfast, left a small tip, and headed out for work at the John Deere plant in Waterloo.

Pogo began counting the time until all the hoopla of graduations and proms and end-of-school-year activities began. He had already checked Sky High's calendar online. Students at Sky High were scheduled to graduate June 11th, 2005. Today was January 15th. Graduation for the Sky High Class of 2005 was just five months away. At this rate Pogo could possibly lose another sixty-five to seventy-five pounds. That would mean he'd lost an entire person weighing one hundred and fifty pounds by then.

The way Pogo had it figured, May or June would be the optimal time to strike.

Too bad the hundred pounds lost couldn't be Tad McGreevy or that twit Stevie Scranton, thought Michael with menace.

With changed eye color, different hair and some new clothes, Tad McGreevy would never know what—or who—hit him when it happened. It could happen at Prom on May 7th. It could happen at graduation on June 11th. It could happen any time that Pogo didn't have to contend with a nosy police officer pulling him over on his way to stop the kid who could see the future. And it could happen anywhere. Pogo liked the sound of the end of the school year, when the weather was not as godawful as it had been for the past two months.

It'll be the end, all right. Good luck with seeing THIS crime before it happens, he thought.

Michael Clay smiled a secret smile as he cracked another egg and wiped the sweat from his brow.

Chapter Ten:
January 17, 2005, Monday

Cozy Conversation

Charlie Chandler turned over in bed. He looked to his right. He was still amazed every time he saw a beautiful woman lying there next to him. The beautiful woman wasn't sleeping soundly, as Charlie imagined she would be. She was up and fastening her bra. Putting her clothes back on.

"Andrea…Andrea! Why don't you just move in with me? We're sneaking around like we're sixteen years old, when I'm closing in on sixty!" Charlie sat up in bed. The sheets fell to waist-level, revealing a rugged physique that belied Charlie's comment about his age.

"Charlie—you know I can't do that now. Jenny graduates in June. We can talk about living together after Jenny's gone off to college."

"What if she decides to stay in town and go to the University of Northern Iowa? THEN will you come live with me?" Charlie brushed a lock of hair away from his eyes. One thing Charlie Chandler had not lost was his full head of hair, though he was graying at the temples more every day.

"Here? In the Regency Suites Apartments? With your daughter Belinda just two doors down?" Andrea laughed. "I don't think so, Charlie." Then she paused in the process of buttoning her blouse. "I'm a realtor, you know, Charlie. Either you can move in with me, or I can find us a new place."

Charlie—who always slept in his underwear— walked around the bed to Andrea's side of the bed. He towered over her as he gave her an affectionate bear hug.

"How long have we been going out, Babe?" he asked Andrea. She was impatient to be on the road to the SanGiovanni Real Estate office.

"That's exactly my point, Charlie. We've only been seeing each other since Abe died." Andrea was referring to the untimely death of Dr. Abraham Eisenstadt at her house on October 28th, 2004. That crisis had drawn the couple together when Charlie helped Andrea move Abe's body from her bedroom into the car in his own garage next door.

"That was only three months ago. I'm no prude, but I'd like to think that we really know each other well before either one of us gives up our independence. I'm a two-time loser, Charlie. First, Jeff. Then, Greg. Neither of my marriages ended well." Andrea shot Charlie a pained look from under dark lashes. "I'm not looking to become a three-time loser with men any time in the immediate future. Why spoil what we have?" Andrea grabbed her briefcase. Put on her coat. Got ready to face the day.

Charlie shrugged. "I'm meeting Evelyn for dinner tonight. She wants to run some ideas past me about those two girls who disappeared."

"You mean Heather and Kelly, right?" said Andrea, hand on the doorknob.

"Yes. They've been missing since noon on Saturday. Evelyn called me right after they disappeared, but everyone thought they would return on their own before now."

Andrea shook her head. "Those two were both cheerleaders with Jenny. Heather was with Jeremy when he was murdered. In fact, Heather had Jenny over for a sleepover the very night that Abe died. Jenny is very upset. I sure hope you DO have some good ideas. After all, you and Evelyn got Stevie back. If anyone can figure this out..." Andrea trailed off. She smiled at Charlie, still preparing to leave for work.

"I just wish that Rita Cernetisch was back in town. If two heads are better than one, then three heads would be better than two," said Charlie.

"Where is Rita?" asked Andrea.

Charlie grabbed his watch from the nightstand. He pulled on a pair of jeans as he answered, planning on walking Andrea to her car.

"Well, you know she was pretty shook up about the Earl Scranton shooting," he answered. "But that was only part of it."

"What do you mean? Rita was essential in the police siege of MY old house. Why is she suddenly squeamish?" asked Andrea.

"If you remember," said Charlie, "and I know that you do—Rita was mainly providing cover for some of her fellow officers that day— like me. She didn't actually watch one of the bullets she fired strike a man she knew right between the eyes. She had never watched a man she knew personally die, in front of a stadium full of football fans, while that man's son cradled his father's bloody head in his lap. The Earl Scranton thing hit her hard.

Then, too, there was the fact that Rita didn't make the Olympic shooting team this time around. The U.S. had twenty-one competitors on the squad in Greece. Rita wasn't one of them. She made the Olympic team in 2000, you know. Took the silver medal in 10-metre air rifle. Said she was going for the gold next time. Instead, DuLi of China got the gold. Rita *really* wanted to be in Greece in August. She said she felt like a failure when she didn't make the team. Then, after the Earl Scranton thing…"

Here Charlie stopped speaking and looked out the window at the swimming pool below. He reached in his pocket for his handkerchief and took a long time folding and re-folding the small pocket-sized square. He seemed to be composing himself. Regrouping.

"Well, she just up and said she was going to take six months off— *if* the department would let her. Wanted to go visit Greece, anyway— even if she didn't get to take part in the Olympics. Said she wanted to see Panathinaiko Stadium up close and personal. She left immediately after the shooting. From what I heard from Evelyn, the department shrinks were pretty supportive. They thought Rita needed to get away. Needed the time off. She's not due back until the middle of May."

Here Charlie moved towards the bathroom, changing his mind about the walk to Rita's car and deciding to shower instead. Charlie turned to speak to Andrea just before she exited.

"I mean, it was a righteous shoot. The department agreed. But afterwards, Rita said it felt like an execution: her being up in the press box like that, just waiting. Armed. Ready to take out anybody doing anything crazy. But nobody knew it would be Stevie Scranton's dad, Earl. I think that got to her more than anything—watching Earl's kids freaking out as Earl lay there dying. Knowing she was responsible for shooting a man dead in front of his kids. I think it hit her hard."

Charlie coughed. Or was it a cough?

Andrea shook her head. Thinking about Charlie's words, she looked disturbed. Conflicted. She glanced down at her knuckles and then made a quick decision.

She walked back to Charlie's side and gave him a quick peck on the cheek. It helped make them both feel slightly better.

The troubled look on the face of the man she loved bothered her. It was the look of a person with a conscience. Someone who knew he was responsible for inflicting emotional damage on a friend.

That emotional pain would haunt Rita Cernetisch forever.

Chapter Eleven:
January 18, 2005, Tuesday

Stevie and Janice Speak

At school on Tuesday, everyone was talking about the missing girls.

Zack Porfino told Stewie Truitt how the Amber Alert worked. Or didn't work.

"They won't put out an Amber Alert on Kelly and Heather because nobody saw them being taken. It's the stupidest thing ever. Who is ever around to actually SEE somebody being snatched?" Zack shook his head back and forth with an expression that said, *Can you believe this shit?* The two were standing in an alley near school smoking one last cigarette before the start of the school day.

Stewie responded, "W-w-well, what good is it then? I-I-If they won't use it? I mean, even N-N-N-Nora C-C-Crompton didn't s-s-see anything. And she was r-r-right at the t-t-top of the hill above where they were s-s-skating!"

Stewie's stutter usually was made worse by excitement. The disappearance of the two girls was big news on the state and national scenes. CNN had sent Wolf Blitzer to town. All three major networks were on the prowl. There hadn't been this much excitement since Stevie Scranton was returned to his parents on September fourth. Everyone was on the lookout for Brian Williams to come calling again, as he had then.

In the midst of all this chaos, Stevie and Janice found a quiet spot to talk about their own troubles. It was right after school. The gym was temporarily deserted. They sat on the bottom level of the empty bleachers.

"Janice, your parents can't keep us apart forever. You'll be eighteen on May third. We can get married then, whether they like it or not." Stevie looked hopefully at Janice. He wanted confirmation that Janice was onboard with his plans. He hoped against hope that the resistance from the Kramers encountered last night would not doom their relationship.

Janice hung her head. She looked thoroughly dejected.

"I know what you're saying, Stevie. I *do* want to marry you. I also want to keep this baby. I didn't, at first. But seeing Melody in the hospital, fighting for her life, struggling to stay alive to buy her baby boy time. Well, let's just say that, even if this *IS* Jeremy's child—and maybe even more so, because Jeremy's child may be the only legacy he'll leave behind—I decided while sitting by Melody's hospital bed that I want to keep my baby. And I want to marry you, too. But how? When? Where?"

Stevie's mind was tumbling like out-of-control dice in a state lottery basket, with ping pong balls caroming madly around the interior of his skull as his thoughts skittered from one possibility to another.

"I don't know the laws of all the states around us, Janice, but I can find out. There may be a state where we can get married without parental permission at seventeen? I turned eighteen when—well, you know—when I was in Chicago. Back in August, when I was a captive. I'm old for our class. I was held back once in Kindergarten."

Janice hesitated. "It's not that I don't want to marry you, Stevie. Ideally, we'd be able to get married before this child is born. Give him your name. But I have to stand up to both of my parents. It's just—hard." She started to tear up. Stevie reached for Janice's hand to comfort her.

"I know, Janice. I know. We'll have to give your folks some time. Although I will say that your mother seemed more positive than your father did."

Stevie didn't want to come right out and say that he thought John Kramer was going to knock his block off, but Janice had been there. She knew what Stevie was describing.

"Yes, I think my mom might come around. For one thing, I can't believe that my mom is cool with my dad *MAKING* me give away my child. This is 2005, not 1965. Give me a break! Girls don't give up their babies any more. Not unless they have overly Catholic parents like mine, that is," she added in a glum tone. "But my dad is very old-fashioned. He's living in the past."

"Nobody's making you give up your baby if you don't want to, Janice. That is *your* decision and nobody else's." Stevie's voice was strong. Assertive. He'd grown up a lot since November when his father died. Now, Stevie did not back down just because he might have to take a beating. Janice raised her head and glanced at the sweet blonde boy, her savior.

"Thank you, Stevie. I needed to hear that. I'll fight for this child. Melody is fighting for little Adam right now, and she doesn't even know it. I refuse to abandon my own child just because my dad thinks I should." Janice sounded determined and looked Stevie in the eye, "And I'm so sorry about what my dad said about your father. I know you loved your dad. That wasn't right." Janice squeezed Stevie's hand to emphasize her support, simultaneously shaking her head from side to side to fully emphasize her words.

"I guess the Winter Formal this weekend is off," Stevie said, declaring the obvious. The Winter Formal seemed petty and unimportant compared to all the obstacles the two now faced.

Both laughed at Stevie's remark. Self-conscious laughter.

Then Janice said, "I didn't have a dress that fit, anyway. Maybe we can figure out a way to meet at the movies that afternoon? See each other then?"

"Okay. I'll talk to you later in the week. We'll figure out what we want to see," Stevie said. "I'd better get going. I have a job interview at the Target store where I met you. Part-time for now, but who knows? They might go for a guy like me."

Stevie smiled a crooked grin and rose to leave, walking out of the gym with the girl of his dreams.

Chapter Twelve:
January 18, 2005, Tuesday

Stevie Talks to Tad

After his successful job interview, Stevie felt like sharing the good news. He had been hired for a part-time after-school position. He wanted to tell someone. That someone would have been Janice, if not for the embargo her parents had imposed on their communicating. He couldn't call Janice.

Thank heaven for computers! Stevie thought. At least he could reach Janice via AOL. They talked that way every night.

When he realized that he couldn't talk "live" to Janice, he thought of Tad. Although the two had drifted apart, Stevie's return to Cedar Falls and his new position as water-boy for the team had brought Tad and Stevie closer together again. At least they saw each other because of football, while their class assignments never coincided. In fact, Stevie suddenly realized that he needed to let Tad know that he and Janice would no longer be double dating with Tad and Jenny for the Winter Formal. Stevie decided to stop at Tad's house.

Jeannie McGreevy answered the doorbell. She was genuinely glad to see Stevie.

"Stevie! We haven't seen you here nearly enough lately. How are you doing? Are you okay?" Jeannie was aware of Stevie's troubles, including his kidnapping, his parents' divorce and his father's death. She was worried for Tad's oldest friend.

That's a lot for anyone to deal with in a short time, Jeannie thought. She smiled again at the teenager and then said," Tad's in his room studying. Why don't you go on up and surprise him?"

Stevie smiled at the thought of "surprising" Tad. He hadn't set foot in the McGreevy's home for months, if not years. He couldn't remember the last time he and Tad had camped out together or had a sleepover, but he was pretty sure it pre-dated freshman year. Now they were seniors, five months away from graduating.

To Jeannie McGreevy he said, "Thanks, Mrs. McGreevy. I'm fine. I just wanted to tell Tad about a job interview I just had and talk to him about this weekend. We sort of had plans to do something together. Now I can't." Stevie set his book bag down on the floor by the front door.

"Where are you going to work, Stevie? It's part-time, right?"

"Target. But not the Target I used to work at. The bigger one just across the bridge in Waterloo. I got the job." He smiled.

Stevie climbed the stairs to his old friend's bedroom. Tad usually studied at a desk that sat in front of a window overlooking the street. Stevie often thought that if he ever did have a desk, he would never be able to get any studying done if it overlooked anything interesting. To Stevie, almost everything was more interesting than schoolwork.

As he entered Tad's bedroom following a light knock on his door, Stevie said, "Hard at work or hardly working?"

It was an old joke. Tad used to respond, to Stevie, "How goes the battle?"

Tad put down his calculus textbook and swiveled in his chair to face Stevie, who took a seat on Tad's twin bed. The room was small, with a slanting ceiling that echoed the roof of the old house. The wallpaper on the walls was of roses. It was not a very "manly" room. Stevie had once said so, to Tad, who merely shrugged and said, "My mom likes roses. She won't let me take the wallpaper down, so I'm stuck with it, I guess. I'm secure enough in my own masculinity to deal with it, Stevie," he said, with an effeminate mincing tone meant to be funny.

"What's up? What's new?" asked Tad.

"I just got a part-time job working alongside Big Bertha at the Target store in Waterloo," said Stevie. "But that's not the main thing I came to tell you."

Stevie launched into the story of the scene with Janice and her mother and father.

"Wow!" Tad said, when Stevie had finished. "Did John Kramer physically throw you out?"

"Naaah. He just made sure I was gone. He wants me to *STAY* gone. But I love Janice. I'm going to find a way for us to get married and keep the baby." Stevie said this as though it were as simple as buying a sandwich at McDonald's.

"How, exactly, are you going to do that?" Tad asked, his brow furrowed with concern for his oldest friend.

"Janice turns eighteen on May 3rd. If we try to get married before that, we'll have to find a nearby state where a couple can get married without parental supervision if one of them is under eighteen."

"Not likely," said Tad.

"Yeah. I know. To be honest, I already checked. There's NO state that let kids get married if they're seventeen and don't have parental permission. I only found one state with a different law—and they make you be even older!" Stevie looked chagrined as he shared this last bit of information. Stevie added, "They don't even make allowances for girls who are pregnant. You've got to have parental permission or be eighteen, and that's that." Stevie looked glum. Then he added, "And we can't double date with you and Jenny for the Winter Formal." He said it almost as an after-thought. Getting a job and talk of marriage was far more serious than a stupid dance.

"What other major news developments do you have for me, Stevie," Tad said. He was still digesting all the information that Stevie had related in less than ten minutes. "And how are you going to pay for a baby? Or, for that matter, for a wife?"

Stevie looked miffed.

"I'm not lazy, you know," he said. "I can work. I just got a job! If they want me to go full-time, I can quit school. Finish later. Get a GED. Plus, I have another idea. Wanna' hear it?"

"Is the Pope Catholic?" Tad asked, deadpan. Another old clichéd joke between the two fast friends, borrowed from Tad's dad Jim.

"Well, you know about Heather and Kelly? Their disappearance?"

"Yes, it's horrible. How does that help you and Janice?"

"Well, the families—the Carters and the Cromptons—have offered a $25,000 reward for any information leading to the recovery of the girls. That's where you come in," Stevie said.

"ME?" Tad was genuinely nonplussed. "How? Why?"

"You're going to have to learn to harness your super power. Figure out who took those two and where they are now. Then, we rescue the girls and collect the reward and we split it." Stevie said this as though he had just suggested that lottery ticket winnings would be the answer to his prayers.

At first, Tad was tempted to laugh. Then he truly thought about what Stevie was saying. It was the first time Tad felt optimistic about learning to control his Super Tetrachromatic nightmare visions.

After all, I used my power to 'see' the deaths at the stadium on Homecoming night. I have to try to 'see' those two missing girls. Perhaps I CAN help. It can't hurt to try. I'd be helping Heather, Kelly, Janice and Stevie.

Instead of rejecting Stevie's outrageous proposal outright, Tad said, "Let's talk about this some more."

Chapter Thirteen:
January 15, 2005, Saturday

Camp Wapsie "W"

Declan Hunter's van turned down the gravel road that led to Camp Wapsie "W."

The two teen-aged girls in the back seat were gossiping about the upcoming Winter Formal.

"Tad McGreevy asked Jenny SanGiovanni to go, you know," Heather said to Kelly.

"I know. He's always had a thing for her. What did she say?"

"I guess she said yes. She hasn't dated anybody for months. Really, her last boyfriend here in town was Jeremy Gustaffsson," Heather answered. "And we both know how THAT ended." Heather looked glum.

"Yeah, but that was way last year. It was first semester of our junior year, because Jenny wasn't even here for second semester. She was out in Boulder at her dad's house."

"True," said Heather. "And we don't know if she had somebody steady out there."

"She seemed weird when she came back," Kelly added. Kelly turned to face Heather straight on. "Didn't you think so?"

"Yes. She seemed sort of strange and distant then. I think she's over that now. Maybe she had a hot boyfriend in Denver and had to give him up to come back here. Broke her heart and all that rot."

"Well," Kelly said, "Tad McGreevy is pretty hot—now. Have you taken a good look at him any time recently?" Kelly smiled at Heather's comment. To herself, she was thinking, *If any girl in school would notice a cute boy, it would be Heather.*

"Tad's okay," Heather responded with disinterest. "Not my type."

"So, what's your type?" Kelly asked.

"Tall, dark and handsome, of course," Heather answered, with a laugh.

The van lurched to the side. Heather shouted to her Uncle Dec, "Are we almost there?"

Uncle Dec didn't respond.

"Seems like we've been driving for a long time. I'd forgotten how far out of town this camp was. I haven't been here since I was about ten," Heather said. "If I had remembered how far out it was…" She trailed off, her thoughts left unexpressed.

"I've never been to Camp Wapsie W," Kelly said. "My parents never sent me to *any* summer camp. They needed me at home to babysit, until…well, you know."

Kelly's younger brother, Jason, had died of leukemia three years ago, when Kelly was fifteen. Up until his death, Kelly was chief nurse's helper and seldom missing from Jason's side. She had developed a dark view of life during the years spent helping to care for her younger brother. A fatalistic view. *Que sera, sera.* But Kelly had also become stronger in the way that the death of a loved one will prepare you to handle future grief.

The van was approaching a long, low-slung log cabin-like building, one of twenty on the grounds. The crunch of gravel beneath the tires lessened as the van slowed to a halt and pulled into a parking spot immediately in front of Cabin Number One.

Declan Hunter got out. He invited the girls to follow him. Some would say he ordered the girls to follow him.

"Girls—follow me!"

Kelly and Heather walked a few paces behind the jacketed figure, into the darkness of an unheated log cabin. There were two bunk beds. Primitive. Army blankets on each. Thin, much-used mattresses that looked like they would be just as at home in a drug house.

Declan Hunter flipped the light switch. The light bulb remained dark. There was a bit of afternoon light filtering in through the open door. It was very dim, because the windows of this particular cabin were covered with plywood.

"Why are the windows all boarded up, Uncle Dec?" Heather asked her silent uncle.

He turned to face them and said, "We're doing some repairs. That's all. The glass got broken. The glass company can't get out here to replace the windows for a few days."

"Where are our skates?" Kelly asked. "Should we put them on in here?" She gestured towards the bunk beds. The upper and lower beds were joined with primitive looking metal scaffoldings.

"Don't worry about your skates," Dec said as he approached Kelly. "Be seated."

To Heather he said, "Heather, run out to the van and bring your skates in from the back of the van." Declan was fumbling with the mattress on the bunk bed that Kelly was preparing to sit on. He tested the bed's stability.

"I made this support myself—to join the upper and lower bunks. Just want to make sure it is stable." Declan's weathered face sported a fleeting smile, as though he took pleasure in the evidence of his labor. Then, his attention returned to the present.

"Heather, hurry on out to the van now." Dec shot his niece a peremptory glance.

Heather usually did as she was told, especially if the authority figure was an older relative.

As Heather cleared the doorway and the door slammed shut, Declan Hunter quickly grabbed Kelly's left arm. He slapped metal handcuffs on her arm, fastening the other end to one of the metal poles he had been testing for stability just a moment prior.

Kelly, startled, began shouting, "What are you doing? What are you doing to me?"

Hearing the commotion, Heather Crompton came running back. She had made it all the way to the vehicle. Opened the back door. Checked in the trunk. Found no skates. Now, she was hearing loud screams from the interior of the cabin.

As Heather entered the barren, primitive structure, Declan Hunter, hypodermic needle in hand, waited behind the door. Lurking. As his niece entered—responding to her friend's cries for help—Declan plunged a hypodermic filled with a powerful tranquilizer into Heather's neck.

Heather collapsed into his arms, mumbling, "Uncle Dec...what's going on? What are you doing?" Before Heather could repeat the question, she passed out, Kelly's cries echoing in her ears, an urgent soundtrack to the unfolding drama.

Declan Hunter carefully picked up the unconscious girl and laid her on the second bunk bed, approximately six feet away from the one on which Kelly Carter sat, watching, transfixed with horror.

Heather's uncle placed a similar handcuff on Heather's right hand and fastened it to the metal struts that attached the lower bunk to the upper bunk of her separate bed.

With the door closed, it was dark inside: an eerie dimness. The late afternoon sunlight infiltrated. Sepia-toned light crept around the barriers of irregular, rough wood covering the windows. Cracks of light filtered in at odd angles. The half-light barely illuminated the surreal scene.

The bare light bulb hanging from the ceiling in the center of the room had not gone on when Declan flipped the light switch. *Must be burnt out*, Dec thought, absentmindedly.

He turned to Kelly, who was dumbstruck at what was happening.

He said, "I'll get a new bulb for that. In the meantime, watch out for Heather. I don't want anything to happen to her. I don't want anything to happen to either of you girls. You'll only be here for a little while. I'll have better accommodations for you soon. Safer ones. Then nobody will leave me ever again."

Declan Hunter's tone was plaintive. Mournful. Robotic.

Declan Hunter walked from the dim dinginess of the interior of the cabin as though in a trance.

Chapter Fourteen:
January 15, 2005, Saturday

No Way Out

A few minutes passed. Declan Hunter returned, carrying a 100-watt light bulb.

Kelly glanced at the unconscious form of Heather. Heather was passed out on the bunk across from her. Kelly was too frightened to scream. She had screamed for help and Heather had ended up unconscious on the bunk next to her. Kelly made a conscious decision to sit quietly and act as though she were not totally terrified. It was a difficult choice, but she could tell that Declan Hunter was not "right" in the head. (If he ever had been).

Dec moved like an automaton. He pushed a chair from along the wall underneath the overhead fixture. He climbed atop the chair, light bulb in hand. He removed the dark bulb, inserted the new bulb. It lit up the dingy interior of the cabin.

Kelly thought, *How many lunatics does it take to screw in a light bulb? Answer? One: Declan Hunter.* She saw the vacant look on his face. Declan was emotionless. Mentally absent. Strange. Weird.

Kelly noticed a room approximately twelve feet from the foot of her bunk, although she could only see a small part of it. It was a bathroom. A sink was visible. Kelly's eyes were still adjusting to the gloom created mid-day by the boarded-up windows.

Finally, Kelly decided she would calmly question her captor.

"What are you doing, Mr. Hunter?"

It was a logical question.

Declan Hunter climbed down from the chair. He fixed his attention on the young blonde girl handcuffed to the homemade scaffolding. There were ready-made bunk bed sets. But Declan Hunter wanted the supportive material to be of metal, not wood. He wanted to save money for the always cash-starved facility. And Declan wanted a metal rod or pole to which handcuffs could be attached.

Declan fixed a baleful gaze on Kelly Carter.

"I don't want you girls to leave me. Everyone always leaves me. I want you to stay."

Kelly was not sure what she should say to something so obviously loony. Just the way Declan Hunter looked when he said it made it clear that he was deranged. His hair was disheveled. His hands shook. His eyes had an absent look. It was as though he were physically there, but psychologically, he was a million miles away. Periodically, a sound from outside the still-open door would cause him to twitch. Finally, he approached the door. Slammed it shut, causing Kelly to involuntarily jump. She was trying to get as far away from this madman as possible.

"Why did you do that to Heather? She's your niece!"

Kelly was unable to stop herself from asking.

"I had to give Heather something to help her sleep. She's been having trouble sleeping, you know." Declan totally ignored the question about his motives for kidnapping the two friends and drugging his niece.

He wandered over and stood above the inert form of the lovely blonde girl, his sister's child. Then Declan returned to face Kelly, six feet away.

"Heather has bad dreams about watching Jeremy Gustaffsson die. I have bad dreams about watching people die, too. I know how it is. When she wakes up, we'll talk about it. We can help one another. I want to help her. You girls can help me."

Kelly gave the frazzled-looking man a sharp look and said, "We have to be home for dinner, you know. They'll be looking for us. Our parents won't know where we are. Do you want your sister to worry about the safety of Heather? Don't you think you should let us go now?"

Kelly's comments were rational, but she was nearly shrieking by the time she finished making them.

"Oh, no. You can't go. Everybody goes. Sooner or later. You're going to be the ones who stay. Heather knows I won't hurt her. I don't want to hurt anyone. I didn't sign up to hurt anyone in Vietnam, either. They made me. Don't be afraid. It'll be all right." Declan smiled. It was a grimace that did nothing to reassure Kelly Carter.

Declan Hunter had a strange expression on his face. He walked towards the door with a halting limp, nerve damage sustained when Earl Scranton shot him on Homecoming Night.

Declan opened the door and walked out. He resembled a member of a zombie Apocalypse, slouching towards Armageddon.

Chapter Fifteen:
January 16, 2005, Sunday

Blessing or Curse?

When Kelly Carter finally drifted off to sleep Saturday night, her wrist was chafed raw from trying to free it from the handcuffs pinioning her to the metal rod. Although Kelly had not succeeded—yet—she thought she might be able to when daylight came. It was hard to see what she was doing in the darkness of the unheated cabin.

She was cold. Tired. Panicked.

Stay calm, thought Kelly. *We have to figure a way out of this mess.*

Right now, with Heather unconscious on the bunk across from her, it was up to Kelly to formulate a plan.

She had one significant ray of hope. Although Kelly never thought her hypermobile metacarpo-phalangeal joints would help save her life— (she considered the condition a curse, not a blessing) —she now realized that it might come in handy.

Kelly's classmates used the layman's term: "double jointed." That was a misnomer. Kelly was able to move her joints—especially her hands and fingers—in ways that were definitely abnormal. She had much greater flexibility than the average person. She could bend her thumb back to her wrist, for example.

Declan Hunter did not know this. In fact, Kelly generally tried not to mention it. It was a chronic, painful, hereditary condition. Kelly had made up her mind not to dwell on painful things in life, like her little brother's tragically inevitable death.

The drawback to Kelly's ability was that joint hypermobility was linked to panic disorder. Kelly definitely felt panicked. She tried very hard in her daily life never to worry. She always attempted not to think long or hard about troubling matters she couldn't do anything about. She followed a version of the old Serenity Prayer that advised people to know what they could control, to have the courage to change the things they could change, and to possess the wisdom to know the difference.

That last category included Stevie Scranton's disappearance, Joe Jamison's obsession with Kelly adopting his surname (which had yet to be resolved), her little brother's fatal illness, and this hereditary condition which often caused those who had it to feel anxious and depressed. Her coping mechanism caused Kelly to adopt a lackadaisical attitude towards life. If she let her true inner feelings have free rein, she'd be inviting hysteria and depression.

On the other hand, another successful coping mechanism was to tone the patients' muscles. Many of those with hypermobility syndrome took up activities like yoga. However, if you were an athlete or a gymnast—both of which applied to Kelly—you could acquire hyper mobility from exercises such as those Janet Sloan, their phys ed teacher and cheerleading coach, insisted the cheerleading squad perform during cheerleading workouts. So, as with everything in life, there were pros and cons of stepping up her already rigorous exercise regimen.

Kelly remembered reading a study while waiting in her doctor's office. The study on hypermobility syndrome, conducted in 1998, found that there was a 70% correlation between patients with joint hyper mobility syndrome and panic disorder. That was a very high correlation, when compared to a control group that had only a 10.1% correlation.

As treatment, Kelly meditated. She breathed deeply, as her therapist had taught her to do, to relieve the panic attack she felt coming on right now. Her heart beat loudly in her chest. The sound pounded in her ears. The sensation beneath her ribs felt like a closed fist growing tighter and tighter. She was beginning to hyperventilate.

In response, Kelly visualized a sunny day and a field of flowers. She tried to pretend that the field was right in front of her. She could lie down in the flowers any time she wanted. She could almost smell the scent of clover and new-mown hay. A musky dandelion scent reached her nostrils.

So, Kelly thought, *the joint thing may help. For once. When I can see what I'm doing, that is; I'm feeling too panicked at the moment.* She smiled in spite of herself. *Some weird guy I don't know just handcuffed us to bunk beds in a dilapidated freezing cabin in the middle of nowhere and left us here all night. No wonder I feel panicked! It would be strange if I DIDN'T feel panicked.*

Nightfall. One day later. Sunday.

Heather Crompton was stirring.

Chapter Sixteen:
January 17, 2005, Monday

Images

Tad had not had a bad dream for months. Tonight was different.

The police called to ask Tad if he knew anything about the whereabouts of Heather Crompton or Kelly Carter. Jenny called Tad first.

"Tad—Heather and Kelly are still missing! It's been two whole days!" Jenny sounded upset. "Where could they have gone? What could they be doing? They didn't have a car. They'd have to be on foot, unless…"

Here she trailed off, not wanting to articulate her worst fears.

"The cops asked me if I knew anything, but I don't. I did hear that the Cromptons and Carters are offering a $25,000 reward for information leading to their return," said Jenny.

"You should help the police find them, Tad. You know more than anyone about looking for a missing person. Get Charlie and anyone else who helped find Stevie. Don't wait." Jenny said all this in a rush, as though she had to get it out quickly or she'd choke on the words. "Please don't wait. Every hour they're gone the trail grows colder."

"That's not a bad idea, Jenny, as long as the police don't mind. I'll give Charlie a call right away. See if we can mobilize a few people to pass out flyers. I'm sure the police department will help us. Let me get off the phone and call Charlie."

The first call to Charlie Chandler's Regency Suites apartment went unanswered. It wasn't until the second or third ring that Charlie picked up. He sounded out-of-breath.

"Charlie—is that you?" Tad hoped he hadn't interrupted anything. It was late to be calling his old friend. The two had talked constantly during the search for Stevie, so Tad dove right into the conversation without identifying himself.

"Yes, Tad. It's me. I live here—remember? I was in the shower. What's got your panties in a bunch?"

"I want us to help find Heather and Kelly. Let's put the old team back together. We should help the police any way we can. Are you in?"

"Sure. Why not? I always appreciated citizen support when I was a cop. I can get Evelyn to lend us the full support of her current status as a Lieutenant." (*Evelyn had received a promotion for being instrumental in Stevie's return.*)

"We'll meet tomorrow at your place—okay? I'll stop by after school," Tad said.

"Sure thing, Kid. Whatever you say."

January 18, 2005, Tuesday.

The next school day flew by.

All anyone could talk about was the disappearance of Heather Crompton and Kelly Carter. Yellow ribbons were tied around trees. Students and teachers were buzzing.

As night fell, Tad decided he'd turn in early, since, after school, the old team that helped find Stevie would meet again. He was nervous, but in a good way.

January 19, 2005, Wednesday, Midnight.

Flashes of color. White snow. Bare trees. Crunching gravel. Brown. A man. Hunched over. Carrying a slender girl in his arms. Tad tried to identify the man in his dream. No luck. The dream was fragmented. The effect when your color television signal breaks up in bad weather.

Tad saw the man's hands placing the limp form of Heather Crompton on a bed. Brown blanket. The same anonymous man's hands placed her right wrist in a handcuff. A hypodermic needle lay on the floor.

What is happening? Where are they? Is Heather alive?

The man with the gray-green aura limped from the room. What room? Where are they? Who is the man?

Tad could see nothing specific to help him identify the setting. The room was dark. He heard screaming.

He awoke to the realization the screaming was the sound of his own voice.

Chapter Seventeen:
January 18, 2005, Tuesday

Heather Awakens

"Heather! Heather!" The urgency in Kelly Carter's voice conveyed itself to the half-conscious girl. "Wake up!"

Heather's eyelids fluttered as she awoke to the dimly lit interior of a rustic cabin. Uncle Dec entered.

"Uncle Dec, what are you doing! Let us go! Why do you have us handcuffed? My wrist is killing me. And I really have to pee."

To emphasize this last statement, Heather squirmed atop the faded, brown blanket of her bunk bed prison.

Declan began fumbling with Heather's right wrist. He used the key to the handcuffs to free her, so she could use the primitive bathroom.

"I told you. I told you when you came. I want to help you. I know you experienced what I did. Murder. Violence. It's given you insomnia, just like it did me. Nora told me. That's why I gave you the shot. To help you sleep. And to keep you calm until I could explain. You two will stay with me. Nobody ever stays. But you two will."

Declan Hunter said all this in a flat monotone. Emotionless. Passive. A detached tone of voice, as though he were commenting on something ordinary. He looked at Heather with a hopeful half-smile.

"No! We can't stay here! We have lives, Uncle Dec. I live with my mom and dad. You know that. You've been at our house, for heaven's sake."

Heather seemed to be pleading one minute and angry the next. "Just let us go. Just let us go. Take us back. We'll never tell anyone about any of this. We promise. We'll say we were going to run away, but we changed our minds. Won't we, Kelly?" The frantic look in Heather's eyes gave the lie to her promises.

Heather looked across the space separating the twin-sized bunk beds at Kelly, who seemed to be trying very hard to keep it together. Kelly said nothing. She just shook her head vigorously in silent agreement. There were murmurs of, "We won't tell a soul!" from both girls.

"I'll take you to the bathroom, Heather. But you have to promise me you won't try to do anything stupid. Your friend is out here with me. If you try to escape, I might have to hurt her. I don't like hurting people. I never wanted to hurt anyone. But that was my job. It will be my job to hurt your friend if you don't come right back here when you're finished." Declan glared at Heather.

Heather wondered where her uncle thought she could go? The bathroom had no window. The rest of the cabin had windows, but they were boarded up, with only gimlet-sized cracks of light filtering in around the edges of the plywood that covered the glass.

Dec helped Heather to her feet and escorted her to the rest room, almost gallantly.

Kelly was now alone in the larger room with the madman. She tried to avoid eye contact. She had read once that you should never make eye contact with a wild animal. The creature would consider it a signal to attack. Kelly was frightened. Her fear was not allayed by Declan Hunter's promise to hurt her if Heather did not behave herself.

Heather shut the door to the bathroom. The two waiting outside could hear the toilet flush, followed by water running in the rust-stained old white pedestal-style sink. The door opened. Heather walked back into the larger room very slowly, cautiously eyeing her uncle.

Declan turned to Kelly. "Now it's your turn." He re-fastened Heather's right wrist to the metal scaffolding and moved towards

Kelly to release her left hand. Kelly cringed. She tried to pull away from the odd stranger. She also needed to use the rest room. She finally shut her eyes and waited. Declan Hunter used a key to unlock the handcuffs that pinioned her left hand in place. As with Heather, Dec helped the girl to her feet in an almost courtly fashion. Kelly was unsteady on her feet, her blood pressure temporarily unstable as she stood for the first time since Saturday, seventy-two hours ago. Declan Hunter escorted her towards the rustic cabin's bathroom. Kelly entered and shut the door.

While Kelly was gone, Declan Hunter sank down on her bunk, facing his niece. He spoke. "You have to realize, Heather. I don't want to hurt you. I want to *help* you. You and I are alike in many ways. One similarity is that we both have watched people die. Right before our eyes, they died violent deaths—and we couldn't do a damned thing about it."

Declan was comparing his Vietnam combat experiences to Heather's wild night on Lover's Lane, watching Jeremy Gustaffsson die and running for her life from Pogo.

Heather regarded her uncle like a cat watches its prey before it pounces. She listened intently. Her life might depend on it. She didn't speak. Uncle Dec looked upset as he continued to talk about the violence each of them had witnessed.

"What you have to realize is that I brought you here to *help* you. And to help *me*. We can talk about how you felt when you saw Jeremy die. I can confide in you about what I saw and heard in 'Nam. Kelly can lend moral support. I can help you adjust to a new life. A life where we help each other, not hurt each other. A life where we forget about all the bad things and concentrate on the good things." Declan's frozen weird smile made his strange statement frightening to his young niece.

"But, Uncle Dec—Kelly doesn't *have* any post-traumatic stress disorder, like you and I have. Let her go. She's not part of this. Let her go home." Heather pleaded for her friend's life.

"Oh, I can't do that, honey. They'd come, you know. They'd come to take you both away from me. And I've already had almost everything taken away from me. My humanity. My compassion. Very nearly my life. Did you know I was wounded five times in Vietnam? I got the Purple Heart when I was shot in the back the first time. And the Silver Star, too. Highest civilian award after the Medal of Honor. But it's all crap. They give you a hunk of metal for screwing up your life. I don't have anyone to talk to. To be with. To care for me. You and Kelly can change that. You are going to stay. You can help me. And I can help you."

The glittering zealot look in Declan Hunter's eyes was completely terrifying both girls.

Heather hoped that the look in her own eyes didn't give away her true feelings. She had always known her Uncle Declan was "different," but she did not know that he was completely insane.

Just then, Kelly returned from the bathroom.

Declan Hunter re-handcuffed Kelly's left wrist to the metal strut. He said, "I'm going to bring you some food now. You can use your free hand. It's just pizza. But when I get your new lodgings finished, you both can cook for me. There'll be a kitchen and everything." Declan smiled. A twisted, wan smile full of pain.

"I just need to finish putting in the ventilation ducts. And I want to make sure that the television works underground."

When Heather heard the word underground, she looked at Kelly, seated behind Dec. Kelly shook her head "no" vigorously, urging Heather not to say anything.

Declan Hunter left, then returned with a pizza. He placed one-half of the pizza on a plate on Heather's bunk bed and one-half of it on Kelly's. He gave each girl a cold Diet Coke in a plastic bottle.

The girls were ravenous. They fell upon the lukewarm pepperoni pizza like starving forest creatures.

Which, in a way, they were.

Chapter Eighteen:
January 18, 2005, Tuesday

Tad Speaks to Charlie

Tad took the steps up to Charlie's second-floor Regency Suites apartment two at a time at four o'clock, right after school let out for the day.

This meeting wasn't like the one held around the swimming pool last fall, when the two were planning how best to find Stevie Scranton. It was the dead of winter now. The days were long and cold and gray. A blizzard was sweeping in from Canada to the north. It was expected to hit northern Iowa by nightfall. That made the urgency of the search for the two missing girls even greater.

What if the girls were lost outside? They could freeze to death in weather like this. It had been twenty below zero last night. With the wind chill, tonight it was even colder.

Tad knocked twice. Charlie answered the door immediately. He was dressed—unlike Tad's visit to Charlie's place two months ago. There were papers and maps spread out on the kitchen table behind him.

"Come on in, young man! Long time, no see," said Charlie. "How goes the battle?"

The old running joke, the phrase borrowed from Tad's dad, Jim McGreevy. It always made Tad smile when Charlie used it.

Tad noticed a woman's blue cardigan sweater draped casually across the back of one of the kitchen chairs. He wondered if it was

Belinda's, Charlie's daughter who lived next door, or Andrea SanGiovanni's. The rumor mill had Charlie and Andrea going steady—if that outdated term fit when the couple in question was as old as Charlie and Andrea.

"So, how is school going?" Charlie eased into the conversation.

"It's fine, Charlie. I asked Jenny SanGiovanni to the Winter Formal this coming weekend. She said yes." Tad smiled.

"I know," said Charlie. "Andrea told me." His craggy eyebrows lifted. Steam rose from his coffee cup.

"What's up with you and Andrea?" Tad asked. Then he quickly added, "If you don't mind me asking, that is."

"Naaah. I don't mind you asking. But ask me no questions and I'll tell you no lies," Charlie said, followed by a short laugh. "How's that for an answer?"

"I guess it's as good an answer as a lie would have been, Mr. Chandler."

"Oh—so it's MISTER Chandler now, is it?"

Charlie reached across the kitchen table and pulled off his young charge's stocking cap.

The last time he could remember Tad sitting in his kitchen, wearing that same cap, was shortly before the gunfight at the O.K. Corral, as he called the events of November 12th, 2004, when Earl Scranton died, along with Daniel Malone and Principal Peter Puck. Tad had come to this very kitchen the day after the election of George W. Bush. The two had talked about W's election. Tad had warned Charlie there would be a shooting at the Homecoming game. Charlie then set Rita up in the press box, just in case Tad's premonition came true.

Remembering that morning led to Charlie's next question.

"Have you seen anything in those nightmares of yours? Anything that might help us locate Kelly and Heather, I mean. You *do* know that the town thinks they either fell through the ice and drowned or ran away? Doesn't seem likely, since there are no holes in the ice and the cops have scoured the area. Plus, their skates were found on the riverbank. And they had no vehicle."

"Yes. I heard that. And I have had a dream. I can tell you that at least one of the girls is still alive."

Charlie, hearing the news, relaxed noticeably. It was as though he had been sitting at attention. Now all the starch went out of his posture. He slumped in his kitchen chair, looking relieved.

"Really? You saw that?"

"I did. Last night. In a dream."

"What else did you see?" asked Charlie.

"I only saw Heather Crompton. Someone was carrying her body. She was either dead or asleep. For sure she wasn't in the river."

"Where do you think she is?" Charlie suddenly became completely serious.

"I don't know. And I don't know who was carrying her. It was a man. He set her down on a cot or bed with a brown blanket covering it. I didn't see his face. I didn't see Kelly, either."

Charlie thought about this for a moment. Then he lifted his omnipresent coffee cup and took a sip. He made a noise. It was a "harrumphing" sound, as though he were startled and thinking over this new information.

"Weird. I wonder if the girls are still together? Maybe whoever took Heather has separated her from Kelly."

Charlie's eyes darted from side to side, as though pondering all the options. You could almost hear the gears in his head turning, silently examining different possibilities, a computer processing information.

"Did you see anything else that might help us find them? Find her?"

"You know how my dreams are, Charlie. Flashes of color. Disjointed images. Whoever this guy is, though, he has the color of evil. He *has* killed people. I know it." Tad shivered.

"Do you think he's already killed Kelly?" Charlie asked.

"I don't know, Charlie. I don't know much of anything—yet."

"Don't worry, Kid. We'll figure it out, just like we figured out where Stevie was. Don't forget: we got him back. I'll give Evelyn a buzz. She'll be off work in fifteen minutes. She wants to join us."

With that, Charlie speed dialed Evelyn Hoeflinger's number.

Chapter Nineteen:
January 18, 2005, Tuesday

Kelly's Plan

When Declan Hunter left the two girls imprisoned in the dimly lit cabin, they were eating pizza. Both girls were ravenous. It was the first solid food they had eaten in three days. Aside from eagerly sucking down some water from the faucet of the rusty sink during their bathroom breaks, the Diet Cokes were the only liquid they'd drunk in days.

At one point, Heather looked over at Kelly, held up the empty Coke bottle and said, "Do you think this could be made into some kind of weapon?"

"No idea," said Kelly, mumbling, her mouth full of pizza.

When the two finished their food, Heather asked Kelly, "What are we going to do now? How are we going to get out of here? He's obviously nuts! I'm scared, Kelly."

Kelly had been waiting for Heather to wake up for over twenty-four hours, so she could explain the plan she had concocted while Heather slept. Heather was unconscious all of Sunday and most of Monday. Only now had the drug's effects worn off. Kelly was afraid to try to explain her plan to a groggy girl who might not remember what you said to her five minutes later. Now was the moment.

"Do you remember that I have hypermobility syndrome?" Kelly finally asked. She looked at Heather carefully, trying to determine how alertly she was listening.

"What? Oh! You mean you're double-jointed, right?" Heather responded.

The cheerleaders all knew this about Kelly. They would tease her about it sometimes, suggesting that Kelly's boyfriends probably would appreciate this talent one day.

"You can call it that, if you want. It's not right. But everybody calls it that." Kelly seemed miffed for a moment. "Anyway, I think I can get out of this handcuff. I didn't want to do it before you were awake. I figured Nut Boy would probably come back in here to give us a bathroom break. Maybe feed us. Both of those things have happened. So he should be gone for a while. I'm going to try to get out of this handcuff before it's feeding time at the zoo again. Then, I'll try to break you out. One of us needs to get out of this room and go for help." Kelly looked around at the shabby cabin. "I can't wait to get out of here. This place gives me the creeps!"

Heather said. "Go for it!"

Kelly sat up straight on her bunk bed. She used her free right hand to bend her thumb back all the way flush with her wrist. Watching it made Heather groan. It looked absolutely impossible and excruciatingly painful.

"Don't worry," Kelly said. "If you inherit a shallow joint socket, instead of a deep one, you have a big range of movement. My doctor says I have shallow joint sockets. I think I can bend my thumb back far enough that the cuff will pass over four fingers. Or what will *feel* like four fingers. Stretching the ligament so that my thumb moves back against my wrist should help my hand fit through the handcuff opening. That's what I'm hoping, anyway. That's my plan. Did I mention that panic attacks go along with this disorder?" Kelly gave Heather a harried look. "Please help keep me calm."

"I can't watch!" Heather said, after a few minutes of Kelly's contortions with her hand. Heather wore the look that teen-agers get during horror movies when the killer strikes: a mixture of terror and shock. Kelly's hand was bent at an awkward angle. The way she was tugging on her thumb with all of her might, using her right hand to

76

pull the thumb of her left hand as far back as possible, was a gruesome sight.

"We're in luck on another front, too, girlfriend. I'm more flexible right before my period. That's another reason I'm anxious to get out of here ASAP. Almost that time of the month. My doctor tells me I have hands like Indian people. Not American Indians— Indian Indians. Indian people's hands are more flexible than European people's hands. Anyway, I never thought this was something I'd be glad I had. It hurts like crazy most of time when we're working out or when the weather changes. And the other cheerleaders always tease me about it. But it just may set us free."

Heather nodded. She said, "Do your best, Kelly. I don't think reasoning with my uncle is going to help. He acts like he's gone round the bend. He and Mrs. Eisenstadt should be sharing a cell in Independence."

In spite of herself, Kelly chuckled. Sarah Eisenstadt had been locked up in the Independence Mental Health Institute's dangerous felons' wing ever since murdering her two children. She'd never get out. But she would go to trial soon. Heather Crompton had just pronounced Declan Hunter to be a logical roommate for Dr. Eisenstadt's insane wife.

Kelly kept pulling on her left hand thumb until a horrible noise, similar to the cracking of a knuckle, but louder, echoed in the stillness of the room. Kelly's thumb had bent all the way back to her wrist. She slipped her hand through the restraint.

Kelly got to her feet and approached Heather's bunk bed. She was unsteady and in shock from all that had happened. She looked closely at the handcuff securing Heather's wrist to the metal supports. Then she shook her head in the universally understood gesture for "no."

"I don't think I can get you free, Heather. But if I escape, I can bring help."

"Do it! Do whatever you have to do. I'll be all right. After all, I'm his niece! He keeps saying he just wants us to stay with him. It will be better if it's me who gets left behind." Heather looked solemn. "We'll keep it all in the family." She looked at Kelly, wide-eyed, and said, "Boy! You can't trust anybody any more, can you? This is *my own uncle!*" The emphasis on the final three words conveyed her utter disbelief.

"Don't worry. I'll bring help. Somehow, I'll get out of here. I'll find a road. There'll be someone who'll help us. The whole town has to be looking for us."

Kelly was right about that.

"How are you going to get out of here?" Heather asked. "He's got the door locked. I heard the deadbolt."

"I think I can break out a window. One window has the plywood nailed to the inside of the frame, not the outside. I'll pry that off. Find something to break out the glass—assuming there *is* glass to be broken out."

"Won't he hear?"

"Maybe. Maybe not. We don't know where he is. He said something about going underground. Did you hear that?"

Heather nodded yes. "I heard it. I didn't like the sound of that. Please bring help! Fast!" The look of fear in Heather's eyes mirrored Kelly's own.

Kelly nodded and approached the window that she intended to turn into Freedom Road. She began prying up the plywood nailed to the logs of the inside of the log cabin window, starting from the bottom right corner and struggling to pry the plywood off and up.

Chapter Twenty:
January 18, 2005, Tuesday

Charlie's Place

The team gathered at Charlie's Regency Suites condominium had swelled to seven: Charlie, Tad, Andrea and Jenny SanGiovanni, Evelyn Hoeflinger—who had come straight from her police shift—Stevie Scranton and Janice Kramer. For Stevie and Janice, it was an opportunity to meet without Janice's parents realizing that Stevie was part of Charlie's group.

"Do you think we should order some food?" Evelyn was hungry. She had arrived at five thirty. It was now close to eight o'clock. Nobody in Charlie's overcrowded kitchen had eaten dinner.

When no one objected, Evelyn moved to the phone. She called in an order for Kentucky Fried chicken.

"We need flyers and lots of them," Charlie told the troops. He looked over at Stevie. "When you went missing, Stevie, we distributed close to fifty thousand flyers. There wasn't a telephone pole or store window that didn't display your picture."

"Gee. I didn't know I was such a major celebrity," Stevie said, ruefully. Janice punched him in the shoulder.

"No. Seriously. We need to get these out. And when I say 'out,' I mean distributed within at least a one-hundred-and-fifty mile radius, if we can. Evelyn, can you see if the police department will help us make flyers?" Charlie remembered how his small Canon copier burned out from overuse. The Canon was in no condition to take on another desperate rescue mission.

"Sure thing, Boss," Evelyn said, giving a mock salute.

"What about using the Internet?" Tad asked.

"You kids take care of that, okay? We old fogies don't use the Internet much. Do whatever you can."

Tad nodded his head, committing to spreading the word electronically with the help of Jenny, Stevie and Janice.

Stevie didn't have the experience the others accumulated from rescuing him, but he now made a suggestion.

"You know, Lenny McIntyre is our Officer Friendly at school. I'll bet he'd help us distribute some of these flyers to outlying communities. He could drive them to places like Dysart, Jesup, Independence, Hazelton, Evansdale, Waterloo—really, any place we ask. Lenny likes to be in on what's happening."

"Good idea, Stevie! The banks and stores will pay more attention to a cop. I do remember that Lenny was very fascinated with the siege of your house, Andrea. He seemed to want to be more involved. Ask him, Stevie. Excellent suggestion!"

Stevie beamed. Janice smiled at Stevie's enthusiasm. This time, he was one of the rescuers—not the person who *needed* rescuing.

Andrea spoke up, asking a question. "Do you think we should continue searching for some sort of break in the ice where the girls might have fallen through? Or will the police have covered that angle thoroughly?"

Evelyn answered Andrea's question. "I'll see to it that the department investigates the entire riverfront area. Personally, I think it's unlikely the girls are in the river."

"Why do you say that, Evelyn?" Andrea asked a logical question.

"Well, for one thing, I read the police report over just before I joined you. There is evidence that some sort of van was parked on the road near where the girls' skates were found. Three sets of footprints in the snow lead to the van."

"Did it look like the girls went willingly?" Charlie asked his old partner.

"There was no sign of a struggle or of anyone being dragged by force, if that's what you mean, Charlie." That was exactly what Charlie meant.

"So, the department is checking to find out what sort of vehicle made the tire tracks, I assume?" Charlie and Evelyn lapsed into an easy camaraderie indicative of their years together on the force.

"Yes, but the road was pretty heavily traveled. There is really no definitive way to determine which of the many sets of tire tracks might be the right vehicle. That's a pretty busy road down below the Cromptons' house. It's really surprising that nobody saw the girls get into any kind of car or truck or van." Evelyn shook her head slowly from side to side. The gesture conveyed a feeling of helplessness at the lack of solid information in the case.

The chicken arrived. A brief break while the Starving Seven, as Stevie had dubbed the group, ate. It was close to nine o'clock on a school night.

Charlie said, "Okay, Kids. Let's get going. You all know what you have to do. We'll meet back here at five o'clock on Friday. In the three days between now and then let's get the flyers made and out everywhere we can. Is that time okay with everybody?" The group agreed. The meeting broke up.

Stealing a line from an old television show that had been one of his favorites during its run eighteen years earlier, Charlie said, "Be careful out there."

None of the four young people realized Charlie was quoting Sergeant Phil Esterhaus from "Hill Street Blues."

Only Evelyn and Andrea laughed, which puzzled the four young Sky High seniors.

Chapter Twenty-One:
January 18, 2005, Tuesday

The Escape

Kelly worked feverishly. She pried the lower corner of the plywood square covering the window nearest her bed up with her hands until a nail broke. A loud "Ouch!" caused Heather to ask, "What happened?"

"Never wear Lee Press-On Nails when trying to escape from a maniac," Kelly muttered under her breath.

Of course, the nail that had just sheared off at fingertip level was Kelly's *real* fingernail. Breaking it hurt like hell!

No point in whining about it to Heather, thought Kelly. *She's still got a wrist in handcuffs. That can't feel good after three days.*

Nevertheless, Kelly took a moment to suck on her sore finger, which burned with pain. She grimaced slightly, then went back to work.

Kelly grasped the now-loosened bottom right corner of the piece of plywood firmly in both hands and pulled up on the board with all her might. She was grunting like Maria Sharapova during a close tennis match.

"You're doing great, Kelly!" Heather tried to encourage and calm her friend.

Kelly looked around the room and saw the rickety chair. Declan Hunter had used it while changing the cabin's light bulb. She realized that once she successfully removed the plywood from the window, she'd need something to break out the window itself—whether glass or screen. The only piece of furniture in the bare cabin, other than the two bunk beds, was the chair.

Kelly walked to the chair. Grasped it firmly in her hands. Smashed it as hard as she could on the wooden floor of the cabin. It took three such efforts to dislodge a leg of the straight back chair. Once Kelly had this lever, she inserted it under the now-loosened plywood corner, to finally, triumphantly, bring down the wooden barrier. Kelly remembered some Greek philosopher they had studied in history class—Archimedes, she thought— said all you need to move the world is a lever.

I hope Archie was right, she thought, grasping the chair leg firmly. She had a determined look on her face.

The glass in the window was gone, but a screen still barred the way to freedom. Kelly took the leg of the broken chair and used it like a baseball bat, swinging at the screen with all her might.

The screen never had a chance. It gave way on the first blow. Kelly experienced an adrenaline rush. Fight or flight. Flight, in this case.

Her bunk bed was close enough to the window that she could stand on the bottom level bunk. She could use it as a stepping stool to gain access to the window, now gaping wide. The plywood covering was on the floor beneath the window. Kelly was athletic and in the best condition of her young life. She grabbed the coarse brown scratchy Army blanket from her bunk. She placed it over the bottom of the window where the screening had been attached. As the finger with the broken nail made contact with the coarse cloth, the pain was excruciating. She didn't want to cut or scratch herself on the pieces of wire screening that protruded from the window frame, which might gouge her when she climbed through the window.

"Good work, Kelly!" Heather said. "Keep going. Don't worry about me. Remember: I'm Declan's niece. He might not let me go, but he isn't going to hurt me. Go get help!"

"I'll be back for you. I promise," said Kelly. She stepped onto her bed and prepared to hoist her slight frame over the edge of the broken-out window. The window opening was five feet up from the floor of the cabin.

Kelly felt the scratchy blanket on her knees as she teetered on the edge of the open window frame. It was not dark out yet. Dusk was coming fast, a good sign.

Once I get out this window, it'll be harder to find me in the dark, she thought.

She prayed that Declan Hunter would not hear the sound of the plywood falling back inside the cabin nor the noise of the window screen falling onto the grass outside.

Kelly took one last deep breath and heaved her small body over the edge of the window frame as though performing a gymnastic maneuver on the balance beam. She dropped headfirst to the ground below, holding her hands out to break her fall. When she was perched in the open window briefly and looked down, there was no glass or gravel visible beneath the window frame. For this, Kelly was grateful.

When she landed, she had the wind temporarily knocked out of her. She gasped. Struggled to quickly catch her breath.

Calm. Remain calm, she cautioned herself. *Remember what Heather said: he's not going to hurt us. He's just nuts. Oh? Is that all? Just crazy? No worries, then.* Kelly breathed deeply, trying to overcome her mounting hysteria.

Stress was Kelly's excuse for her political incorrectness. She would never normally use inappropriate terms for mental illness. If she hadn't been kidnapped and held captive against her will for days and weren't under extreme duress, she would never resort to calling a mentally ill person "nuts" or "crazy." Kelly's own sanity was teetering just this side of outright panic.

Stunned and out-of-breath, Kelly got to her feet. She ran as quickly and quietly as she could around the corner of the shoebox-shaped cabin, heading towards the road that ran alongside the entrance. Kelly planned to follow the gravel road out of the compound.

Too bad it isn't Heather who's *double-jointed. She's been here before. She'd know which way to go,* thought Kelly, feeling hassled.

As she rounded the corner, a hand grabbed her left arm roughly. "Just where do you think you're going, young lady?"

Declan Hunter had placed a tray holding the girls' evening meal on the ground. He had heard the sound of Kelly landing outside the window.

He dragged the terrified young girl back inside the cabin, while Kelly futilely screamed and struggled.

Chapter Twenty-Two:
January 18, 2005, Tuesday

Darkness Falls

"I'm sorry, Heather," Kelly said, as she and Declan re-entered the cabin. She was choking back tears. So close. And yet so far.

Heather looked up, alarmed.

"Uncle Dec. Let her go! Let *us* go!"

"I can't do that, Heather. You're here so that I can help you and you can help me. I told you: I'm tired of everybody leaving me. I just caught your friend Kelly trying to leave me. Why would she do that? Can't I trust you two girls? Isn't anybody trustworthy any more?" Declan's voice sounded outraged.

"This isn't right, Uncle Dec. Our parents are worried. I'm your own niece. Don't you care what my mom must be thinking and feeling? Don't you have any empathy for your little sister Nora's feelings?" Heather sounded desperate as she spoke. "We've been gone for three days! We want to go home!"

"Of course, you do. And perhaps you will, in good time. One thing is for sure. You two can't stay here in this drafty old cabin."

By now, Dec had handcuffed Kelly a second time to the metal supports of her bunk bed. The disconsolate girl sat there, wide-eyed. She felt like whimpering, the same way a beaten dog might, but she didn't want to give her captor the satisfaction.

Declan Hunter spoke. "It's a good thing that leaving you two here was just temporary. For one thing, Kelly here ruined the window."

(Declan gestured towards the gaping maw of the screenless frame). "Now it'll be even colder at night." This was the least of the girls' worries.

"It can't get much colder, Uncle Dec. We damn near froze to death in here the past two days." Heather sounded angry. She *was* angry. "It's absolutely frigid in here. My arm is about ready to fall off from being handcuffed for so long. I can barely feel it. I think your handcuff has cut off all the circulation. I'm not kidding." Heather was beyond angry.

"I know. I know. I'm sorry about that. But this cabin was never intended to be your permanent residence," Declan explained.

As he said that, Declan motioned around at the room. He stood in front of the door. The room with the now-broken-out window was letting the harsh wind of January blow freely into the interior. It was below zero outside with a thirty-mile per hour wind blowing slushy snow across the rudimentary roads. No one with any sense was out in this kind of weather.

"I've been working on your real room for a long time. Ever since I came back to Cedar Falls, in fact. I just had to get some more PVC pipe and a few other things. I've been trying to make sure that you two will be able to watch your favorite TV shows while you're with me." Declan looked momentarily peeved. "You two should be thanking me for going to all this trouble to make your new accommodations much better than this cabin. I never intended for you to stay here (*gesturing around the room*). This was always meant to be temporary."

Declan Hunter walked back outside. He picked up the tray he'd placed on the ground when he heard Kelly's fall. Hamburgers in a McDonald's bag. French-fry containers. Ketchup packets.

"I don't know what you girls like on your burgers. I'll find out as we learn to live together. It'll be fun—just like camping out in the woods!" Declan gave the girls a goofy grin.

Totally out-of-touch with reality, Heather thought.

"We're going to move you to a warmer, cozier place than this. And yes, Heather, I need to get you out of those handcuffs. Now that I've installed the wider pipe in your new home, I can do that. I'll take your handcuffs off permanently just as soon as you finish eating."

He turned to give Kelly a stern look. "Kelly: don't try that handcuff escape trick again. I'm not going anywhere. I'll wait here while you two finish eating. Then I'll show both of you to your new home." Declan Hunter gave each girl one of his strange bird-like stares, with an eerie smile. "I'm taking you there one at a time. You first, Kelly."

Declan handed each girl a cold bottle of Diet Coke. He had unscrewed the cap of each Coke bottle before handing them off to the girls.

Declan didn't get the feeling that Heather and Kelly appreciated his efforts to be a good host, but he felt confident they'd come around in time.

Chapter Twenty-Three:
January 21, 2005, Friday

New Recruits

At the second meeting of the ad hoc committee formed to find the missing girls, two new recruits showed up.

Belinda Chandler learned about the group from her father, Charlie. She showed up with her fiancé, the school's chemistry teacher, Kenneth Kellogg.

Kenny Kellogg was 38 years old. Belinda was just about to graduate from the University of Northern Iowa, where she was a senior, majoring in Phys Ed. She was twenty-two. Coach Kellogg had recommended her for her college volleyball scholarship. Then he had recommended some other extra-curricular activities just for the two of them. Belinda had been down with the program for a long time. The two had been dating secretly for years. Belinda was one of Cereal Man's few former students who actually enjoyed getting his phone calls.

Belinda didn't mind that Kenny was sixteen years older than she was. Cereal Man bought her a two-carat diamond ring and promised he was ready to settle down. Belinda was now degreed to work as a Physical Education teacher, but not until she gave birth to Kenny's first child, due in seven months.

Kenny Kellogg had changed a lot in the past two years since he had been seeing Belinda Chandler. When Belinda told him that she was pregnant with his child, he was happy.

"That's great, Belinda! We'll get married. We'll find teaching positions in the same school district," Kenny said.

"Something tells me I won't be doing much coaching *or* teaching for at least a year, Hon. We're having a baby, you know." She smiled at the thought. Ever since her mom's death, despite her dad's attempts to spend more time with her, Belinda had felt lost and alone. She looked forward to starting a family of her own.

Kenny Kellogg, for his part, had finally grown up. He thought to himself, *There's only so long a man can chase tail. Everybody has to mature, sooner or later. It's time. Belinda's a good girl. As an added bonus, she's a terrific lay. She's having my kid, for Chrissakes! I'm not going to abandon her when she needs me most. She's already had some tough stuff to overcome in her life. First, her mother was murdered. Then that maniac Pogo held her hostage. I'll step up. I'll do the right thing, for once.*

Belinda told her father about the engagement and his impending status as a grandparent. He hugged his daughter and smiled. Then, he turned to Kenny Kellogg and said, half in jest, "If you hurt my daughter, I'll kill you. And I don't think you want that." After he made that speech, he punched Kenny Kellogg in the arm and gave him a big bear hug. But Kenny "Cereal Man" Kellogg thought: *Note to self. Do NOT piss off Belinda's father!*

As the conversation continued and the subject of the missing girls, now gone nearly a week, was discussed, Charlie told his daughter and her fiancé about the committee meeting that very night to try to help find the girls. Both instantly volunteered to help.

"I had both of those girls in my chemistry class," Kenny Kellogg said. Secretly, he was glad he had never hit on either of them. "I'd like to help."

Belinda echoed, "Me, too!"

At the meeting in Charlie's kitchen, with the usual suspects present, Belinda sat next to Janice Kramer. Janice couldn't help but notice Belinda's brand new sparkler. Her engagement ring was so large it almost hurt to look at it.

"Wow! That is a gorgeous ring!" Janice said. "Are you two engaged?"

Belinda smiled happily, confirming the news. "Yes. Yes, we are. The stork will be visiting us soon, too."

Later on, leaning in close, Janice confided to Belinda, "I'm pregnant, too."

The two girls made their way to Charlie's bathroom together on a break, and Janice confided in the older girl, "Could you tell I was pregnant before I told you?"

Actually, Belinda could. By this point, Janice was showing. Even though Janice was wearing baggy sweat pants and a sweatshirt to hide her condition, she had that rosy pregnancy glow. Plus, as she was seated next to Stevie, the two could barely keep their hands off one another. It was their only chance to see one another outside of school.

Belinda didn't know whether to answer truthfully (yes) or to jolly the younger girl along. She decided she'd deflect the question by asking a question of her own, an old politician trick.

"When are you due?" Belinda asked.

"May 28th," Janice answered.

"When are you two getting married?" Belinda asked.

A cloud passed across Janice's face. "That's the problem. My parents don't like Stevie. Because of what his dad did. You know."

Belinda nodded. Of course she knew. Everyone in Cedar Falls knew. Everyone in the Midwest who read a newspaper or watched television knew.

"What are you doing to do?" Belinda asked. Janice had her attention and the young girl was obviously in need of someone to talk to about her situation.

"We can't get married in Iowa until I turn eighteen. I don't turn eighteen until May third. Stevie looked up the laws for other states about marrying without parental consent. It's eighteen everywhere. My parents want me to give up my baby. I think they want me to give it to my married sister, Claire, who can't have kids. She's twenty years older than me. They just think I should be *thrilled* at the prospect of giving up my firstborn to Claire. I'm not."

Janice looked glum.

She continued, "My entire idea about this baby has changed since Melody's accident. Before, I didn't know if I wanted to have the baby or not. Now, I know. I wish my parents would support me in my decision. I love Stevie. I want to marry him. I'd want to marry him even if I *weren't* pregnant. He's been wonderful to me."

"You turn eighteen about three weeks before you're due..." said Belinda.

"Yes. My eighteenth birthday's just four days before the Senior Prom," said Janice. She sounded sad. "I'm missing the Winter Formal tomorrow because my parents had a cow about me dating Stevie. My dad kicked him out of our house. If we do get married before the prom, I'll be nearly nine months pregnant."

Janice didn't sound overjoyed at that prospect.

"There's nothing more beautiful than a pregnant woman," said Belinda. She smiled. "I should know. I am one." Both girls laughed. "You should just go and be the sweetest little mama there. And I'll help you out any way I can," said Belinda.

Belinda was thinking how lucky she was to have a man with a good job who could support her, to have completed her college degree, and to have a father who had given his blessing to her marriage.

Belinda said, "This must be tough on you. Not having anyone to talk to about everything, I mean. Feel free to call me any time."

With that, Belinda got one of Kenny Kellogg's business cards out of her purse (*Kenneth Kellogg, Chemistry Department Chairman, Cedar Falls SCI High School*) and wrote her contact information on the back of the card for Janice. Before they left the bathroom, Belinda squeezed Janice's hand and said, "True love will find a way."

"Well, right now, we're both just trying to finish our senior year of high school. Stevie is going to need a full-time job to support me and the baby."

"He seems like a good guy," said Belinda. "Remember: any time. Just call. Or send me an e-mail." Belinda was moved by Janice's tale of her friendship with Melody, the injured cheerleader who still lingered in a coma at Cedar Falls Memorial Hospital.

This girl needs a friend, thought Belinda. *Been there. Done that. After Mom died, I could have used someone older and wiser to talk to. I'll try to do for her what my dad did for me.*

The two returned to the strategy session in Charlie's kitchen.

Chapter Twenty-Four:
January 22, 2005, Saturday

The Winter Formal

Angie Yancy and her steady boyfriend Chris Turgasen double-dated with Jenny and Tad, since Stevie and Janice couldn't.

Angie was the Big Cheese. She had chaired the committee for "Snowflakes are Singular." Everyone was well aware that Kelly Carter—now missing an entire week—had also been a key committee member. The talk at the dance was all about the two missing cheerleaders. Aside from that concern lurking in the background, the dance was a roaring success.

There were just a few mishaps.

The staircase leading to the band balcony, specially constructed to provide a truly grand entrance for the Winter Formal, fell apart almost immediately. Fortunately, the couple using the staircase at the time, Zack Porfino and a girl from Columbus High School he had talked into accompanying him on a first date (Betty Whetty), were on the bottom step when the entire structure came crashing down.

Although the collapse was loud and potentially dangerous, no one was seriously injured.

Some of the dance attendees, including Chris Turgasen and Tad McGreevy, helped the school janitor move the boards and debris to the side of the gym floor. One of the chaperones was stationed at the entrance to the band room from that point on, to deny other arrivals the dubious pleasure of falling to their death while descending the ramshackle structure.

Stewie Truitt, in typical Truitt fashion, marched over to Zack Porfino and his date and said, "I c-c-coulda' been killed. You s-s-saved my l-l-life, Man. Thanks for that! Are y-y-you okay?"

Zack assured the distraught Stewie that neither he nor his date was hurt. Betty Whetty knew no one and had now nearly been killed by a faulty staircase. She would talk about this dance at Sky High for years. And not in a good way. For her, it would be her first and last date with Zack Porfino. She'd only accepted in the first place because Zack drove a hot car.

Much was made of the fact that it was Heather's father, Chris Crompton, a partner in the local building company, who authorized the construction. The carpenters were actually at fault. Normally, Chris Crompton would have been on top of the project. Inspecting it. Making sure that everything was done properly.

Unfortunately, instead of being at the top of his game, Chris Crompton, whose daughter Heather had now been missing for a week, was running on empty. His partner in the construction company was Heather's grandfather, Robert "Bob" Hunter. Neither of the owners of the construction company was paying any attention to the temporary staircase leading from the band room balcony to the gym floor.

Prior to Zack's arrival with Betty Whetty—whose name Stewie Truitt immediately began making fun of —the committee members, including Jenny, Tad, Angie and Chris Turgasen had safely descended using the faulty staircase. Zack was in the wrong place at the wrong time. Or the wrong place at the right time, depending on your point-of-view.

The dance proceeded without further incident.

When Tad dropped Jenny off at her mother's house, the two sat on the porch swing for a while, before she went in for the night. This particular January night was unseasonably warm. They sat there on the porch swing watching their warm breath form small frozen clouds in front of their noses. It was their first "real" date.

"I had a really good time, Tad," Jenny said, breaking the silence.

"Me, too, Jenny. But I'm glad that staircase didn't collapse while we were on it." Both of them laughed. Nervous laughter. Not so much about the staircase as about the two of them finally being alone together on a real date.

"You know—Tad—I'm glad you asked me out again. The first time, I was kind of messed up."

Jenny looked down at her gloved fingers, clutching her hands tightly in her lap.

"I didn't have a very good time at my dad's place in Boulder. When I got back—well, I just wasn't myself for a while."

Jenny left it at that, not mentioning her bouts of cutting, the condition School Counselor Randall had helped her overcome.

"I know, Jenny. It's okay. We're here now, and I'm glad we are. I would have waited even longer for you, Jenny. Surely you know that?"

Tad looked at the girl who had stolen his heart years ago. She smiled back at him. Her eyes brimmed with unshed tears.

"Yes. I know. You've been a good friend to me, Tad. Probably my *best* friend."

Jenny put her gloved hands around Tad's neck and moved to give him a peck on the cheek, but Tad had other ideas.

He turned and kissed Jenny full on the mouth. Warm. Sexy. Smooth. She liked it.

Tad has developed some moves, thought Jenny.

Jenny kissed Tad back. A long lingering kiss. A heartfelt, sincere exchange of emotion.

Tad rose from the porch swing and helped Jenny to her feet.

He put his arms around the much shorter girl. His face leaned down to inhale the exhilarating fragrance of her freshly shampooed hair.

"Call me tomorrow, okay, Jen?" he said. He started to leave.

"Sure thing," she responded. She enjoyed being held in the comforting arms of this tall, handsome boy she had treated so indifferently all these years.

What was I thinking? Where was my head?

Tad held the front door to her house open for her and said, "Thank you for going to the Winter Formal with me. It was perfect. Except for Zack and Betty nearly getting killed and Stevie and Janice not being able to double-date with us." His amused look showed he was kidding.

Both of them laughed.

Tad pecked Jenny on the cheek one last time before descending the porch steps.

Chapter Twenty-Five:
January 18, 2005, Tuesday

Underground

Declan Hunter had secured an old unused gondola railroad freight car. It was cheap, since it had been out of service since the seventies, and perfect at roughly 5,000 cubic feet. Sixty feet long. At least the size of many mobile homes. Dec had considered burying an actual mobile home, but the used freight car was cheaper. It was, quite literally, abandoned.

Free is always good, Dec thought. Dec learned in conversation with the lot owner that a different railroad car on his lot cost $14,500. It was newer and in better shape. It was also out of Declan Hunter's price range.

The business on the edge of Waterloo, Happy Times Sales Lot, had unused freight cars like this one stacked to the skies. The business tried (unsuccessfully) to hide the unsightly stacks of brick red and black freight cars behind equally unsightly fences, attempting to shield the mostly rust-colored eyesore from passing motorists on the nearby highway.

Declan sold the owner of the business a tall tale. He'd be doing a good deed for all the little campers by donating the battered-looking freight car. He'd be helping out a wounded war veteran. Storage, Dec said. He promised to make sure the local newspaper learned of the Happy Times' Lot's magnanimous owner/operator.

Of course, that never happened.

Back when the weather had been warm, but Camp Wapsie "W" empty because the season had ended, Declan made arrangements for a friend who worked for Hunter/Crompton construction locally, to come dig a large hole. He told the friend it was for a new swimming pool for the camp. The friend didn't care. It was a weekend project, for him. A little extra money in his pocket using the Bobcat bulldozer he owned and operated.

A different man with a crane lowered the empty railroad car into the hole prepared for it. That is when Declan Hunter's real work began. Not only did he have to install ventilation and electricity, he had to make sure that the structure would be difficult to enter or leave, except through one trap door.

Anyone wanting to enter or leave had to climb down the fourteen steps to the floor of the former railroad car. Declan intended to conceal the underground lair's very existence from the outside world. This wasn't difficult. The camp was way-the-hell-and-gone away from town. Nobody visited Camp Wapsie "W' in the fall after school started or in the winter. Fewer and fewer young people were signing up for summer camp at all. Video games were more popular. Going camping was for squares.

Declan put in a toilet and shower, with special pumping mechanisms to empty the waste. He made sure that the already-in-place water tower of Camp Wapsie "W" was hooked up to the underground railroad car, to provide running water for bathing and cooking.

Declan had to be very careful that the PVC pipe was of the appropriate size. He intended to place an IED—an improvised explosive device— in the PVC pipe that would bring air to the car's inhabitants. That was his most recent delay. He wanted to plant a "grenade in a can," as they had called them in Vietnam, in the PVC pipe. This was a simple method used in Vietnam by the Viet Cong, who placed a hand grenade with the safety pin removed and the safety lever compressed inside a tin can and attached a length of string or tripwire attached to the grenade. If the grenade was pulled out of the can, placing tension on the string, the spring-loaded safety lever would release. Dec didn't expect to be discovered any time soon, but he wanted to be ready to defend his underground fortress.

Nobody's going to take my new home away from me. And nobody's taking the girls. If they come for the girls, they'll have to come through me, thought Dec as he rigged the grenade in a can and placed it in the PVC pipe.

So, the arming of the cabin (he had another device below ground, plus guns), and the addition of Kelly to the mix, making three inhabitants, instead of the two he had originally planned for, caused the three-day delay in moving the girls from their temporary holding facility: the boarded-up cabin.

Then came the decorating challenge.

Declan wasn't much on interior decorating. There must be beds, dressers, tables, and chairs. All the comforts of home. To provide for privacy, he constructed temporary walls every fifteen feet (the bathroom was smaller), separating the railroad car into a makeshift kitchen area, bathroom, family room and two small bedrooms. Each of these areas save the bathroom was fifteen feet by fifteen feet. The height of the bunker was only six feet, which was just about Declan's height (and less than either girl). Declan moved bunk beds from one of Camp Wapsie "W's" cabins into one half of the bedroom area, for the girls. The two bedrooms and the bathroom were smaller than the other areas. The extra space gained was given over to the family room.

The other side of the underground bunker was Declan's bedroom. It was there that he placed the single twin bed removed from the girls' side. It was there that he kept his .308 Winchester, also known as a 7.62 x 51 mm NATO. His Vietnam weapon, an M-14, was never far from the head of his bed. Declan was in the Army before the change-over to the M-16 in 1970. Since he completed more than one tour of duty, he had both an M-14 and an M-16, kept from his days of reluctant soldiering. As a munitions expert, he also had some other destructive toys, including the grenades he used in his IEDs. He could and would use them against intruders if he had to.

Realizing that he now had two girls, instead of just Heather, he thought it was probably a good thing.

They're just like cats, he thought to himself. *Girls like company. They like to talk more than I like to talk.* He smiled as he thought back to the girls in the van, chattering away as he drove them to their new home.

Declan had no intention of sexually molesting either girl. He would never do that to his own niece.

She's my sister's child. My own flesh-and-blood! he thought to himself. The contradiction of taking his sister's child and holding her hostage didn't occur to his deranged mind. Of course, Declan also would have denied that he would ever molest any child, male or female. But he had.

That was something that only happened because I felt threatened and alone, he thought as he justified his past actions. He wasn't proud of his past. He was sorry he had interfered with Stevie Scranton. Stevie was just a little guy then.

I told Stevie that I loved him. Did Stevie reciprocate? No. He just wanted to leave. Like all the others.

Declan felt intense anger as he thought of the multiple times he had been left.

So many people. Always leaving me. Never staying. Never standing by me.

Declan swore off any vestigial homosexual urges after he got the Camp Wapsie "W" job. He felt it was unbecoming to a war veteran and he had never really considered himself to be gay. He felt ashamed of his past actions in regard to Stevie Scranton, especially after Earl Scranton shot him at the stadium. He was certain Earl was gunning for him because he knew. Declan told himself, *I'm not "twisted" The Bible says it's wrong.* Declan swore off such behavior with underage boys after he was appointed to the Camp Wapsie "W" position. He had honored that pledge. He considered it his "one step at a time" program. Like AA.

Declan did not kidnap Kelly Carter to become his sexual partner, either. She just happened to be with Heather. *It is true,* he thought, *there'd be none of the incest accusations if, some day, Kelly and I were to become a couple. After all,* he thought, *we'll be together forever.*

Declan honestly believed that the end of the world might come at any time. He thought that by being underground, he and the girls might escape the devastation of a nuclear attack. He had plenty of survival supplies on hand. *If the attack comes, somebody will have to repopulate the planet,* he thought. *It might be me.*

Declan Hunter had some serious issues. He lived in a fantasy world. He'd had these problems for a very long time.

January 18, 2005, Tuesday, 2 A.M.

Tad awoke in a sweat. He'd had one of his dreams. The special power, Tetrachromatic Super vision, which allowed Tad to "see" the actions of those with the color of evil (khaki) was working overtime. He was "seeing" the crimes of the unknown evil-doer who had kidnapped Heather and Kelly. The powerlessness of seeing, without the ability to intervene, was unsettling and scary.

Auras. Colors. Extraordinarily bright hues. A reliving of the crimes of killers he saw in his nightmares. Khaki = Killer. Tad shivered.

Underground. Stairs going down. Girls screaming. Who are the girls? Heather? Kelly?

Tad saw a flash of faces. He recognized Kelly and Heather.

Later, Tad would ask himself, *Did I 'see' Kelly and Heather because of my power, or did I see them simply because everybody in town is talking about them and looking for them. Did my subconscious dictate it?*

The wind kicked up outside to near-blizzard conditions. Tad opened the window. The wind blew everything off his bookshelf. His books and papers and picture frames and CDs landed on the floor with a loud clatter, totally awakening him. He closed the window, teeth chattering. Tad shivered like a wet dog climbing from the cold water of a Canadian lake.

Even though this might not be a real vision, I'll tell Charlie, he thought. *At least it proves both girls are alive and together.*

He went back to bed, tossing and turning in restless slumber.

Chapter Twenty-Six:
January 19, 2005, Wednesday

Aftermath

"Charlie?" Tad thought the sleepy voice at the other end of the phone sounded unconscious.

"Yeah. Tad? What time is it?"

"It's early. I'm just getting ready to go to school. I hope I didn't wake you up."

Charlie looked over at the still sleeping form of Andrea SanGiovanni and said, "Well, you did wake me up, Kid. But it's okay. I don't have to get up early, but you do. So tell me: to what do I owe the pleasure of this early-morning wake-up call?"

"I had a dream…a nightmare."

"Okay. One of *THOSE* dreams?"

"Yes. I wanted to let you know what I saw. It's not much to go on, but…"

"Shoot."

"It was definitely Heather and Kelly. No idea who else. They were being forced down some stairs. Underground."

"Any other visual clues to the surrounding area or to the person with them?"

"None. So, like I said, it's not a very informative dream, but I wanted to tell you before I left for school. Before I dismissed it as stupid and not worth bothering to mention at all."

"You're not bothering me, Tad. And your dreams are not stupid. Weird, maybe. But never stupid. Don't ever think that."

"Have a nice day, Charlie. If I remember anything else, I'll call after school."

Charlie crawled back into bed and curled up close to the sleeping form of Andrea SanGiovanni.

January 19, 2005, Wednesday, 7:00 A.M.

Janice made a practice of stopping at the hospital on her way to school whenever she could. During Lent, her parents always made her go to St. Joseph's Church every morning before school. She treated this hospital visit much like that. It was like going to church. She owed it to Melody. If she had commitments at school early, she didn't stop at the hospital, but most of those commitments had ended with the cheerleading season.

Ironic, she thought. *Cheerleading stopped and so did Melody. I can only visit her because cheerleading is over. But for Melody, it's really over.*

The thought depressed her.

Every time she entered Melody's room, it was the same. Family members hovered nearby. Melody kept breathing. Her feeding tube continued to nourish her body. There was no sign of real life.

Things were heating up in Florida with a similar case. Terry Schiavo's parents were fighting with her husband over whether to disconnect her feeding tube. Like Melody, Terry was in a vegetative state. Like Melody, she was being kept alive by a PEG (percutaneous endoscopic gastrostomy) feeding tube, but was breathing on her own. Unlike Melody, Terry Schiavo sometimes made weird facial contortions that her mother and father described as "smiles." Never mind that the MRI showed Terry's brain to have atrophied. There was no brain wave activity, another similarity with Melody's condition.

Melody made no Schiavo smiling life-like movements. She resembled a rag doll. A beautiful, motionless rag doll, as inert as her cloth counterpart.

Unlike the Terry Schiavo case, Melody's husband, Sean Carpenter, sided with her parents in wanting to keep Melody alive, no matter what. Sean's parents felt that Sean and the Harrises should let the poor girl go. Not before her baby had a fighting chance, though. Six months pregnant when she fell in December, Melody needed to keep breathing and to continue being fed intravenously until the end of March.

Every time Janice sat by Melody's bedside, brushed back her hair, touched her hand, she thought, *You have three months to live, Melody. Three more months. Then, who knows? They may pull the plug and you'll be gone. Hang in there, Mel. I'm praying for a miracle. For you and for your baby.*

Janice gathered up her books, wiped her eyes, and prepared to go to school.

Chapter Twenty-Seven:
February 25, 2005, Friday

Melody

"I can't believe they're going to remove the feeding tube from that poor woman in Florida," Ruth Harris said to her husband Harold. The Harrises and Carpenters and Sean were seated in Melody's hospital room. Melody remained motionless, just as she had since December 28th. She was a mute witness to the conversation.

"It's a crying shame. That's what it is!" Sean Carpenter exclaimed.

The Carpenters, Linda and Paul, exchanged glances. "You do know that Terry Schiavo has been in a persistent vegetative state for fifteen years, right?" Paul asked his son.

"That doesn't mean miracles can't happen!" Sean protested. "They need to try some of the techniques the doctors here say they'll try."

"Like what?" asked Sean's mother, Linda.

"Well, one is called VitalStim. It's a swallowing therapy. There's another one called vasodilation therapy. There's some kind of nerve therapy. Something called the Thalamic stimulator. They implant something in her brain…" Sean trailed off before mentioning other courses of action.

"Sean…you know that those therapies are not proven. Tests have already shown that the Schiavo woman can't swallow on her own. How long does she have to suffer in the condition she's in while her family deteriorates around her?" Linda walked towards her son to hug him. He was seated in a straight back chair on the opposite side of Melody's hospital room. "Sean…"

He backed away from his mom, rejecting her overtures.

Paul Carpenter spoke up. "You heard that there is a bill proposed by Rick Santorum and Mel Martinez, didn't you? In Congress? They even got Tom Harkin, our very own liberal Democratic Iowa Senator to come aboard to sponsor this thing. Martinez is running against a Democrat in Florida, Bill Nelson, a Democrat. Brian Darling, Martinez' legal counsel wrote a memo. It was leaked. Darling wrote, 'The Schiavo case offers a great political issue that will appeal to the Republican Party's base.' Those guys just want to use that poor woman to beat the Democrat in the race, the Nelson guy. When there's no hope, you have to learn to accept that there's no hope." Paul threw the paper with this information in it down and walked from the room, clearly disgusted.

"But how do they know she won't just wake up?" Sean asked of no one in particular.

Linda Carpenter looked at son Sean over the inert form of her daughter-in-law. "Well, for one thing, they've done computed axial topography—a CAT scan. It shows severe cerebral atrophy to the hippocampus, the cerebellum, the midbrain, the cerebral cortex, the thalami, the basal ganglia. Shall I go on? Terry Schiavo has severe anoxic brain injury."

Sean's mother hesitated before adding the stark truth, but it had to be said: "Terry Schiavo is basically dead already, Sean." Linda Carpenter returned to her seat on the opposite side of the bed, rebuffed by her headstrong son, his countenance grim.

Ruth Harris, Melody's mom, spoke up.

"But that poor woman's been in the hospital for fifteen years. Melody's only been here for eight weeks. We should try everything we can to bring her back." Ruth's lips quivered as she spoke.

"Ruth. I agree with you," Linda was sympathetic. " We should try everything that is medically possible and proven to work. But medicine isn't infallible. Doctors reach a point where they can't do anything. We have to be aware of that. We have to be ready."

Sean just looked at them, eyes blank. Defiant. Then he said, "Trust no one. Nobody knows what can happen. Miracles do happen, you know. I still believe in God. I wish you did." He delivered the last two lines with the choked sound of helpless rage.

Linda Carpenter was doing her best to try to help the Harrises and her son recognize and possibly accept the inevitable. It wasn't going to be easy.

Sean abruptly re-entered the hospital room and spoke again, hurling the words like stones.

"All I know is that I love Melody, and I love our baby. By the time Adam is delivered, the doctors may find a way," Sean said. " They can't stop trying."

No one contradicted the obviously distraught young man.

Everyone dropped the topic.

Chapter Twenty-Eight:
March 1, 2005, Tuesday

March Comes In

"What's that old saying about March?"

Stevie was escorting Janice from her English class on the top floor to Kellogg's room on the basement level of Sky High. He was carrying her books for her and insisting that Janice, now six months pregnant, hang onto the railing as she climbed.

"Something about it coming in like a lion and going out like a lamb, or vice versa? The way this winter has dragged on, I'd say it has come in like a grizzly bear and it will never end. It's going to go out like a polar bear, if it *ever* leaves."

"Stevie, I swear. You're treating me like I'm a little old lady! I'm only seventeen, you know. I can still WALK," Janice protested.

Janice, too, had an independent streak a mile wide.

"I know. I know. But I read somewhere that pregnancy can throw your center of gravity off. I don't want you to take any chances." Stevie shifted Janice's book bag to his other shoulder.

"Oh. By taking chances, do you mean, like getting knocked up in the first place?" Janice answered derisively. "It's too late for that, by the way. About six months too late.'

"Janice, I just worry about you. I want to help," said Stevie.

Janice softened. "I know, Stevie, and I appreciate it. Really I do. It's just that I'm beginning to feel and look like a beached whale, and I still have three months to go."

"How much longer before Melody's due date?" Stevie asked.

"End of the month," said Janice. "I'm worried for Melody, and I'm worried for her baby."

"It's in God's hands now," said Stevie.

"I'm worried that if Sean and the Harrises don't get a grip, it could wind up in the hands of the Circuit Court, like the Schiavo case. They ordered that woman's feeding tube removed four days ago, you know. But then there was some court ruling or other and it was put back in. They have similar brain injuries. The EEGs of brain waves are identical. Poor Melody." Janice paused as she reached the bottom of the staircase.

"Don't think about the Schiavo court case now, Janice. Think positive. At least Melody's baby is doing all right," said Stevie, hopefully.

Janice nodded her head. "Yeah, the baby seems to be doing fine from what they can tell, and nowadays, with sonograms and all the rest of it, they can tell a lot. The doctors are really concentrating on keeping that baby alive and well. I hope they are half as dedicated to delivering me safely when it's the end of May and I'm due."

Janice headed towards Kellogg's classroom door, turning to wave at Stevie as she disappeared inside.

***

On the top floor of the building, Tad McGreevy was taking his leave of Jenny SanGiovanni as she entered Miss Nicholson's class.

"Be good," he said, to the beaming Jenny.

"I will. See you after school?" Jenny asked.

"Sure thing. I'll pick you up outside Kellogg's class last hour."

Tad hurried down the hall to his locker.

Chapter Twenty-Nine:
March 31, 2005, Thursday

Melody's Time

The surgical team assembled to deliver the full-term baby boy via Caesarean section.

The operation was performed quickly and efficiently. A healthy seven-pound baby boy, Adam Sean Carpenter, entered the world. He cried quickly, scoring a seven on the APGAR scale at the one-minute mark. After five minutes, Adam's appearance, pulse, grimace, activity and respiration were still strong. He rose to an eight. Nevertheless, because of the extraordinary circumstances surrounding his birth, Adam was immediately placed in an incubator and moved to the neonatal ward to be monitored.

At the exact moment that Melody was delivering a new life into the world, Terry Schiavo was dying. Schiavo's feeding tube was removed March 18th at 1 p.m. The President of the United States, George W. Bush, flew from his ranch in Texas on March 21, 2005, to the White House to sign a special bill known as the Palm Sunday Compromise. It was in response to the removal of Schiavo's feeding tube and an attempt to capitalize on the right-to-life movement within the conservative base of the Republican Party.

It was a remarkable use of executive power. The president removed the court decisions from the circuit court level to the federal courts. Legislation was even passed in Florida. The precedent set by a sitting president in attempting to circumvent the circuit courts' decisions, however, only applied to the case of Terry Schiavo. Despite the extremely irregular nature of Bush Junior's actions, the legislation did not offset right-to-die legislation and decisions from past years. Those previous court decisions stemmed from the cases of Karen Ann Quinlan, who died in 1985, and from Nancy Cruzan, who died in 1990.

The irony of Melody giving birth the same day that Terri Schiavo died was not lost on Janice Kramer who, as usual, stopped at the hospital on her way to school. The media circus surrounding the seven-year Schiavo case that involved fourteen appeals and five suits in district court came to a close with Terry Schiavo's death. Only her autopsy remained. It would be performed on April first.

Melody was wheeled back to her room after the delivery. The debate over whether to remove her feeding tube began in earnest amongst doctors, her parents, her husband and Sean Carpenters' parents.

When Janice left the hospital, Sean Carpenter was holding his newborn son. Both were crying.

April 1, 2005, Friday

The autopsy of Terry Schiavo's brain on April Fool's Day showed the loss of a massive number of neurons. Hydrocephalus ex vacuo of her brain matter showed up as black liquid portions on an MRI. Her brain weighed only 21.7 ounces (615 grams). This was half the weight expected for a woman her size, age and weight.

Linda Carpenter approached her son, Sean, in the hospital nursery, where Sean spent his time rocking and feeding his newborn son. Sean spent less and less time in the depressing atmosphere of Melody's hospital room. He was focusing on the needs of Adam, their child.

"I can't handle it any more, Mom," he said, when asked. "I just can't. I have to take care of Adam now. Melody would want me to be here for him." He continued giving Adam his bottle of infant formula.

When Linda approached Sean, carrying the morning paper that outlined the facts of the Schiavo case, she sat next to him in a second rocking chair.

"Sean, they did an autopsy on that poor Schiavo woman in Florida. Read this."

Linda Carpenter laid the folded newspaper with the details of the Schiavo autopsy on the broad, flat arm of Sean's rocking chair. She continued, "We all loved Melody, but you have to turn your attention to Adam. Let her go. For the love of God, ask yourself what you'd like done, if it were you. Let her go."

Linda got up, leaving the paper behind, and returned to Melody's room.

Later that day, Sean Carpenter, red-eyed and visibly shaken, signed papers authorizing the removal of his wife's feeding tube. As he signed the papers, he said, "Somebody's going to pay for this. It's not right. Maybe it's the UNI Dome's fault. They shouldn't have trusted the safety of that new turf they installed. Not without testing it first. Maybe it's Janet Sloan's fault."

Sean was defiant. He wanted to blame someone. Anyone. He was heartbroken. The Harrises, especially Ruth, sobbed quietly as doctors disconnected Melody's PEG feeding tube, which was removed on April 2nd, 2005.

The Harrises accepted Sean's authority to make the decision for their daughter, his wife.

Only later would trouble surface between Sean and the Harrises, when the University of Northern Iowa, owners and operators of the UNI Dome, the only indoor facility of its kind in the state of Iowa, was ordered to pay a settlement of $6.8 million in a lawsuit lodged by the Carpenters. The amount, which was covered by the university's insurance company, was ultimately reduced to only $2 million, because Melody had taken part in the human pyramid willingly. She had signed documents at school allowing her participation in cheerleading, documents that confirmed that she understood the risks involved and would hold the school harmless if injured.

However, "the school" that was held harmless was Sky High and the Sky High athletic field. At the time of her accident, Melody was neither on Sky High's athletic field nor on the field of any participating member of their athletic conference, as the crafty lawyers pointed out. The accident occurred on a field owned by the State College of Iowa (later renamed the University of Northern Iowa.). That signaled deep pockets to the Carpenters. They filed suit. Eventually, Sean would receive one million dollars. The Harrises would sue Sean Carpenter and receive half of the insurance settlement.

Trust no one.

It took Terri Schiavo thirteen days to die a peaceful death in Florida.

It was April second when Melody's feeding tube was removed. How long would Melody Harris Carpenter survive?

Back at Sky High, when Melody's classmates learned of the removal of her feeding tube, Zack Porfino repeated his favorite movie line to Stewie Truitt, once again, the Kevin Kline line from his 2001 film *Life As A House*, "We're all dying. Melody just got moved to the front of the line."

The countdown began.

Chapter Thirty:
April 1, 2005, Friday

April Fool's Day

Lenny McIntyre, Sky High's Officer Friendly, had joined the group searching for Heather Crompton and Kelly Carter. Now the group numbered ten. They were meeting at Charlie's apartment on Friday, as usual. It had been eleven weeks since the two girls disappeared. Vanished into thin air.

After Tad McGreevy shared his dream of the girls descending stairs to an underground lair, the town made an extensive search of all the town's sewers.

"This duty sucks," said Tom Tolliver, Sergeant with the Cedar Falls Police Force. At the time, he was slogging through a sewer pipe large enough for a person to walk through, hunched over. He was not enjoying it. Listening to Tom's non-stop bitching, his partner just gave him a dirty look.

Privately, Charlie and Evelyn expressed fears that Kelly and Heather had been buried alive. However, no one had contacted the Cromptons or the Carters about the reward money and no kidnapper had demanded a ransom. There had been no tips or sightings. The police and Charlie's crew of volunteers were no closer to solving the mystery of what had happened to the two teen-aged girls. The Cedar Falls Police Department was actually discussing bringing in a psychic well-known on the national scene. Charlie scoffed when he was told.

"We have our own home-grown psychic. If Tad can't see the girls, nobody else is going to do a better job." Charlie was a believer. He recognized that Tad had unique abilities.

Periodically, there would be a report that the girls were seen in different cities: Las Vegas, New York, Chicago, San Francisco, Los Angeles. All the reports were checked out. All turned out to be false. Neither the Cromptons nor the Carters believed that their daughters had run away. Where they had gone and why was still a mystery nearly three months later.

The town rallied around the search. Pink and yellow ribbons were tied to trees. Pink, because it was the girls' favorite color; yellow as a tribute to the old "Tie A Yellow Ribbon" song. Signs were mounted in store windows. Bake sales and other fundraising efforts were held to raise money to continue the unofficial search by the team of ten. "Welcome Home" signs appeared in many windows with Heather's and Kelly's names prominently displayed.

"I dropped some flyers off in Dysart yesterday afternoon," Lenny reported. "They had them up in the bank window, the Walmart, the grocery store and the theater before I left town." Lenny seemed pleased with his efforts and eager to do more.

"Good work, Lenny!" Charlie Chandler said, clapping him on the back.

Lenny resembled Don Knotts. It was hard to take Lenny seriously as an officer of the law. Charlie always had sympathy for Lenny because of that.

"Anybody have anything else to report?" Charlie asked.

Janice spoke up. "This isn't about Heather and Kelly, but they delivered Melody's baby yesterday. Adam. Seven pounds, three ounces. He's doing good. I'm not so sure that Sean is, though."

Janice looked down at her hands, clasped in her lap.

"And Melody? What about Melody?" Evelyn asked.

"I don't know. There is talk of another CAT scan. But the ones they've taken so far don't look good. Sean and the Harrises won't give up. The Carpenters have no legal say. They seem to be hoping that the doctors can convince Sean of the truth."

"What is the truth?" asked Evelyn.

"Melody suffered severe cerebral anoxia. Severe deprivation of oxygen to the brain. Absolutely devastating if it goes on too long. Remember: her heart actually stopped in the ambulance? I was there. It was scary. Plus, she hit her head really hard on the UNI Dome's new Astroturf. I'm just glad she was able to hold on and carry little Adam to term. If there's a silver lining to this story—and there isn't—it's that Adam is alive and well tonight. Sean has a healthy son."

Janice looked very sad as she concluded her update on Melody.

"How is Sean taking—everything?" asked Evelyn, always the maternal Mother Hen.

"Not well. Last time I saw him he was holding his son and they were both crying. Everyone feels so helpless. There's nothing that anyone can do. 'The Lord giveth and the Lord taketh away.'" Janice lapsed into Bible-speak, quoting a line she'd studied in her Baltimore Catechism days at St. Joseph's Elementary School.

"What do the doctors think the family *will* do?" asked Charlie. Andrea slipped her hand through Charlie's arm as he stood in his kitchen, arm cocked on his hip, a pose movie stars from John Wayne through Steve McQueen, Tom Cruise and Ryan Gosling sometimes affected.

"The doctors want to disconnect the feeding tube. Melody delivered Adam. It's been over three months since she fell. She's not getting any better. She hasn't regained consciousness. The doctors don't think she'll ever come out of the coma. Sean is in denial about it. Nobody's been able to reach him, so far. The Harrises aren't doing much better. The tension is so thick in that hospital room, you could choke on it. It's really depressing."

Janice let out a sigh. Of all Melody's classmates, she had been the most faithful in visiting the comatose girl and keeping abreast of developments in the ongoing family saga. She looked stricken and exhausted.

"Lordy," said Andrea under her breath.

The two pregnant women in the room, Belinda and Janice, appeared more upset than the others present.

"Anybody have anything good to report?" asked Charlie, attempting to change the subject.

Various group members reported where they had dropped off flyers. Then, Charlie said, "Let's brainstorm a bit. Tad here (*gesture towards Tad*) saw the girls in a dream. They were descending some stairs. Possibly going underground. No other identifying characteristics as to where the stairs might be. No other faces he recognized. Anybody have any ideas on this? We shouldn't dismiss Tad's nightmares. He's always been right before."

"Well, it could be just a basement. Maybe somebody is holding them prisoner in a basement," Lenny McIntyre said, stating the obvious.

"Yes, Lenny, but how do we figure out *WHICH* basement?" Charlie asked.

Lenny had no answer. He just looked befuddled.

The group fell silent.

Chapter Thirty-One:
April 15, 2005, Friday

R.I.P. Melody

It was Friday, April 15th, thirteen days after her feeding tube was disconnected, when Melody died. She died peacefully, never regaining consciousness. She looked as pretty in death as she had in life. The family members and medical personnel had a good idea of about how long a person could live without food or water. Melody was right on schedule.

Melody's parents and husband and newborn son. Her in-laws. All were present at her bedside. Janice was not there. She was too upset by the inevitable death of her closest friend. Stevie urged her to take care of herself, for once.

"You can pay your respects at the funeral. It's going to be too hard on you. Too hard on our baby," Stevie told Janice.

Janice smiled privately at Stevie's referencing her unborn child as "our" baby.

"Remember, when you had your cat put down, you couldn't even be there for that. You told your folks to make it happen some time when you wouldn't know about it."

This was true. Janice was very softhearted and the death of her beloved cat Snookums upset her immensely. The death of her best friend was one million times worse. A terrible, tragic and sobering thing.

The funeral was arranged for the very next day after Melody's death, Saturday, April 16th. Since the two families had been keeping a Death Watch for nearly two weeks, during that time they had selected Melody's casket, made arrangements with Green's Funeral Home, debated about what Melody would wear *if*, and began putting together photographic tributes to their daughter, daughter-in-law and wife. Unlike most visits from the Grim Reaper, which often come with little or no warning, the family had time to prepare.

Evelyn Hoeflinger reached out to Rita Cernetisch, sharpshooter heroine of the SanGiovanni shoot-out, the woman who put Earl Scranton down at the Homecoming game, to tell her the sad news. Rita decided to cut short her trip to Greece and return to the United States for Melody's funeral.

"I've had about all the Greek food I can stand," she said. "And I've seen the Olympic Stadium where I *didn't* get to participate." Evelyn thought she detected a slightly bitter tone when Rita said this. "It's time for me to come home. I've got some things I'd like to take care of. Maybe I can help with the Crompton investigation."

Rita was on a plane that landed at the Waterloo/Cedar Falls airport late on the Friday that Melody died.

The entire town turned out for the funeral. It was held at the same Methodist Church where everyone had gathered to celebrate the marriage of Melody and Sean just seventeen weeks earlier. Four months and one week from marriage to birth to death.

The funeral was as sad as the wedding had been happy. It was so crowded with Melody's classmates that the choir loft was pressed into service for the overflow spectators. Some mourners who arrived slightly later than the ten a.m. funeral start time couldn't gain admission to the church. They huddled outside in the crisp spring air, waiting for Melody's coffin to be carried outside to the waiting black hearse. The bitter weather did not deter them.

The visitation at Green's Funeral Home late Friday night was extremely sad and poignant. Melody was wearing a beautiful white dress. She looked like Sleeping Beauty, a princess waiting for her prince to awaken her with a kiss. Sean carried their son, Adam, to the side of the coffin. He bent to give her one last kiss. There wasn't a dry eye in the house.

Floral tributes kept arriving. The entire high school was in an uproar over the events of the past winter, including Melody's injury and death and the continuing mystery concerning the whereabouts of Heather Crompton and Kelly Carter.

The Crompton and Carter families were in church. The interment at Cedar Falls Memorial Gardens was as sad as anything Janice Kramer had ever experienced. Everyone in Melody's Sky High senior class was either crying or dabbing at tears they were unsuccessfully trying to hold back. Teenagers don't accept death well.

"This isn't supposed to happen to *us*! We're *young*!" said Angie Yancy, huddled outside the church with long-time boyfriend Chris Turgasen. It was a long day. Young people have no tolerance when the Grim Reaper comes for one of their own. No comprehension or understanding or acceptance. Death was for other people. Death was for old people, for those who had lived full lives. Into the ground. No distinction. No reprieve. Death does not honor human distinctions.

At the end of the day, Evelyn Hoeflinger called Charlie Chandler at his Regency Suites condo. The usual pattern of meeting on Fridays had been suspended. Everyone was too upset by Melody Carpenter's death, the visitation that night, and the funeral the next day to carry on with business as usual.

"Charlie, when are we going to meet again to go over the Crompton/Carter case?" Evelyn always got right to the point in her phone calls or during her occasional lunches and dinners with her old partner.

"Evelyn—there isn't much new to go over. The girls have been missing now for over three months. Nobody has seen them. Nobody has heard from them. What more can we do?"

The frustration in Charlie's voice was palpable.

"Well, Rita called. She came back early from her trip. You probably saw her at the funeral. She wants to help. Can you call a meeting for this week some time? Maybe Rita will have some good ideas. It's always helpful to put fresh eyes on a problem."

"Sure thing, Evelyn. If Rita is going back to work on April 18th, on Monday, how about we meet on Friday, the 22nd, like always? She'll have a week to get acclimated, get over her jet lag. Check her mail. All that good stuff."

Charlie had no idea what Rita Cernetisch would find in her mail.

Rita's surprising discovery would change the entire investigation.

Chapter Thirty-Two:
April 18, 2005, Monday

Rita Returns

"Hey, Rita! I thought you weren't due back for another month?" Lenny McIntyre greeted the one true celebrity on the force with a cheerful smile.

"You're right, Lenny. I came back early because I knew you missed me."

She grinned. Rita had a soft spot in her heart for the nerdy officer.

"Plus, I heard you guys needed me back here. After all, somebody has to help you cope with the out-of-control Cedar Falls crime wave."

This was a joke. Cedar Falls had just been named one of the safest cities in America, slightly ahead of Marion, Iowa.

"How was Greece?" Lenny asked.

"Yeah. How are Zeus and the boys?" echoed Tom Tolliver, walking up behind Rita at the front desk.

"Greece was Greece. It is what it is--or was what it was. I enjoyed seeing the stadium and the sights. But I'm ready to get back to work. I hear you have a couple of missing girls, for one thing."

Rita looked around inquiringly at her two fellow officers. "Anybody know where my mail from the last five months is?" Her quizzical look suggested she knew that saving her mail had not been a top priority in her absence.

"I do," offered Lenny.

Lenny smiled a toothy grin that revealed his diastama, the big space between his two larger-than-normal front teeth.

Lenny often inherited jobs that the more macho members of the squad felt were beneath them. The others—the Tom Tollivers—felt clerical work was nerdy. It should be relegated to secretaries. But the budget for clerical help had been severely curtailed; guys like Lenny inherited those duties. Plus, Rita was always nice to Lenny. He'd looked out for her mail while she was gone. Payback.

Keeping track of incoming and outgoing mail was not a routine job for any officer, but if the mail was addressed to a specific officer, that was unusual. That called for special handling. Lenny liked Rita. He admired her marksmanship skill.

After the SanGiovanni shootout, Rita got fan mail. Plus she was easy on the eyes. Lenny had nursed a bad case of heroine worship ever since Rita saved the day at both the SanGiovanni house during the shootout with Pogo and, again, during Earl Scranton's rampage at the football field on Homecoming night.

Lenny pulled a large box with built-in handles from beneath the station house desk. He presented it to Rita, almost as though he were offering her a "Welcome Home" gift.

Rita groaned aloud. "Oi vey!" she exclaimed.

"I thought you went to Greece? Did you visit Israel, too?" Tom Tolliver was smiling as he asked. He had never heard Rita use a Yiddish expression. In fact, he had never heard *anyone* anywhere in Cedar Falls use the common Jewish exclamation.

Cedar Falls was a lily-white bastion. The mixing pot element of U.S. society, while not totally absent, especially with the influx of Hispanic meat-packing workers, was not as prevalent as in larger cities.

Rita laughed. "It was a pretty international group of tourists in Greece. I made some new friends. Some of them may have influenced my speech," she explained, arching an eyebrow in Tom's direction. Tom had the hots for Rita, and she knew it.

Rita grabbed the handles of the full-to-the-brim box Lenny had stored her correspondence in since her departure after the November Homecoming shooting. She began the climb to the second floor of the police department, lugging the box, trudging to where her desk was located.

Tom Tolliver hustled alongside her, volunteering," Here, Rita. Let me help you with that."

Rita was grateful. Her Coach purse was the size of a small suitcase. The box was heavy. She was tired from the flight, the funeral, and jet lag.

When she reached the second floor, other co-workers greeted Rita. They asked her about her trip. Rita had been gone part of November and all of December, January, February and March. Her return to Cedar Falls on April 18th was one month earlier than her May 12th planned return. Recutting her ticket to come home earlier had cost her. She was anxious to get back in the swing of things. She dumped the full box of letters and manila envelopes onto her clean desk surface.

"This may be the last time my desk is completely clear," she said with a certain degree of wry amusement. She made the remark to Joe Clark, sitting across from her in the detective division.

Joe nodded. "I hear you," he said, without looking up from his work, chewing on a piece of gum that he'd probably been masticating for hours. Joe was trying to give up cigarettes.

Tom Tolliver said, "Well, I'll let you get to it. Catch you later for a drink, maybe?"

"Maybe." A preoccupied response not promising for Tom Tolliver.

As Rita sorted through the accumulated correspondence, she put in one pile the mail that appeared to be the equivalent of computer spam. Anything that looked important or different received priority handling.

That was what led her to pick up a strange-looking hand-addressed standard brown manila envelope marked "media rate."

The envelope had no return address. That, in itself, was unusual. It looked as though the person addressing it had been in a hurry. The writing was more scrawled than carefully printed. Rather than using a magic marker or a pen, the sender had used a pencil. Odd.

She tried to open the manila envelope with just her fingernails. It had several layers of reinforcing tape. Finally, Rita reached in her desk drawer for a scissors to cut the package open. Inside was a black-and-white composition notebook—the kind kids in school use to take essay tests.

"Curiouser and curiouser," she muttered, under her breath, stealing a line from *Alice in Wonderland.*

On the cover of the black-and-white composition book, in bold block print, was the name of its owner: *Stevie Scranton.* Stevie's printing on the cover of his journal was far more legible than the writing on the exterior of the package. Rita's detective instincts told her that two different authors were involved.

Why is somebody mailing me Stevie Scranton's composition notebook? was Rita's first thought. Then she saw the short note, again handwritten in pencil, which accompanied the book.

First, she saw the signature: *Earl Scranton.*

Her heart dropped to the floor. She had spent nearly half a year trying to forget her feelings when Earl Scranton began shooting spectators at random at the Homecoming game in November. She had shot him to death in front of thousands of people. Cheering football fans. Family members. She would never forget the sight of Earl's children huddled beside his body on the football field. Stevie cradling the dying man's head in his lap. Earl's daughter, Shannon, wailing. Rita shook her head to clear it of the painful images. She steeled herself to read through Earl's note: a message from beyond the grave.

"Rita: please read this journal carefully. Do for my boy what I was not able to do for him. Seek justice for Stevie."

That was all. It was a cryptic message signed with Earl's scribbled-in-pencil signature.

Rita began reading Stevie Scranton's journal

Chapter Thirty-Three:
April 22, 2005, Friday

The Meeting

"So, who's got something new to report?" Charlie silenced the volunteer investigators assembled in his kitchen on Friday, April 22nd, at 5:30 p.m.

A new face in the group spoke up. Rita Cernetisch accompanied her friend and colleague Evelyn Hoeflinger to the meeting. Also present were Andrea SanGiovanni, Lenny McIntyre, Belinda Chandler and Belinda's fiancé, Kenny Kellogg.

None of the young folks were present this night because a special memorial was being held for Melody Carpenter at the high school. It would focus on all the good times in her brief life. It was Janet Sloan's idea, but quickly embraced by school authorities as a way for the traumatized friends and classmates of Melody to heal. Closure. Focus on the positive. A celebration of life service. Stevie, Janice, Jenny and Tad were all attending the special memorial in Sky High's gymnasium. The absence of the high school students turned out to be a blessing in disguise.

Clutched in Rita's hand was a black-and-white composition notebook. A sober look crossed her face as she stood up to speak.

"I think I might have something, Charlie," Rita said.

"Shoot, Rita. Spill!" Charlie and the others turned their attention to the only former Olympic athlete any of them had ever met.

"As most of you know, I've been out of the country." There was a murmur. It had been spreading through the small kitchen as the regulars acknowledged the unusual presence of Rita in their midst and welcomed her back.

"While I was gone, this piece of mail came for me. It was mailed to me by Earl Scranton before he died."

A buzz began among the listeners.

Rita cleared her throat. She tugged at the corners of her mouth, a nervous tic that surfaced when she felt ill-at-ease.

"I've been reading and re-reading this journal. It's Stevie Scranton's."

The eyes of the assembled volunteers widened.

"I think it might contain some clues as to why Earl did what he did. It will almost certainly paint a new picture of some of the pillars-of-the-community we all knew. Or thought we knew. It might even give us a clue regarding the whereabouts of the missing girls. Or, at least, who might have taken them."

Rita continued, "A lot of people thought that Earl was there that night to kill Sally, his wife. Earl and Sally were getting a divorce. Even Sally wasn't sure if that was why Earl came to the game and shot so many people that night. He *did* wound Sally. But ballistics has proven that Sally's injury was accidental. The bullet wasn't even from Earl's gun. Sally was not the reason Earl grabbed a gun and shot and killed two men. He only wounded Declan Hunter. And Earl shot Rodney Black in the leg. School authorities confirmed that Rodney and Stevie had a fight in history class the day Stevie disappeared. In fact, Stevie was sent to the office for smarting off to Rod, who apparently had spent a fair amount of time picking on Stevie from grade school on. Stewie Truitt got shot, too. Pieces of plastic from the bass drum. They hit him in the ass—not to put too fine a point on it."

Rita was a person who called things as she saw them. The group tittered nervously at her use of the word "ass" and the image.

Rita continued, "Ballistics determined that Stewie Truitt was hit by plastic fragments from gunfire aimed *AT* Earl Scranton, a round fired by Daniel Malone. The bullet passed through Rich Cromwell's bass drum on the field. Pieces of the plastic rim went airborne. In other words, Earl was responsible only for the two adult fatalities. Two of the three people wounded by Earl's bullets were intentional targets. The two non-fatalities Earl *meant* to shoot were Rodney Black and Declan Hunter. Sally was hit by a misfire from Daniel Malone's returning fire. It ricocheted off the metal bleachers. Read this journal. You'll find out why Earl picked his targets, why he selected some for death."

"Wow! When you return, you return with a vengeance," said Charlie. "What's in the book? Was there a note or a message with it?"

"There was a note with it, Charlie. It was from Earl, sent before he died. It was brief. It simply asked me to—and I'm quoting here— 'Seek justice for Stevie.'"

"What was Earl talking about? Justice for what?" Charlie asked.

"This will shock some of you. I know it did me. But Stevie recorded incidents that involved child abuse not only by Daniel Malone, his Chicago kidnapper—which we all knew about—but by the principal of the school, Dr. Peter Puck, and by his Scoutmaster from third through fifth grade."

There was an audible gasp from Kenny Kellogg at the mention of the name of the deceased principal of Sky High, his former boss, Dr. Peter Puck.

Rita continued, "One victim was Daniel Malone, Stevie's captor in Chicago. It's easy to see why Earl would have it in for Malone. And, if Stevie's charges are true, it explains why Dr. Puck was shot. But there is *another* name in this book."

Here, Rita waved the book dramatically, capturing the attention of the already-spellbound listeners.

"Declan Hunter. Stevie says Hunter abused him during Boy Scout camping trips at Camp Wapsie "W" from third through fifth grade when he was Stevie's Scoutmaster. Abuse. Fondling. Pedophile crap. Not stuff that anybody wants to hear happened to their child."

Rita's face wore a stern expression. Her voice lowered several decibels and was barely audible as she outlined the case against Stevie's tormenters.

Charlie and the others were stunned. In characteristic fashion, thinking like a police officer and the lead investigator he had been on many cases, Charlie looked first to his ex-partner Evelyn.

Charlie asked, "Do you see a pattern here, Evelyn?"

"Of course. Everyone Earl shot that night is someone who abused Stevie. But only Declan Hunter, Earl's ex-wife Sally, and Rodney Black survived. And, of course, Stewie, who was really unintentionally shot by Daniel Malone's round in a ricochet."

Charlie was nodding his head in agreement.

"So, we know from this book that there were at least three sickos who preyed on Stevie at different times in his life. Three pedophiles Earl plotted to take out at Homecoming. Stevie's journal confirms that. It gives Earl motive. Earl seized the opportunity. It tells who he wanted dead and why."

Here Charlie looked back at Rita and asked, "Were there any other creeps besides Puck, Malone and Hunter specifically mentioned in the book, Rita?"

Rita answered, "Well, there were a couple of high school bullies who were unkind—the steal-your-lunch-money kind of thing— but nothing like the abuse Stevie details with Puck, Malone and Hunter. If you think back to the casualties that night—the night Earl died—it's clear that it was probably Earl's goal to kill those three. He wanted justice for his son. He succeeded two out of three times. He also wounded a small fry bully, Rodney Black. But Declan Hunter escaped. Declan either moved at the right time, or the bullet ricocheted. Something went awry. Rodney and Declan got lucky. We need to find and question Declan Hunter. Apparently, he's more deranged than even his loner persona suggests. Stevie mentions how Declan told him he wanted him to be his 'Li'l buddy, forever.'"

Rita shook her head at the phrase in astonished disbelief, spitting out the phrase with disgust.

" Declan had a real fear of abandonment, this guy. And I think we all know a little bit about his post-Vietnam history. The guy's definitely got issues. Most of them, as Stevie tells it, are about people leaving him. Not staying with him. Not loving him back, when he declares his love for them."

Rita sat down. The room buzzed with hushed conversations amongst the listeners.

"But, Rita," said Belinda Chandler, "isn't Heather Crompton his niece? Isn't there a family relationship there of some kind?"

Rita nodded her head and said, simply, "Yes."

"Have you told anyone within the department about this notebook yet, Rita?" Charlie asked.

Charlie's eyes were alight with curiosity and the fire of the hunt.

"No. I just finished reading it late last night. I wanted to check in with this group first. Everyone in town knows that you found Stevie Scranton when the police department had given up. If anyone deserves to know this first, it's your group, Charlie."

Secretly, Rita thought of her disillusionment with new Chief of Police Larry Mullin and all the powers-that-be like him. They were the most sexist bunch of bullshit artists she had had the misfortune to be bossed around by for the past five years. She knew Charlie would work long and hard on any tip she gave him.

She wasn't so sure about her colleagues on the force. They hated to be one-upped by a woman. She was willing to risk disciplinary action to let Charlie in on the ground floor of the Stevie Scranton composition notebook break in the case.

Charlie put his hand to his chin, deep in thought.

"I think we need to be very careful about this information leaving the room. We need to coordinate our efforts with the police, of course. But each of you must swear not to mention this to anyone else until I tell you differently." He had a look in his eye that went with his computer-like processing of information.

Everyone present nodded.

Belinda spoke up. "I'm glad Stevie and the other high school kids—Tad, Jenny, Janice—weren't here tonight. I'll bet Stevie's embarrassed beyond words to think people might know about all of this. I don't think he ever said a word to anyone, unless it was Dr. Eisenstadt. I know Abe counseled Stevie after he returned to Cedar Falls. Maybe the good doctor even advised him to keep this journal?"

Unwittingly, Belinda had correctly deduced exactly why Stevie—who hated to write anything—would pour out his secret, innermost thoughts and feelings in a journal.

Kenny Kellogg added, "What about Principal Puck? To think that someone in a position of authority over the entire high school could get away with this! That no one even knew or suspected! It's sickening, is what it is. I'm ashamed to admit that I went to Puck's funeral, instead of Earl's. They had Dr. Puck laid out in the gym. Had all the students walk by and pay their respects. Earl's was at the same time, across town. Remember?"

Kenny made a derisive sound. "I'd like to pay my respects to him right now with the toe end of my boot."

Kenny seemed to completely miss the irony of his expression of outrage. After all, it was Kenny Kellogg who had bedded numerous underage female students. But Kenny Kellogg, in the warped way of many, thought that what *HE* did was "normal."

If Cereal Man had been accused publicly of taking advantage of his underage female students, he'd have said, "It's just sex. They all wanted it. They all knew what they were doing. They were all sixteen going on twenty-one."

It is always those least pure of heart who denounce others and overlook their own misdeeds. How many times has an Evangelist preacher, tears streaming down his face, begged for mercy from his flock after some sex scandal? It made perfect sense that Kenny Kellogg would articulate the disdain and disgust all present were feeling. It was fitting because he was only slightly less guilty than his former boss. Kenny had not taken to heart the Biblical injunction, "Let he who is without sin cast the first stone." Another bit of scripture that might have served Kenny well was "Judge not, lest ye, also, be judged."

"Rita and Evelyn—please stay behind. We'll discuss the best way to make the department aware of this new information," said Charlie. " We have to plan the next phase carefully. We don't want to let the word get out and frighten Declan out of town. Remember: not a word of this to anyone."

Everyone nodded his or her agreement. The meeting broke up.

Chapter Thirty-Four:
April 22, 2005, Friday

After the Memorial

"So, what do you think? Would Melody have liked the ceremony?" Stevie asked the group as they walked away from the gymnasium towards Tad's car. Stevie and Janice and Jenny and Tad had ridden together in Tad's car.

"I think she would have liked it, yes," said Janice, wiping a tear away. "She always loved music by Maroon 5 and Michelle Branch. When they played 'She Will Be Loved' I just kept thinking about Sean and Melody's wedding. That line 'He was always there to help her' really got to me." Janice sniffled.

"I know," said Jenny. The song *Goodbye to You*. When the lyrics said feels like I'm starting all over again, I thought of Sean, and I felt so bad."

"It's so sad," Stevie said. "Sean couldn't even bring himself to attend. He's lucky he made it through the funeral. *Goodbye to You* got me, too, Jenny. I always thought Melody looked a little bit like Michelle Branch—only tinier. I'm glad Sean wasn't here. He'd have lost it on the line, 'Goodbye to the one thing that I tried to hold on to' Melody really was Sean's shooting star. And he was hers. That last line just tore me up."

Stevie wiped his sleeve across his eyes. "How is Sean holding up, Janice?"

Everyone looked to Janice for the most recent news about Melody's progress. Janice had become Melody's most faithful friend from their high school class. It had been Janice who accompanied Melody to the hospital in the ambulance. It was Janice who visited almost every day before school. It was Janice who watched the family dynamic play out in Melody's hospital room over the agonizing three months of her hospitalization.

Now Janice answered the group this way: "I think Sean will be okay. But it's going to take a long, long time. He's thrown himself into being a hands-on father to Adam. That consumes him.

It's like people who go back to work immediately after a death in the family. Sometimes they get criticized for it. Taking care of Adam helps Sean forget for a little while. Who knows how long it takes for grief to work its way through your system? One year? Five years? Never? There've been entire books written on the subject by people a lot smarter than me.

The feeling I got from being around Sean in the hospital near the end, when he finally signed the consent papers to remove Melody's feeding tube, was that he consciously willed himself to look forward, not backward. For Adam's sake. When he turned his attention to Adam full-time, he began to separate from his all-consuming grief. He had to. It was destroying him.

You know, he told me this. He said that what made it possible for him to even be there for her funeral, with the open casket and everything, was that he knew this was not 'his' Melody. The body lying there was just a husk. An empty vessel. The real, true Melody had gone on ahead.

Many times, during her hospitalization, Sean said he believed in God and heaven. He thinks he'll see Melody again some day. That sustains him.

What makes death so horrible is that you know you can never ever have a conversation with that person again. You can never ever be with them again. Or talk to them. Or laugh with them. It's so...."

Here, Janice searched for the exact word she wanted. "So final," she said, quietly.

Everyone was subdued. Somber.

They reached Janice's house. With Tad driving, Janice did not fear her parents' wrath. Tad was not banished from the Kramers house; Stevie still was.

"See you guys tomorrow," Janice said, as she headed for her front door.

Tad drove off. The three occupants of the car discussed Janice's comments.

"It's good that Sean is concentrating on little Adam. Adam's a boy without a mother now. Will Linda Carpenter help take care of him?" Stevie said this with a questioning tone. He didn't know what sorts of arrangements were being made to take care of the newborn baby boy.

Jenny said, "I hear that Sean insists on doing everything for Adam when he's home from school. But during the day, Linda is watching him some of the time. Ruth Harris is also helping out.

The Harrises didn't have any other children. Melody was their whole life. They're taking it hard.

Sean and his parents are talking about suing somebody over Melody's death. I think Sean's grief is so great that he's just looking for a scapegoat. He wants someone to blame for the randomness of life. Seems like that happens all the time," Jenny added.

Tad joined in. "I'm glad to hear that Sean is sharing Adam with the Harrises. They really need support right now. It's not that Sean doesn't need help, but his folks have four children. The Harrises' entire life was Melody. It's tragic."

Tad and Jenny dropped Stevie off at his mother's Hilliard Arms condo. Stevie gave a small wave as he turned and entered the building in Shantytown.

As the trio in the car watched him enter his mother's door within the Hilliard Arms near the bridge—a recent purchase that Andrea

SanGiovanni had helped Sally buy with insurance money from Earl Scranton's insurance policy—Jenny said, "Is Stevie all right?"

"What do you mean?" Tad asked.

"I mean—he lost his dad. He was kidnapped. His parents' marriage fell apart. He was abused by at least three adults he trusted. His dad went bonkers and shot a bunch of people. Then, his father died. Right in front of him. Now he's got Janice's parents trying to keep them apart. And he loves Janice. Is he okay?"

This concern for others was typical of Jenny. She always tried to take care of others before taking care of herself.

Tad idled the motor in front of Jenny's small robin's egg blue Cape Cod home on Cherry Wood Lane. He finally said, "Well, Stevie's got Janice. It's like that line we were talking about in the Michelle Branch song, 'The one thing that he tries to hold on to.' Their relationship counts for a lot to Stevie. He's trying to look forward, too. He's trusting and believing that things will improve. Even though her parents disapprove of Stevie now, I think it will all work out in the end. Stevie will make a really good father to Janice's child. You know that he already has a part-time job, don't you?"

"No!" Jenny said. "When? Where?" This latest news flash came belatedly to Jenny SanGiovanni.

"He came over to my house practically busting his buttons. Wanted to share the news that Target in Waterloo hired him, part-time. Said the potential for full-time work in the future is there." Tad smiled at the memory of Stevie's proud enthusiasm when he told him the news.

Tad got out and went around to open Jenny's door, a social etiquette nicety his mother had impressed upon him. Old School values. Good breeding.

Jenny got out of Tad's car and turned to him with a slight smile. "That makes me feel better, somehow, Tad. It's good that Stevie is looking to the future. Not the past. And Sean, too. There's a lesson there. For all of us."

Jenny pecked Tad on the cheek, turned, and headed for her front door.

April 22, 2005, Friday, near midnight.

After Tad finished his homework, he turned off the bedside light. Slumber came quickly. Almost immediately, Tad was plunged into a world of bright colors. Flashes of brilliance.

Stairs. Walls. Screams. A man's face. Tall. White beard. Brown eyes. Declan! Declan Hunter!

For the first time, Tad was able to 'see' the faces of all three occupants of a trailer of some kind. Tad didn't know Declan Hunter well, but he did know his face. Everyone in town did. Declan was such an odd figure that once you saw him, you didn't forget. A loner. Thin. Tall. Solitary. Weird.

Tad woke with a start. The first thing that sprang to his mind was how worried he knew the Cromptons and the Carters were about their girls. He went to the phone. Despite the lateness of the hour, he dialed the Cromptons' number, in his cell phone from the group's investigation of Heather's disappearance.

Nora Crompton answered on the second ring.

"Hello?" Tad could tell that Nora had not been asleep from her alert tone of voice.

"Mrs. Crompton? This is Tad McGreevy. I think I know who might have your daughter and Kelly Carter. I know that they're still alive."

Nora Crompton exclaimed, "Who is this? Who has Heather?"

"This is Tad McGreevy. I just saw the girls in a dream. They were being forced down some stairs by your brother, Declan."

There was a long silence on the other end of the line.

"Is this some kind of cruel joke?" Nora Crompton asked. "What do you mean, you saw them? Were you *with* them?"

"I see things in dreams, Mrs. Crompton. That's one of the ways Charlie Chandler and Evelyn Hoeflinger and I got Stevie Scranton back. I saw him in Chicago. And I just saw Kelly and Heather.

The girls are both alive. I don't know where he has them, but I think it's somewhere underground. I just wanted to let you know, before I call the police. They're alive. They're okay. But they're scared."

With that, Tad hung up. He had already said more than he intended to. He needed to alert Charlie and the Cedar Falls Police Department, although he'd go through Charlie and Evelyn for that. They knew the department procedural ropes better than a lowly high school senior did.

Tad dialed Charlie's number.

Chapter Thirty-Five:
April 25, 2005, Monday

One Week Later

It was just one week since Rita Cernetisch returned to the Cedar Falls Police Force. It was her first workday since the reading of Stevie's journal. Upon her return, the search for Heather Crompton and Kelly Carter broke wide open. New information contained in Stevie Scranton's journal pointed towards a possible suspect. This was the first glimmer of hope in nearly four months of searching.

Charlie Chandler, Evelyn Hoeflinger, Tad McGreevy and Rita Cernetisch were sitting with the Chief of Police, Larry Mullen, in his office. Larry had succeeded Paul Nicholson as Head Honcho of the Cedar Falls force; Larry Mullen and Rita did not always see eye-to-eye.

Rita was running down the latest theory as to why Earl Scranton murdered two people back in November at the Homecoming game. She was detailing the contents of Stevie Scranton's journal for the others, who had not yet read it.

It was the very same journal that Dr. Abraham Eisenstadt had told Stevie to keep. Abe had told Stevie to "pour out his thoughts" and deepest feelings by writing them in the journal. It was the book that Stevie meant to be his suicide note, the night he tried (and failed) to hang himself. It was this same journal that Stevie left inside the refrigerator for his father to find. The same journal he'd removed from the refrigerator after his failed suicide attempt. The same journal that Stevie's father Earl found and sent to Rita Cernetisch the day before he began his quest to even the score and avenge Stevie at the Homecoming game.

After limping back from the woods near Ike Isham's cabin, Stevie took the small black-and-white book to his room, stuck it in a bottom drawer underneath his underwear and forgot about it. Dr. Eisenstadt was dead. Stevie was busy with his new duties as equipment manager for the football team. And then he met Janice. Writing down suicidal thoughts went out the window when Stevie visited the Target store and rescued Janice Kramer from Big Bertha and a potential shoplifting charge.

Earl Scranton took the small black-and-white book from Stevie's room (never letting on that he had ever removed it from the refrigerator, read it, and replaced it).

After that, Earl—perhaps aware that he might not live to complete his self-appointed Homecoming task— mailed the journal to Officer Rita Cernetisch (now Lieutenant Rita Cernetisch), to document the abuse of his son by both his principal and his Boy Scout troop leader. Dr. Peter Puck and Declan Hunter were monsters, even if they were camouflaged as respected educator and brave veteran.

One of three survivors of bullets fired by Earl Scranton, Declan Hunter definitely now was promoted to the head of the pack of "persons of interest" in the Crompton case, once Rita read Stevie's words.

The next step was to bring Stevie in and tactfully confront him regarding his accusations. That move was now under discussion. Tad was there because of his precognitive dream of Friday night. He had already alerted the Crompton family, via late-night phone call. The Cromptons were on Chief Mullen's case immediately about raiding Camp Wapsie "W." It was all the Chief could do to persuade them not to go off half-cocked and ride out to the camp themselves.

The Chief pointed out that the FBI should be contacted. If the girls were there, their safe extraction required specialized expertise and hostage negotiators. The raid of an underground bunker was going to be difficult—perhaps deadly for the officers involved. It was definitely not in the normal line of duties performed by the Cedar F alls Police Force. The local police were better prepared to arrest drunks and answer routine domestic violence calls.

Could even the FBI rescue the girls if they were held prisoner in a heavily fortified underground bunker? How would *that* work? The Chief FBI investigator, Shawn Van Slyke, whom Chief Mullen had consulted, said, "Best case scenario, we rescue one or both girls. Otherwise, we lose some people. Be prepared for a double murder/suicide."

That was not the good news Chief Mullen wanted to discuss with Nora Crompton, so he held off on calling the families of the missing girls until experts decided upon a course of action. The exact location of the underground bunker Tad saw in his dreams—if it even existed—was still not known. The best guess was that it was somewhere on the grounds of Camp Wapsie "W" near both water and electricity.

Nora Crompton only half believed the charges leveled against her older brother. His long and troubled history, post-Vietnam, made her believe the charges *could* be true. Nora didn't want to believe that her own brother would kidnap his niece and hold Heather against her will, but stranger things had happened in Declan Hunter's life. Nora had been witness to many of them.

When she spoke with Chief Larry Mullen, Nora said, "We tried to get help for Dec. He came back from Vietnam a changed man. We tried everything. But he's always been out-of-step with society. You need to bring the Scranton boy in. Question him first. My brother may not be a saint, but Stevie Scranton's father was a cold-blooded killer. We shouldn't just take the word of a felon's son before we find out if any of this is true."

Nora sounded self-important. Defensive. Angry. Upset. Almost outraged. The Cromptons were a big deal in Cedar Falls. Stevie Scranton and Earl Scranton were not. Stevie would be brought in and interrogated. But, first, Chief Mullen wanted to talk to Stevie's best friend, Tad McGreevy, not only about Tad's mysterious 'visions,' but also about the veracity of his longtime best friend.

When Tad was brought to his office, the Chief appeared uncomfortable. He leaned back in his swivel chair and started the conversation.

"Now, I'm not suggesting that your friend is a liar, Tad. I'm just asking you if he has a vivid imagination. Maybe an overly creative one? Do you think Stevie might be making some of this stuff up, just to get attention?" The Chief had the craggy face and demeanor of actor Sam Shepard. Lined weather-beaten face. Mustache. Bright blue eyes. The look of a man who has spent a lot of time in the sun.

Tad just stared at Chief Mullen, sitting there in his uniform with his big desk and his bright shiny badge. Tad was incredulous.

"Why would Stevie do that? He's already had more attention *of the wrong kind* in his life than any of us. I don't think Stevie is a liar, if that's what you're asking me. And, besides, I doubt if Stevie even knows his journal is now police property. I doubt if he wrote down his innermost thoughts hoping everyone in town would get a good look at them. Stevie probably doesn't even know that his dad mailed it to the cops." Tad was truthful. He was also sticking up for his best friend, who was not present to defend himself.

Chief Mullen turned to his secretary. "Okay, Dawn. We bring Stevie in. Set aside that small conference room. Contact the department psychiatrist. We have to handle Stevie's questioning delicately. He's already been through a lot. Make sure it's all videotaped, but in an unobtrusive way."

"Yes, Sir," Dawn responded. She left the room to make the necessary arrangements.

"If Stevie's story checks out—and your tip, too, Tad—about the underground bunker—first, we have to find it. Then we have to practice with a model to figure out how to breach it without putting the girls in danger. Kidnapping is a federal offense. There's no statute of limitations on kidnapping. The FBI has hostage negotiators and experts in this sort of thing. But, again, that's if Stevie confirms the charges against Declan Hunter that he made in his journal. The statute of limitations on prosecuting Hunter for molesting Stevie seven years ago also applies. Hunter can be prosecuted for that within ten years of the victim turning eighteen, and Stevie's just eighteen now. So, the kidnapping of two teenagers—if Declan Hunter's guilty of that— that's now! That's ongoing. That's big. We're taking this all very seriously. First, we have to find this bunker you saw in your dream. We don't want Declan Hunter to know we're even looking for him. We have to be careful. If you can think of any other details that would help us locate it, tell us now."

"Chief," interjected Charlie, "Tad here has a very rare ability. It's called Tetrachromatic Super Vision. Check it out. Ask your shrinks. Ask your other experts. He was instrumental in helping us find Stevie when Daniel Malone kidnapped him. He probably saved the lives of both Heather Crompton and Jenny SanGiovanni on two other occasions. Through his dreams. Through his visions. I don't blame you for sounding like you don't believe him. I didn't believe him, either—at first. But, now I AM a believer."

Tad followed Charlie's lead. He appeared calm and unruffled. *Never let them see you sweat*, Charlie once told him. Tad was bored. He wanted to get back to school. He had a calculus quiz last hour.

"Are we done here?" Charlie asked. Tad would have echoed this, but he felt it best to keep still.

"Tad can go. I think he's told us all he knows," said Chief Mullen. "But I'd like you to stay on and help Evelyn and Rita and the task force that we're assembling. Will you do that? I know you're not on the clock any more, Charlie, but we'd appreciate it."

The Chief gave Charlie a hopeful look.

Then Chief Mullen turned to Tad and said, "And, Tad, if this tip checks out, the Cromptons have said that you'll qualify for the reward money. Twenty-five thousand dollars will pay for a lot of college expenses." The Chief smiled.

Tad immediately thought, *Or it could pay for Janice and Stevie to start life together with a new baby, until Stevie can graduate and go to work full time.*

Tad rose to return to Sky High and take his calculus quiz.

Chapter Thirty-Six:
April 26, 2005, Tuesday

The FBI

The advance guard of the FBI arrived in Cedar Falls, Iowa on Tuesday, April 26th. Yellow crime scene tape went up everywhere, barring access to roads and sensitive areas. There were cars and media and helicopters. Everything short of tanks and bazookas! It looked like a war zone.

Chief negotiator Shawn VanSlyke immediately formed an elite team under the field command of Walter "Wally" Ohlsen. The advance team—a small group of four men— would approach Camp Wapsie "W" and locate the hidden bunker.

There was a small rural Presbyterian church two miles from Camp Wapsie "W." The FBI appropriated the structure as their command post. They began outfitting the four men for the task. They'd try the search after dark, wearing night goggles and protective gear.

"Look for a PVC pipe. There has to be air. If he built this himself, it's probably a fairly simple-looking white pipe. If the structure is large enough, there might be more than one." Shawn VanSlyke's last instructions to the team.

Wally Ohlsen consulted the map one final time. Dressed in camouflage gear, with night goggles, shielded helmets, bulletproof vests, the four-man advance team set off on foot. With the heavy equipment and protective gear, they'd be sweating and uncomfortable, despite the cool temperatures of the spring night. It had rained a few hours before. There was discussion of both looking for tracks leading to the structure and also covering their own tracks by dragging brush over the telltale footprints as they retreated.

"If you find him, don't engage. Take pictures and retreat to base," said Shawn. By "base," he meant the small Presbyterian Church two miles away. "If he's outside of the bunker and you think you can take him without killing him, do it. But don't kill him. We need to know more about the interior. Any booby-traps he may have set for us? Don't kill him!" VanSlyke was adamant.

As the quartet—all seasoned combat veterans—approached the camp through the wooded terrain, they were in luck. A trap door, concealed with sod and plantings on top, lifted. Declan Hunter's grizzled white head popped up, like a gopher peeking out of a hole. Dec thought he heard something unusual. Something different.

The four FBI scouts froze. Completely motionless. Barely breathing. Hidden behind nearby trees. They stayed quiet, concealed by the foliage surrounding the camp. Dec looked around like an inquisitive bird. He heard and saw nothing. Eventually, Declan withdrew. He retreated underground, closing the hatch to his subterranean world. The FBI agents let out their collective breaths, glad that Hunter had not seen them. The advance scouts took pictures and retreated to base.

"We've got the location, Sir," said Wally Ohlsen. "It's not far from the road, near an area that looks like it was once a garden. There are trellises in place, but no roses growing there. Two clicks away. We only saw Hunter. He stuck his head out through a trap door. We didn't see the girls. But there's definitely a structure below ground."

VanSlyke smiled, a thin-lipped smile, at Ohlsen's confirmation of Tad McGreevy's visions.

"Good work!" said VanSlyke. "Tomorrow we'll approach in daylight. Check out the terrain. Did you see any sign of ventilation...of PVC pipes?"

"Yes, Sir. There are four white PVC pipes located about every fifteen feet. Each one protrudes from the ground about three feet." He indicated the approximate height with his right hand. Wally picked up the map of the area. He pointed to the exact location of the underground bunker.

"We'll put a guard on watching the place till morning. Then we move in," said VanSlyke.

The next morning there were at least twenty cars, trucks, jeeps and police cars surrounding the small church. Helicopters hovered overhead. A large group of men—mostly National Guard part-timers—were outfitted for an all-out assault on the bunker. Camouflage. Protective gear. Gas masks, in preparation for the breaching of the fortress.

" Whose idea was this?" asked Shawn VanSlyke. "This isn't how we're going to play it. Tell those men to stand down." VanSlyke was referencing the National Guard that Governor Tom Vilsack had mobilized.

"We don't really know what we're dealing with yet," said VanSlyke to the twenty to thirty men about to head into the woods. "Let's try to keep this down to a low roar for now," said VanSlyke.

It was near dawn.

"If we get there early, there's a chance nobody will be up yet. We'll go in about five a.m. at first light. But not with all of these weekend warriors."

When he said that, VanSlyke made a sweeping gesture indicating the National Guardsmen.

"First, we'll send in the same four man advance team that discovered the bunker. Chances are the place is booby-trapped. We can't just walk up and open the trap door. He'll have it chained shut. He definitely knows enough about explosives and weapons that we're all at risk. Are you four ready?"

"Yes, Sir!" answered the men in unison.

"Good! Tell those amateurs out there to go get coffee or something," Shawn VanSlyke said this to Chief Mullen, motioning towards the National Guardsmen, who appeared totally inept. VanSlyke looked disgusted. He returned to examining the maps on his desk.

The four FBI special agents set off through the forest to investigate the bunker that Tad had 'seen' in his dream.

Chapter Thirty-Seven:
April 26, 2005, Tuesday

Assault

Declan Hunter had not slept well since Vietnam. Bad dreams haunted his nights. Flashbacks plagued his days.

He had gone to his van to bring in some clothing he bought for the girls (sweatpants, sweatshirts, pajamas) when Declan first saw the heavily armed gunman crouched behind the tree. His militaristic instincts and training immediately kicked in. He drew his service revolver and fired. The bullet glanced off a tree. It warned the approaching FBI team that Declan knew they were coming.

Radio communication with FBI headquarters modified the plans.

Declan retreated to the safety of the booby-trapped bunker. Trapdoor locked. Chained. The walls of the old railroad car were heavily reinforced with brick. The place was a fortress.

Ron Oscow, Declan's target in the woods, did not return fire. His instructions were clear. Bring Hunter back alive. Don't shoot to kill. If the girls were not in the bunker but at some other location, killing Declan Hunter would be a colossal mistake. Declan Hunter then would be the only person in the world who could tell the authorities where to find Heather Crompton and Kelly Carter. True, the girls were probably in the underground prison, but no one wanted to make foolish assumptions.

What if Declan had buried them— alive or dead— elsewhere? Their dead bodies would not be easily recovered if Declan didn't lead authorities to their graves. What if they were alive, but tied up somewhere else? Only Declan Hunter, if he was the kidnapper, could pinpoint their location in time to bring them back alive.

It took only a few minutes for Declan to fire at Ron Oscow, grab the bags of girls' clothes he'd purchased in Waterloo, and scramble back to the safety of his underground hideout. Declan thought, *Let the games begin*!

Shawn VanSlyke instructed Wally Ohlsen to insert a camera in the PVC pipe. A small camera with a flexible neck was successfully inserted in the first pipe. The bunker was twelve feet underground. The camera gave the Feds up top a much better idea of what they were dealing with. The girls were nowhere to be seen. Hunter was lying on an old orange and white plaid couch, watching a television set with a live feed.

The FBI could communicate with Hunter through the pipe. Of course, the danger to Wally Ohlsen and Ron Oscow and the other field agents was very real. There was nothing to prevent Declan Hunter from blowing the underground bunker to Kingdom Come. He could take out the FBI, the girls and himself by detonating the bombs the cameras confirmed were present in Declan's underground compound.

"He's got guns, ammunition, food supplies, water. He could hold out for a long time," said Wally on his walkie-talkie, reporting back to base after the successful insertion of the camera.

"Can you see the girls?" asked Shawn VanSlyke.

"Not yet. So far, we've seen evidence that Hunter has guns in his bedroom area with extra magazines. A variety of firearms. Looks like an M14. An M16. Grenades. Rounds of ammunition. There's a television. It appears to be live." Wally waited for his boss' response.

"Good work, Wally. Report back in person. I have an idea I want to run by the team," said VanSlyke.

Back at the small church, the FBI experts agreed that, since the bunker had live television, appeals to Hunter to give up should be made through the media.

"We'll butter him up. Get the girls' parents on live television. Try to make Hunter see Kelly and Heather as more than just hostages. Declan Hunter should realize that Heather and Kelly are someone's kids, especially since Heather is his own niece. That didn't stop him from taking her in the first place, though. We have to try to stroke him. Get him thinking in terms of keeping the girls alive and well. Of course, that's assuming that they are even there." VanSlyke turned to Officer Oscow. "Have you eyeballed the hostages yet?"

"Negative, Sir."

"Keep watching the feed. If you see either of them, report to me immediately."

"Roger that, Sir."

VanSlyke continued with instructions for his team.

"Wally—I know it's dangerous—but I want you to try to initiate contact with Hunter through that first PVC pipe. Go right up to it. Holler down it. See if he answers. Can you do that?"

"Yes, Sir!" said Officer Wally Ohlsen. He rose to go.

Just then, the voice of Ron Oscow interrupted.

"I've got the girls! I've got the girls! Visual confirmation. They look like they're all right."

Shawn VanSlyke smiled the same thin-lipped grimace of a smile. "Good," he said. "Now it begins."

Chapter Thirty-Eight:
April 27, 2005, Wednesday

Contact

Wally Ohlsen breathed out slowly, to calm himself. He approached the white PVC pipe cautiously. Step by step.

"Declan Hunter! Give yourself up! Let the girls go!" Wally shouted this at the open pipe with the hooded top. He stood there, rooted to the spot, no idea what to expect. Every one of Walter Ohlsen's senses was hyper-alert. He was acutely aware that the next sound he heard might be the last sound he would *ever* hear. Wally hadn't been a demolitions expert all this time without knowing the risks associated with explosives.

"Go away! You're just going to get your damn fool head blown off! Go away! Leave us alone!" The voice was reedy. Determined. "And if you fool around with that pipe, you're going to blow yourself up. There's a bomb in there. You idiots know that I'm smarter than you are. I know this stuff. Go away, leave me alone and nobody gets hurt."

"Mr. Hunter. We know you have the girls. Let them go. Let your niece and her friend go." Wally shouted into the pipe's aperture. He waited.

"The girls don't want to leave. Go away. This is my family. Leave us alone."

"Mr. Hunter. Kelly's parents want to know if they can send down her medicine."

"What medicine?" Declan sounded genuinely surprised.

"A muscle relaxant. It helps her sleep. She's had trouble sleeping ever since her little brother died. Prescription medicine that she takes. It's for her condition. Can we send it down—through the pipe?" Wally waited.

"What condition?"

"Hypermobility syndrome. Ask her."

There was a long pause. Then the answer from Declan Hunter.

"Okay. Send it down. Put it in a pouch. Attach it to a rope thirteen feet long. I'll see that she gets it. Then go away and leave us alone." Declan almost sounded reasonable, although his request that he be allowed to keep two teen-aged girls captive without police interference was naïve.

"I'll be sending it down within the hour, Sir. Let me talk to Kelly."

"I can't do that."

"Why not?"

"She's busy. We're busy. Go away. Leave us alone." Declan sounded as though his frustration was growing.

"Let us talk to Heather."

"No."

"Mr. Hunter—we have to know the girls are all right. Please let us speak with one of them."

"No. Go away."

Wally Ohlsen was getting nowhere fast. He chose to make a diplomatic exit.

"Okay, Sir. I'm going to go get that medicine now. I'll be back."

Wally retreated and headed back to base.

Chapter Thirty-Nine:
April 29, 2005, Friday

Underground; Above ground

It was Friday, the night Charlie's team met.

It was exactly one week since Rita Cernetisch showed up with Stevie's journal at a meeting exactly like this one. Since then, it was like a kaleidoscope of feverish activity had been unleashed. Time almost seemed to collapse on itself during the past week.

Now, the entire town was involved. Ministers were urging their flocks to pray to Almighty God for the safe release of the girls. Fundraisers. Yellow and pink ribbons tied around trees and fences. Signs. Media coverage. You couldn't walk a block without a reporter shoving a microphone in your face and asking for a comment.

As the group gathered, Charlie switched on the television set in his kitchen.

KWWL, Channel 7, Waterloo News at Six was just starting. Top of the hour the Cromptons were on live.

"Declan: this is Nora, your sister. Please, Declan. Let the girls go. Let Heather and Kelly go. We'll get you help." Nora seemed to lose her composure at that point and could not continue.

Chris Crompton finished their message. "Don't hurt them, Declan. We want to thank you for keeping them safe. Please let Heather go." Chris Crompton, too, choked back tears.

With the Cromptons signed-off, the parents of Kelly Carter moved to the microphone set-up outside City Hall. Megan Carter Jamison,

Kelly's mom, did all the talking. She was tearful and nervous. She echoed the Cromptons.

"Mr. Hunter: thank you for keeping Kelly safe. We know you don't want to hurt anyone. Please let them go. Give yourself up. We promise nothing will happen to you if you just surrender the girls." Megan couldn't go on. Joe Jamison stood behind Kelly's mother. He looked shifty and sweaty and nervous. He did not speak.

Belinda Chandler commented on the television appearances of the families. "I don't like the looks of that Jamison guy. Where's Kelly's real dad? Doesn't he want to help get her back?"

Kenny Kellogg drew Belinda aside and answered her question privately. His position as a teacher at the high school meant that he was privy to information about the students' backgrounds that others might not know. Kenny didn't want to say too much about any pupil's parents with high school kids present to hear.

"I heard the Carters had a real bitter divorce. When Kelly's dad left, he just dropped out of Kelly and Megan's lives forever. Never sends Kelly a birthday card. No Christmas gifts. Just wiped that part of his life from his mind. It had a lot to do with Kelly's little brother, Jason, dying three years ago of leukemia. Kelly lost her brother *and* her father.

It seems like, in a marriage, if there's a crisis that big, it either makes the marriage stronger or it destroys it. When Jason died, it tore the family apart. Kelly's dad remarried. He has a second family in Dubuque. Doesn't communicate with Megan or Kelly. Wants nothing to do with what's left of his old family. Megan had to sue him for child support. Then she married Joe Jamison.

That Jamison guy, husband number two, isn't a whole lot better. He looks shifty; I think he *is* shifty. I wouldn't trust him any more than Kelly's real dad. And her biological father is a real piece of work."

"Nice. Real nice," said Belinda, sarcastically. "That must be tough for Kelly, poor thing." She shook her head from side to side sympathetically.

"Oh, yeah. She had panic attacks and all kinds of problems right after her brother's death and her parents' divorce," said Kenny Kellogg, shaking his head in agreement.

Charlie spoke, focusing the group's attention back on the front of the room. "I notice they're promising Declan everything under the sun. He's smart enough to know that you can't trust the bastards. I heard that he asked to speak to a reporter. He wanted that pretty blonde gal who does the noon news. Paula something. The cops told him that if he'd just give up the girls, they'd send her right over. *Riiight!* The FBI isn't in the business of aiding and abetting kidnappers. They're just blowing hot air up his...well, you know."

In deference to the presence of the young people and the women in the room, Charlie curbed his naturally colorful language.

Charlie continued. "It can't go on like this much longer. It's a tough thing. I guess we just have to hope Declan's better angels persuade him to do the right thing. Pray he gives up peacefully."

Andrea said, "It seems like it would be very difficult to pry someone out of an underground fortress that is heavily fortified *and* rigged with explosives. There's only one way in, and that's through the trap door. If the FBI guys go in that way, they're sitting ducks. And if he detonates the bombs he has, they're *all* dead." Andrea sighed heavily.

"I hope this ends well," said Charlie, "but the odds are heavily against it ending with everyone alive."

"As long as Heather and Kelly are alive, I don't care what happens to that Declan guy," said Jenny defiantly. "Especially now that we know what he did to Stevie when Stevie was little. Who knows how many other kids he molested? And now he takes *his own niece* hostage? It's just not right. I can't believe this is happening!"

Everyone nodded his or her head in agreement with Jenny's last comment. The quiet, bucolic rural town of Cedar Falls, Iowa, had become the Center of the News Universe. Brian Williams did an entire special from the local affiliate's studio. Williams had been in Cedar Falls in September, when Stevie returned. He was new on the job then. Now, he knew Cedar Falls well. There were reports that the NBC anchor had been seen dining at Beaver Creek Country Club with Mayor Crew.

The helicopters and news vehicles and FBI alone had filled up every hotel and motel in Cedar Falls, Waterloo and all surrounding communities. The hoopla was twice as loud and long as when Stevie was returned home on September 4th, seven months ago.

The siege continued, showing no sign of abating.

Three days and counting.

Chapter Forty:
May 2, 2005, Monday

Six Days In

"Sir, there's visual evidence that Hunter's losing it. He's handling the grenades and guns more frequently. He appears increasingly upset. Situation's volatile."

Wally Ohlsen reported the latest news from the bunker siege to his boss, Shawn VanSlyke. Wally and his team were monitoring the actions of all three of the underground bunker's occupants via the hidden camera.

"Are you and your team prepared to go in?" Shawn asked Wally. VanSlyke knew that he might be sending four good men to their deaths.

"Yes, Sir. We're ready."

Wally's trio of FBI special teams' agents, standing behind him as he reported, nodded assent.

"Well, you know the drill. By the end of this day, there's going to be a determination. Use the tear gas first. Protect the girls. Shoot to kill. Try to talk him into surrendering before you go in." VanSlyke pushed a pile of papers from the right side of his desk within the small church to the left. Nervous rearrangement. "Do what you've been practicing to do for the past six days. Do it well."

"Sir—we've been trying to talk him into surrendering for almost a week. I'm afraid he'll flip out. Kill the girls. Kill himself. We don't want that. We have to go in." Wally's concern was genuine.

Wally displayed no fear. Inside, he was experiencing all the emotions of astronauts, pre lift-off. Anticipation. Fear. Exhilaration of a sort. Suppression of the "what ifs" of life. Positive thinking. Focus on the task at hand.

The FBI team had been practicing for the past five days on a hastily built life-size mock-up of the bunker. They knew what they had to do. They knew how to do it. Declan Hunter would be waiting at the bottom of the stairs when they entered. Fourteen steps down. While the team would be wearing bulletproof vests and riot gear, Hunter definitely had the advantage. His position at the bottom of the stairs put him in the catbird seat, just as Michael Clay had occupied that position when shooting down on the officers in the street below from the SanGiovanni attic. Michael Clay was like the Indians of old, high on a bluff shooting down at the cowboys. Hunter would be below the men, shooting up at them as they tried to descend into his territory. Unless, of course, the FBI agents were able to totally obscure their descent using tear gas canisters.

"God be with you," VanSlyke said. "Bring the girls back alive."

May 2, 2005, Monday, 2 p.m.

The raid was over in less than two minutes.

First, tear gas. The FBI special agents could hear at least two people coughing and choking. Declan Hunter was wearing a gas mask. He had no such protection for the girls. Declan couldn't see through the fog the tear gas produced.

Heather and Kelly retreated to the farthest end of their prison, the bedroom section, and huddled under the covers, trying to protect their eyes and throats from the chemical assault. That put them fifty feet from the steps leading down to the interior of the underground bunker. A break for the FBI.

The agents used C4 to blow the trap door. It was open within seconds. One of them joked, later, that they should have just "knocked or rung the doorbell."

The men were down, inside the bunker's kitchen/family room area, within thirty seconds. Declan opened fire on the foursome. Fortunately, their bulletproof vests and shields protected them. The FBI was past negotiating. They shot to kill, and kill they did.

Then, the men ran to the rear of the long, shoebox shaped structure to find the terrified girls cowering in their bunk beds. Covers over their heads to protect against the tear gas, the teenagers were like little girls hiding from the bogeyman.

"Heather! Kelly! Come with us! We're getting you out of here!"

The girls would have to step over the bloody body of Declan Hunter to reach the stairs. Heather, who was able to walk, began to cry as she stepped over the dead body of her uncle. A whimpering sound.

Kelly—who had controlled her panic attacks for so long—completely lost it. She began to sob uncontrollably. Ron Oscow picked her up and carried all one hundred and ten pounds of frail double-jointed, sweatsuit clad girl up the stairs as she wept hysterically. With grief. With relief. With tension.

It had been a long siege for the FBI. A long siege for Declan Hunter. A long siege for the Cromptons and Kelly Carter's mother and stepfather.

After one hundred and seven days, improbably, both girls were safe.

Chapter Forty-One:
May 3, 2005, Tuesday

Prom Week; Janice's 18th Birthday

"I heard that Kelly and Heather both spent the night in the hospital," Jenny told Tad. "Neither one of them was—you know…sexually assaulted… or anything like that." Jenny looked embarrassed. She purposely avoided saying the word rape. Even the word had a savage sound.

"They've both got to be strung out, though. I mean…come on…one hundred and seven days stuck underground! I can barely stay in my room for one hundred and seven minutes without wanting to go outside and walk around," Tad said.

Tad said this seriously, but as soon as he spoke, he realized how silly it sounded, especially when compared to what the girls had endured.

"I know!" Jenny said. "I can't figure out how they managed to keep it together. I mean…they look like they've both lost weight. They're as pale as the girls in a vampire movie, but, other than that, I think they're okay. I'm going to go see if they'll let me talk to Heather today. She'll be back home. The hospital was just an overnight check-them-out kind of thing."

Jenny felt guilt over her failure to support Melody during Melody's hospitalization. She had visited Melody in the hospital only once. She wanted to do a better job being a good friend to Heather now. Still, as she had often told her mom when her mother encouraged a medical career, hospitals gave Jenny SanGiovanni the creeps.

"What do Angie and the Prom committee think about the dance this weekend?" asked Tad.

May 7th, Saturday, was Prom for the Sky High Class of 2005. Discussions had been ongoing since January, when the girls disappeared, about having some sort of memorial to those in the class who were missing. Or, in Melody's case, dead. Missing forever.

Jenny was a member of the Prom committee. She'd been working on the details of the celebration for months. As usual, Angie, the President of Madchens, was running the show.

"Angie thinks we should invite Heather and Kelly to be, like, Honorary Grand Marshals or something. She even suggested that all of the cheerleaders attend as a group, to honor Melody's memory. I think that's a good idea, but I wanted to talk to you about it."

Jenny gave Tad a questioning look. She added, "It doesn't mean that we can't go together. It just means that you'd be there after the introductory stuff. We could still go out to dinner beforehand, though. You would still be my date. If you want to be, that is." Jenny smiled.

Tad had asked Jenny to every important dance or social event for four long years. Jenny usually said no. Only this year did she finally say yes. Jenny was glad she had started being positive, instead of negative, where Tad McGreevy was concerned.

"I think that's a great idea, Jenny. Plus, it might solve Stevie's problem. If you girls all go together, it means that Janice will be with the cheerleaders. You know that her parents will never let Stevie be her official date. But if Stevie and I are just there after the opening remarks, we can sit together and escort the two of you." Tad restated the answer to the dilemma.

Tad smiled, thinking of this easy solution to a problem that he and Stevie had discussed several times over the past few months.

"I hope that Janice has something to wear that fits," said Jenny, with a smile. "She's due May 28th, you know. I wouldn't say she's as big as a house, but she's definitely packed on some baby weight. She looks good. Really good. But pregnant. *Really* pregnant. She's afraid her parents won't let her buy a new dress or even let her go to Prom."

"I've got an idea!" Tad said. "Isn't Janice's birthday today?"

"Yes, how did you know?"

"It's about all Stevie has been talking about. Janice turning eighteen. Legally, they can get married without her parents' permission when she's eighteen. Let's go to the courthouse and get the documents. Will you come as a witness, blah, blah, blah. Janice is still hoping her parents will come around. Realize that Stevie's a good guy."

"Not likely," said Jenny.

"You know that Stevie's been working part-time at Target, right?"

"Yes, why?" asked Jenny.

"Why is he working? Or why do I bring it up?" Tad asked.

Both of them knew that Stevie was working to raise money for the time when Janice delivered her child, so he could take care of Janice and the baby. Tad was saving the news of the $25,000 reward money. He planned to give it all to Stevie, but he wanted to tell the couple when they were together—either at Prom or at graduation. After all, the entire reward money idea was Stevie's to begin with. Tad wanted to find the perfect moment to tell his oldest friend in the world that his late-night phone call to Nora Crompton would be considered the "tip" that rescued the girls. Police Chief Mullen had told him so. News of a $25,000 windfall should not be tossed off in normal conversation. Tad was waiting for the right event. The right moment.

Tad said, "Stevie gets an employee discount. Twenty per cent, I think. Why don't you cheerleader types take Janice shopping at Target today for her birthday? Chip in a couple of dollars apiece. I know Stevie's been saving to get her something special. But what could be better than a dress that makes her look and feel like a million bucks for the biggest party night of her high school career? Maybe Stevie and Janice won't be able to do things the traditional way. But, then, Stevie never was much of a traditionalist, anyway. How could he be, with Sally for a mother?"

Tad laughed when he described Stevie as "not much of a traditionalist."

"What's a traditionalist?" asked Jenny.

"I think I just made that word up," said Tad, "maybe." He hugged Jenny around the waist.

"Naah," said Jenny. "You've just been studying for the SATs too long."

"It's the ACTs that I really need to study for," Tad responded. "Most of the Midwestern schools want the ACT. I'd only need a high SAT if I were going to Harvard. That's not likely to happen in this lifetime."

"Are you sorry that you aren't going out East to school? Far, far away?" Jenny asked. Her blue eyes grew serious.

"No, Jenny. I'm not sorry at all. In fact, I wanted to talk to you about *your* choice of colleges. Where do you think you'll end up next year? For college, I mean," Tad asked.

.

"I'm guessing that my mom will want me to stay in town. Looks like the University of Northern Iowa!" Jenny said this last line imitating Tom Cruise in an old movie that she knew Tad liked, *Risky Business*. Tad recognized the joke. Both laughed. Tad and Jenny were Cruise fans. They'd seen him in *The Last Samurai* and *Minority Report*. That led to watching all of his old movies. *Risky Business* was an oldie, but a goodie.

"I've always loved *Risky Business*. But it was the University of Illinois," Tad corrected Jenny. "We should be so lucky as to go to school there. Hard to get into that one. I think my folks will want me to go to Iowa City, anyway. They're both alums, you know. I'd be a legacy."

"Where do *YOU* want to go?" Jenny asked.

Tad looked at Jenny. A searching look. "Wherever you are. That's where I want to be."

Jenny was struck by Tad's sincerity. She was hard pressed to know how to respond. To laugh would trivialize Tad's emotions. To say, "Me, too!" might be premature. *Or is it?* Jenny thought.

More and more Jenny wanted to be near Tad. Now and in the future. She had always considered him one of her best friends. This year, their friendship had deepened into something else. Tad was always respectful. Cared about her feelings. Didn't push things. She felt safe and secure around him. She thought again of the line from *She Will Be Loved*: "He was always there to help her."

She thought, *Tad is MY shooting star.*

Just like in the Michelle Branch song they'd played at Melody's memorial service.

Chapter Forty-Two:
May 3rd, 2005, Tuesday

The Girls Shop Target

"Sheesh. This place gives me the willies," said Janice, as the group of Sky High cheerleaders approached the front door of the Cedar Falls Super Target store.

"Why?" asked Angie Yancy.

"Just because. It has to do with a trip I made a long time ago to the Waterloo store. Ask Stevie about Big Bertha some time," said Janice, waddling a bit in her maternity jeans, and alluding to her ill-fated attempt to secure an in-home pregnancy kit at this very store. The rash action had nearly led to a shoplifting charge.

"Isn't Big Bertha a golf club?" Kelly Carter asked.

"Yes, but not *this* Big Bertha. She's a real-life person. Just ask Stevie. Although he got himself transferred to this store so he wouldn't be working with good old Bertha." Janice answered.

Janice, Kelly, Jenny, Heather and Angie strolled into the store. Only Melody Carpenter was missing from the group of Sky High cheerleaders. Permanently missing.

After ooh-ing and aah-ing over the latest nail polish and lipstick colors on display near the front of the store, the girls headed for the dress section.

"Janice, it's your birthday. We all wanted to go in on a gift. We decided the best gift we could get you would be the dress of your dreams for the Prom on Saturday," said Angie, acting as unofficial chairperson of the cheerleaders.

By now, the invitation to Heather Crompton and Kelly Carter to be Honorary Prom Queens in attendance at the Saturday night event had been extended via their parents. The Cromptons had signed off. Kelly Carter's mom and stepfather had agreed. Each girl's parents would attend at the beginning of the dance. Sean Carpenter, his parents, Linda and Paul, and Melody's parents, Ruth and Harold Harris, would also be present. A second more formal tribute would be paid to Melody. The event at Sky High earlier had been billed as a "Celebration of Life." This would be shorter. More serious.

The Mayor of Cedar Falls, Jay Crew, would make a 'Welcome Home' speech for Heather and Kelly. Mayor Crew took a lot of ribbing over his name because of the clothing line. He had been full-time Mayor of Cedar Falls for twenty-nine years. There were rumblings that the City Council wanted to replace Mayor Crew with a City Administrator, downgrading his position to part-time. As Mayor Crew pointed out in a rebuttal statement, "It's only because I'm full-time that I am able to appear at so many civic events, such as the Sky High Prom on May 7th. I am honored to represent the citizens of Cedar Falls, Iowa, in welcoming back the two missing girls and paying tribute to one of their fallen comrades from the 2004-2005 Sky High cheerleading squad."

Janice selected a silver dress with an Empire waist. Silver beading just above the 'baby bump' area tucked the dress in firmly beneath Janice's attractive décolletage. Janice had gained all of her weight in her tummy. Her arms, face and legs were as slender and shapely as ever.

Angie Yancy, who planned to become a hairdresser after graduation, volunteered to style Janice's long black hair. An "up" do with a sparkly tiara. The silver dress, itself, was very short, showing off Janice's long, slender legs. She looked beautiful in the dress with the rosy glow of a pregnant woman. Her complexion was flawless, plus Janice knew her way around a make-up table.

Each of the four girls (Heather, Kelly, Jenny and Angie) chipped in $15. Stevie said he'd pick up the difference and throw in some shoes and a purse. The look of happiness on Janice's face was worth ever penny.

"Janice, you look like a doll. And you can hardly even tell you're—you know." This remark was from Jenny. She meant it. Once your eyes landed on Janice's ample bosom, the mid-section before her shapely long legs was unimportant. Add in make-up and a striking necklace and Janice would be home free.

Janice looked gorgeous. More importantly, for the first time since her father threw Stevie out of their house, Janice felt truly hopeful. In her happiness at this wonderful eighteenth birthday gift, she was thankful for such great friends.

Stevie approached the group as they were nearing the checkout counter. He was working, but he took time out for one important moment.

Just before the girls got ready to pay for their purchases, Stevie drew Janice aside, produced a ring box from his back pocket, got down on one knee and said, "Janice Kramer, today is your eighteenth birthday. I love you with all my heart. Will you marry me?"

Janice looked at Stevie with tears in her eyes, as the assembled cheerleading squad squealed in excitement. Jenny clapped. The ring was everything Janice could have hoped for and more. A square stone, emerald cut, with smaller baguette chip diamonds at the sides. Janice immediately slipped it on her left hand and said, "I love it, Stevie! And I love you."

"Your answer?" Stevie was smiling but he still wanted to hear it from the girl he loved.

"Yes! Oh, yes, Stevie. Yes, I will marry you," said Janice. She threw her arms around her sweetheart.

Chapter Forty-Three:
May 6th, 2005, Friday

Janice's 18th Birthday Party

Janice's eighteenth birthday party with her family was three days after the actual date. It was a family tradition to have a family dinner to celebrate a birthday, but they weren't always able to have it on the exact day.

Claire and her husband Stephen were not scheduled to work at the bank on Saturday morning. By holding Janice's dinner celebration on Friday night, they could celebrate without having to get up early for work the next day. Claire was twenty years older than Janice and had been married to Stephen Richardson since she was twenty-one. They had met at the bank when both worked there as tellers.

Ever since their wedding on October 28, 1988, Claire and Stephen Richardson had been trying to conceive. They had consulted every fertility specialist in the area, within the limits of their budget. (Bank tellers do not make a lot of money.) Nothing worked. Hormone therapy didn't work. Prayer didn't work. In vitro—the only time they could afford it—didn't work. GIFT (Gamete intra-fallopian transfer) performed at the University of Iowa did not work. They struck out each and every time.

Now, at thirty-eight years old, the fact that Claire Richardson was never going to have a child of her own was closer to becoming a reality. It was a bitter pill. Since the couple had tried this long and hard to have a biological child, they were now considered too old to adopt by traditional adoption agencies. Pushing forty, the odds of Claire conceiving naturally shrank with every passing year. The Richardsons didn't have the money to adopt privately. It was beginning to look like Claire and Stephen would never be parents— and then Claire's baby sister, Janice, announced she was pregnant, although she was still in high school.

No one in the Kramer family was happy about Janice's pregnancy, including Janice, initially. At first, Janice confided in Claire. Janice was devastated by the news of her pregnancy by an ex-boyfriend, the murdered Jeremy Gustaffsson.

The more Claire and her mother talked about what Janice should do about Jeremy Gustaffsson's child, the more the answer seemed to be that Janice should have the child and give it up to Claire and Stephen to adopt. It was too late for Janice to abort, even if the Kramers believed in abortion, which, as staunch Catholics, they did not.

This family adoption idea was suggested to Janice early on, when she was still vacillating about what to do. Janice's early shock at the news of the unwanted pregnancy caused her to say many negative things. These early negative statements gave Claire and her mother, Gina, hope for the adoption plan they developed.

Later, after Melody's accident, when Claire and Gina suggested this solution to Janice again, she had changed her mind on the life growing within her. Then, Janice said, "Absolutely not. I'm having this baby. It's *my* baby. There'll be no giving up of my child to Claire or anybody else. I'll have the baby, and I'll take care of it."

This change in attitude on Janice's part had come about, in part, because she witnessed the struggle by the doctors to keep Melody alive so that Adam Carpenter could be born. Janice saw Melody as a heroic figure. It was true that all Melody did was lie in a hospital bed, comatose. But even Melody's success at breathing on her own when the heart-lung machine was disconnected was considered a minor miracle.

Then, too, there was Stevie as a factor in Janice's life. As Janice grew to know Stevie better and to depend more on him, they became closer. Now, Janice saw a way out of her dilemma that was better than the bittersweet solution proposed by her mother and older sister.

How weird would it be to have to pretend I am my own child's aunt? How upsetting would it be for the child to learn the truth, years later? Janice thought. She had read that Jack Nicholson, the actor, learned late in life that the woman he thought was his sister was really his mother. Janice felt it was unfair to saddle a child with such potentially devastating news. Better to be honest with her firstborn from the beginning. Better to trust her maternal instincts. Best not to trust anyone who advocated giving her child away.

Janice now felt that this was *her* baby. She was going to protect it from everyone and everything that might try to take it from her. Stevie encouraged her to stand up for herself. He had learned that difficult lesson the hard way in life. Because he was a sweet, trusting, naïve young boy, he had been victimized over and over again. The Peter Pucks, Daniel Malones and Declan Hunters of life stole his innocence from him. But that was all over now and a new Stevie had risen, Phoenix-like, from the ashes. That was then and this was now.

Stevie, especially after his father's violent death, became an advocate of fighting for what was right. Never giving up on your own inner self. "If you don't believe in yourself, who will?" he had once asked Janice. "Trust your own moral compass and do what YOU think is right."

Trust no one, Janice thought, as she remembered Stevie's words. Jeremy's child was *her* child and could become *their* child. Without Stevie by her side and in her corner, Janice might have folded in the face of the pressure from her mother and older sister. But she had a different view on the fragility of life after Melody's death. And she had Stevie, whom she loved and who loved her, unconditionally.

Gina Kramer continued to attempt to reason with Janice, trying to convince her to surrender her firstborn child.

"You'll still know your child, Janice. Claire will raise him. It won't be so bad. Some day, when he's older, he can be told the truth. You're still young. You can still go to college. Have a normal life. Have lots of other babies; Claire cannot. Otherwise, you're tied down with a baby at the age of eighteen."

Gina said it. Claire said it. Stephen said it. John Kramer said it. Janice simply sat there, mute. *Some birthday dinner!* she thought.

Janice was careful to remove the engagement ring that Stevie had given her inside the Target store. She carefully placed it in the change pocket of her wallet. She steeled herself for the task of putting on a happy face during dinner. She pretended that she was enjoying the presence of her sister and brother-in-law at her eighteenth birthday dinner. It was one of the trials and family rituals she would simply have to endure. She must stand up for herself against the combined might of all of those in her life whom she held most dear, except one. She felt the emotions of a wounded animal as the vultures circled, waiting for the prey to give up. Waiting for the weakening victim to stop fighting. Fending off vultures ready to swoop in and have their way with the spoils.

At some point they're all going to bring up my baby. Then, they're all going to tell me how much better off my child would be if Claire and Stephen raised it. They'll pressure me. I'm not going to listen. I'm going to do everything in my power to avoid a fight, but I'm not going to give up my baby. I have to be strong.

I'm of legal age. Stevie says we can find a justice of the peace to marry us. Maybe get Sue Ann Raymond. She married Sean and Melody. It won't be a Catholic Church wedding, but that will have to wait till my parents accept me as Mrs. Steven Scranton, if they ever do. They'll come around. I know they will. I just have to stick by my decision.

Stevie and I even got the marriage license. Took the documents to the Recorder's office at the County Courthouse on my birthday. Stevie said it was the two of US set free that day, too. Social Security cards. Picture IDs. $35 cash. Tad came to witness. Someone at least *eighteen had to be a witness. Three-day waiting period. We can get married any time within the next six months. Stevie says we'll get married right before the baby is due, if I want. No matter what Claire and my mother say, this is MY life. I'm going to make a new life with Stevie and my baby. OUR baby. I want my baby born to a married couple: Mr. and Mrs. Steven Scranton.*

She smiled at the sound of "Janice Scranton" and "Mrs. Steven Scranton." She'd been scribbling the names all over her schoolbooks for months now—ever since the Target store encounter with Stevie.

The birthday dinner was a quiet affair. A few presents were given Janice—mostly small things: bedroom slippers, a new curling iron, some earrings. Janice opened them. She thanked everyone politely.

As the conversation was heading in the direction she knew it would, she excused herself.

"I'm sorry. I really don't feel well. I'm going to turn in early." She left to go to her room. This excuse was true. Janice was experiencing indigestion after the heavy Italian meal they had all just eaten. Janice took a Tums. She went to bed. Before climbing into bed, she fished inside the change purse of her billfold. She put the shiny solitaire emerald-cut engagement ring on her finger when under the covers. Janice smiled a secret smile of satisfaction and happiness as she admired her new ring, sparkling under the covers.

I didn't give in, Stevie. You'd have been proud of me. I hope I get the chance to tell you all about it tomorrow night.

Chapter Forty-Four:
May 7, 2005, Saturday

Prom Night

Janice awakened the morning of Prom Day feeling bloated, tired and crampy. The indigestion of her belated birthday dinner had abated, but only slightly.

Janice's mother, Gina, knew that all of the cheerleaders were attending Prom as a group. She was shown the shiny silver dress that the other girls gave Janice on her May 3rd birthday. Gina made all the maternal noises about how nice that was, all the while thinking of Janice's situation.

Janice's due date was May 28th. The day of reckoning grew near. Raising another child was not high on Gina Kramer's list of priorities, but the child would need a home after it was born. John Kramer felt that a stable married couple, not a teenager, should raise the newborn baby. "Not a girl still in high school!" he said to Gina. Janice's father had a point. Unfortunately, the mother-to-be disagreed. Lately, she disagreed vehemently.

Truth be told, Gina Kramer felt bad for both her girls: Claire because she was childless when she wanted a baby with all her heart and soul, and Janice because she was *WITH* child. It was ironic.

If only they could reverse positions, biologically speaking, everything would be so much better, Gina thought.

Gina Kramer sighed and went back to polishing the silver in her small china cabinet. There were many expensive silver pieces, including a silver tea set that John's mother, Angelina Ciccolone Kramer, had given them on their wedding day. The tea set was black with tarnish. Gina had been meaning to get around to this polishing task for some time. Now was as good a time as any to remove the black stain marring the precious metal. John cherished the silver, especially the tea set, because it was a memento from his deceased mother, whom he revered. He often referred to Angelina as "a saint." Removing the tarnish would restore the tea set to the shiny treasured object it was meant to be.

Gina thought, *This tea set's like Janice. It's precious and valuable. It's been ignored and mistreated. People don't know how really beautiful it is. First appearances can be deceiving. If I don't care for it and treasure it, this tea set will remain ignored and unloved. Worst case scenario, someone who DOES see the value obscured by this tarnish, will come along and steal it right out from under our noses. Then where will we be?* Gina Kramer knew that the tea set was worth at least $20,000. Her daughter was infinitely more valuable.

Janice came through the kitchen, passing by her mother, who was at work in the dining room area by the hutch, and headed for the door. It was two thirty in the afternoon.

"Where are you going, Honey?" Gina asked.

"I'll be over at Angie's house. She's going to do my hair for me. I'm taking all my make-up and my dress and stuff." Janice hoisted the garment bag thrown over her shoulder. "Then, we're all going to go out to eat together. We're supposed to be at the school by six o'clock to help set up for the ceremony."

"Do you need any money?" Gina asked.

"No. Thanks to the girls, I've got everything I need to wear, and Heather Crompton is taking us to her country club for dinner. She has to have it put on her family's tab. You can't pay cash there." Janice shrugged.

She knew little about how country clubs worked. Her family was solidly blue collar and working class. While the bakery was successful, there was nothing left over for fancy country clubs like Beaver Creek.

"It's nice that the Mayor and the school authorities are honoring both Heather and Kelly and Melody at the dance. I hope you have a good time with the girls." Gina smiled a tremulous, sincere smile.

"I'll be back late. There's a chaperoned all night party at the Country Club that everyone in the class is invited to," said Janice. She hugged her mother good bye and Gina felt a kick from the baby inside Janice's tummy.

"Goodness gracious! Your baby kicked me!" said Gina.

It was a weird and somehow wondrous feeling for the grandmother-to-be. Gina smiled, in spite of her surprise.

"I know. He or she has been really active all day. It's making me feel kind of queasy, but I'll be okay. It'll be a good excuse not to overeat," said Janice, grimacing.

Although she had tried hard not to gain too much weight, the scales were seventy-two pounds heavier than before her pregnancy. The average weight loss after delivery was nowhere near that much. Janice had been so depressed after first learning the news of her unintended pregnancy that she ate to comfort herself.

Janice really did love both her mother and father. But she also loved Stevie Scranton. The way she saw it, her parents were going to have to come around to her way of thinking. One of the other girls had used an expression about learning to love "the red-headed stepchild." Janice was unfamiliar with the old saying, but she did think it seemed like common sense that, when her baby was born, her parents would love her newborn child, because she knew her parents loved her.

Why wouldn't they love my baby, their first grandchild? And if Stevie Scranton comes along as a package deal with the baby, as my new husband, they'll have to learn to accept him, too, she thought. She grabbed a coat before exiting, as it was still cold outside.

May 7, 2005, Saturday, 5:30 p.m., Prom night.

When Angie finished putting Janice's long dark hair in a fancy "up" do, with tendrils spiraling down the sides, topped off with a sparkly tiara, Janice looked like a princess. Stevie had also given Janice a Swarovski crystal necklace for her birthday. It set off the silver dress and silver drop earrings. Make-up finished, Janice looked beautiful.

But she still felt slightly nauseous. That was nothing new. Being pregnant—even a little bit— produced its fair share of discomfort. Janice had suffered through morning sickness the first three months. Her feet were swelling now. She simply put such inconveniences out of her mind, thinking of the ultimate goal of bringing a new life into the world. Now, with a universe full of possibilities opening up, she was actually beginning to look forward to starting married life with Stevie, although both of them were still very worried about money.

"I think my mom will let us stay with her for a while, but—let's face it—she probably won't want us living with her full-time forever. But, until you get back on your feet and I go to work full-time, it's a solution. What do you think?" Stevie had asked Janice, in a recent conversation.

"I think that whatever it takes to make us a family is what we should do. I know you'll do everything in your power to make that happen. So will I," said Janice, with steely determination.

Janice liked Sally Scranton. Sally was strange, true, but she had been kind to Janice. The fact that the divorce between Sally and Earl wasn't finalized before Earl's death meant that Sally inherited some life insurance from Earl's old employer.

In the old days, when Earl began with Rath Packing Plant and they still had a union to represent the workers, insurance and health benefits and a pension were provided. Earl was such a fossil from the plant's early, more profitable, more democratic days that Sally received $10,000 from the plant's insurance carrier. She used some of it to pay for Earl's funeral.

While the amount left over was not a great deal of money, by selling the original Scranton house and moving into a two-bedroom, two-story apartment at the modest Hilliard Arms (so that Stevie could live with her, as she had always planned), Sally had been able to apply the profit from their old house to their living expenses. The floor plan put two bedrooms and a full bathroom upstairs, with a kitchen/living room/half bath on the main floor, and a basement level for storage and the washer-dryer. Their unit was the first inside to the left, after using a fob to the building's outer door for entry to the stairwell, unit #103.

Sally was not rich. Funerals are expensive. Sally and Earl had not put much aside for a rainy day. Plus, a two-bedroom Hilliard Arms apartment was going to be small and cramped when the baby came. But it would do for now, Stevie and Janice agreed.

Goal: make it to the end of the month of May, since Janice's due date was May 28th. Get married within six months, before the marriage license expired. Set up housekeeping as soon as they could raise the funds. Live happily ever after. That was the master plan.

The living happily ever after part sounded great, but getting there was going to be quite the journey. As John Lennon once famously remarked, "Life is what happens when you're making other plans."

Chapter Forty-Five:
May 7, 2005, Saturday

Prom Night: Girls Gone Wild

The ceremony with Mayor Crew delivering some 'welcome home' words of wisdom and paying tribute to Melody, the girls' fallen comrade, went well. Heather and Kelly still seemed somewhat shell-shocked by their experiences over the last five months, but they were happy to see all of their old classmates. It was the first time the girls had seen anyone other than Declan Hunter since January.

Zack Porfino approached the pair and asked, "What did that crazy guy make you do?" (*Trust Zack to be as tactless as possible.*)

"Y-y-y-yeah," echoed Stewie Truitt, who was functioning as Zack's date.

"He didn't make us *DO* anything. He just wouldn't let us go. He was my uncle, you know," Heather replied. "And he's dead. Have a little respect. He was a lonely guy with issues. But he was also a veteran. It was his service to this country that screwed him up. Why don't you two go be of service to somebody somewhere?" Heather did not want to be quizzed about her Uncle Declan on Prom night.

The two boys shuffled off, looking for unescorted Prom females to hit on.

"Don't pay any attention to those two," said Jenny. "You know how they are." Jenny touched Heather's arm reassuringly.

"Yes, I do," said Heather, sounding angry. "Zack and Stewie: dumb and dumber." The 1995 film had been updated with different actors playing the leads in 2003. It was one of the least cerebral movies of all time. It became even more stupid as a remake. Describing Zack and Stewie with the film title was perfect.

Angie Yancy said, "Consider the source. Don't let inane comments from insensitive people upset you." She could see that Heather was irritated at the bluntness of Zack's question.

Heather smiled. A small, tight nervous smile. She was glad that the other girls from the squad surrounded her. Upon their rescue from the underground bunker, it had come as a huge shock to Heather to learn that Melody Carpenter was dead. Heather was also completely blindsided by the news that Janice was nearly ready to give birth. Heather hadn't known that Janice was pregnant when she and Kelly were kidnapped. And the fact that it was Jeremy Gustaffsson's child, the boy she had been with when he was killed on Lovers' Lane, was an even bigger shock.

Janice hadn't really started to show until the latter part of January. By that time, Heather and Kelly had been prisoners for two weeks. Having Angie and Jenny and Janice around her was a comfort to both girls. Their cheerleading squad together again—except for Melody. Things were so much the same, and yet so different. She remembered that the French had a saying for that: *La plus ca change, la plus ca meme.*

A large round table for ten was reserved for the girls right down front. They headed for it after taking part in the Mayor's opening remarks. The girls were welcomed at the table by their escorts for the night.

Tad and Stevie waited for Jenny and Janice. Chris Turgasen was waiting for his steady girlfriend, Angie Yancy. Hank Henderson and Rich Cromwell had volunteered to escort Heather and Kelly.

Tad pulled Jenny's chair out, as his mother had taught him to do. Stevie followed Tad's lead. Sally had never been much on teaching the social niceties, but Stevie was observant and a quick learner.

"You girls look really beautiful!" said Stevie. It wasn't idle flattery. Stevie was genuine and really meant it. "Especially you,

Janice." He felt so proud seeing Janice wearing the necklace he had given her, plus the outfit he'd helped provide. He just wanted to take care of Janice. Forever.

Janice smiled at Stevie. She opened her small silver bag and slipped her hand inside. Janice's engagement ring was within the small purse. She put the diamond engagement ring on her ring finger. At the table, the other cheerleaders, who had been present when Stevie proposed, began complimenting Janice on the ring and echoing Stevie's praise of her appearance tonight.

Stevie got to his feet. "I'm going to go get us some cake and punch. Anybody want to come with me?"

That was the cue for all the boys at the table to leave, en masse. Tad and Chris Turgasen, Hank Henderson and Rich Cromwell all moved as one, heading towards the refreshment table, where chaperones Kenny Kellogg, with fiancée Belinda Chandler and cheerleading coach Janet Sloan, were chatting while chaperoning the dance.

Back at the table, the girls admired Janice's ring and tried to make Heather and Kelly feel at home at their first school event since their return.

"Janice, your engagement ring is gorgeous! Your necklace is beautiful, too! You just look radiant." Heather spoke with sincerity.

"Thanks," Janice said, acknowledging the compliments. "Stevie picked them both out himself—except the dress, of course. I think he'll be paying on the ring until the turn of the century." The others laughed, but Janice wasn't being funny. She was concerned that Stevie was running up debts at a time when they needed to save for the baby.

Angie Yancy chimed in, "My mom used to sing an old song lyric to me that went, 'First comes love; then comes marriage. Then comes Janice with a baby carriage.' Of course, the name in the song wasn't Janice, but I'm improvising here. Right, Chris?" Angie turned to smile over her shoulder at boyfriend Chris Turgasen, returning from the refreshment table.

"Better Stevie than me," said Chris, none too gallantly. Angie kicked him under the table.

"Yeah, well, I just wish a winning lottery ticket had come first," Janice said. "Having kids is *expensive!*"

The boys returned, holding small paper plates with nuts, mints, and cake. They carried paper cups full of punch, a difficult balancing act since they had to hold two plates and two cups simultaneously.

Stevie had a glass of punch in his left hand and also had one in his right hand. No plates.

"Where's the cake and the nuts and the mints?" asked Janice.

"In my pocket," said Stevie.

With that remark, Stevie fished inside his pockets for the food items, while Tad clapped his best friend on the back, laughing, and said, "I can't take him anywhere!" Tad added, "I always said Stevie wasn't much of a traditionalist."

"You made that word up!" protested Jenny.

"No. It's really a word. I looked it up," said Tad.

"You would!" said Jenny.

"And there's one other thing that's a bit nontraditional that I wanted Janice and Stevie to know about. I hoped there'd be a chance to tell you both at the same time. This is it."

The laughter at Stevie's cake faux pas subsided. "I wanted you both to know (*Tad indicated Stevie and Janice by nodding his head at each*) that you two are going to get the $25,000 reward money for the return of Heather and Kelly."

Heather chimed in. "That's right. Tad actually earned the reward by letting my mom know who was holding us prisoner. But Tad says the entire idea of using his Tetrachromatic Super Vision to 'see' us in his nightmare vision and figure out where we were and then call it in to my folks was *your* idea, Stevie. You get the money. Tad says so." Kelly nodded her head. She was in on the secret, since her mother and stepfather were chipping in half of the reward funds.

"Wow!" Stevie said. "That is GREAT news! But I feel like you earned it, Tad. You shouldn't give it all to us. You should use some of the money for college next year."

"Naaah," said Tad. "I would never have even thought of it. It's yours, Stevie. My folks have been saving for my college education for so long that it feels like they started the fund right after the Civil War. I'm fine. But you and Janice need it. And you need it now. After all," Tad added, clapping his old friend on the back, "what are friends for?"

Jenny looked at the tall boy beside her, her date, with admiration and appreciation in her eyes.

Tad is such a good guy! Jenny thought.

Janice and Stevie were so grateful and overwhelmed that they barely knew what to say.

Janice said, "Thank you! Wow!" Her expression sounded different than Stevie's exuberant tone. She was louder than Stevie. She sounded stressed. Urgent.

Janice didn't feel like eating anything that came out of Stevie's pocket. But she didn't feel like eating anything, anyway. Janice was experiencing sharp pains, increasing in frequency and intensity. She winced with pain.

"What's the matter, Janice?" Stevie asked.

"I hope it's not what I think it is," said Janice. "But I'm pretty sure my water just broke."

This announcement set off near pandemonium at the table. The other girls went crazy. Tad later said, with a laugh, of Janice's girlfriends, "They did everything but start to boil water."

Tad added the famous line from the classic film "Gone with the Wind," that Miss Nicholson had shown their American History class during their study of the Civil War, "I don't know nothin' 'bout birthin' no babies!" All of them laughed at the Hattie McDaniel line from that Clark Gable/Vivien Leigh classic film.

Jenny had the presence of mind to summon cheerleading coach Janet Sloan from the refreshment table. Miss Sloan and Kenny

Kellogg and Belinda Chandler rushed over to help Janice to her feet, Stevie assisting.

As she ran towards the table, Janet Sloan motioned to Lenny McIntyre, assigned to his Officer Friendly duties this night as crowd security. Lenny was standing by the door, making sure that no interlopers tried to crash the party. In the last hour he'd also had to throw Zack and Stewie out for trying to spike the fruit punch with gin.

For tonight, Lenny even had his gun and holster. He wasn't a very big man. In order to reinforce his commands to any thugs who might come on the scene, he needed to be sure they'd listen, so he had brought his service revolver. He also had his trusty nightstick, which he often twirled with boredom when patrolling the empty halls of Sky High between classes.

"Have them send an ambulance right away," Janet Sloan shouted to Lenny. Lenny nodded. Pulled his cell phone from his pocket. Dialed 911.

Janet Sloan took charge. "Stay calm, Janice. If your labor is just starting, you've probably got plenty of time. Let's move you to the nurse's office next door so you can lie down until the ambulance arrives. We should call your parents."

"No!" Janice said, quite sharply. "Don't call my parents yet. Like you said, it's my first baby, so I've got plenty of time. Ouch!" She winced again at another contraction. The pain caused her knees to buckle. "I don't want to alarm them or bother them until I'm further along, further dilated." Janice seemed apologetic after the initially strident tone in her voice, when she said, "It could take all night, and I don't want to have them just hanging around while nothing is happening."

Janice had read up on delivery. She knew that a first child to a primagravida (*first child*) mother usually took longer than later births. She'd already begun timing the contractions (which, originally, she had chalked up to indigestion.)

Seeing how much pain Janice was in, Stevie swept Janice up in his arms. He carried her the rest of the way to the nurse's office.

Chapter Forty-Six:
May 7, 2005, Saturday

Prom Problems

As Stevie carried her towards the nurse's office, Janice whispered to him, "Get the papers. Call Sue Ann Raymond. I want to get married *right now*. Before my folks try to stop us. I want my baby to have a real Dad: YOU! Tell Tad to go get the marriage license. We'll do this before we call my parents. OWWWW!"

Janice said all this to Stevie while wincing in pain. She was practicing the breathing exercises she'd learned in her prenatal class, but the panting wasn't helping.

Stevie nodded. He knew exactly where the marriage license was. He'd left it at his mom's house on top of the desk in his upstairs bedroom. Sally had recently bought a desk for him. Stevie had never owned a *real* desk before. His mom thought it was time.

As cheerleading sponsor Janet Sloan and Heather and the other cheerleaders clustered around Janice, asking her how they could help and if she wanted anything, Stevie drew Tad aside and said, "Tad, here's the key to my mom's house. On top of the desk in my bedroom upstairs is a manila folder. It has the marriage license you went with me to get at City Hall on Janice's birthday. There's also a large box with the wedding ring inside it. Go to my house and bring back the folder and the box. I'll call Sue Ann Raymond. If I can't get her, I'll find a Justice of the Peace. Here's the fob to the outer door of the building. Number 103. First door to the left after you're inside."

Tad took the keys. He nodded his head and drew Jenny aside to explain the duty he had just been assigned.

"And Tad," added Stevie. "I need you to be my Best Man, okay?" Stevie smiled. "Remember: the wedding ring is inside that folder in a big box. Be careful you don't lose it. I'll be paying that ring off until our tenth anniversary," he said wryly.

Jenny asked, "Do you want me to go with you?"

"Naaah. This is strictly a quick run to Stevie's mom's apartment building. The Hilliard Apartments aren't that far away. I'll make it fast. Get what Stevie needs. You find Sue Ann Raymond or someone else who's licensed to marry people. Okay?"

"Will do!" said Jenny, pulling out her cell phone. It was late on a Saturday night. This wouldn't be easy.

Tad ran towards the door to get his car. Then he remembered. He didn't *have* a car. The group had hired a limousine for the night. It wasn't scheduled to pick them back up until midnight. It was only eight o'clock. He bolted for the outside parking lot. No sign of the limo or the limo driver.

Lenny McIntyre, who had walked outside to wait for the ambulance, was standing there, saw the look on Tad's face and said, "What's the matter?"

"Well, other than the fact that we have a woman in labor in the nurses's office, I forgot I don't have my car tonight. I need a ride to Sally Scranton's place at the Hilliard Arms. Normally, I'd just run there on foot, since it's so close. But it's really important that I hurry. I'll be quick. But a ride would be quicker. Can you give me a ride over, Lenny?"

"I can give you a ride over the bridge to the Hilliard Arms, Tad. But I should be here outside in the parking lot to direct the ambulance attendants when they arrive. They're due any minute. They have a little bit longer drive, though. How about I drive you over, drop you off, and you get a ride back from Mrs. Scranton?"

"Okay, Lenny. Give me a ride over and I'll get back by myself. That should work. I appreciate it," said Tad, as the two headed for

Lenny's squad car. You could actually see the bridge over the Cedar River from the school's parking lot and the apartment complex was just beyond the bridge on the right.

Lenny climbed in. Fastened his seat belt. With a big grin he said, "I'm even going to use the siren. I hardly ever get to use the siren." Officer Friendly seemed to be thoroughly enjoying himself. He cranked the siren. The flashing red lights came on and the two were off.

The duo arrived at Sally Scranton's front door in less than five minutes. Her apartment complex was close by, just across the bridge into Shantytown. Two blocks to the bridge from school. Two more blocks after the bridge to the Hilliard Arms. It was a very old complex with a big brown sign planted in the grass outside advertising, "Families and Senior Living."

Tad bolted from the squad car. Lenny took off, driving back to Sky High, to wait outside and direct the hospital EMTs to Janice.

Tad rang the doorbell first. Then he pounded on the door. Nothing. The entryway to the Hilliard Arms was dark. Sally and Stevie had a first-floor apartment to the left as you entered. Sally obviously wasn't there. *Looks like I'll have to run back to school,,* Tad thought.

Tad had hoped that Sally would be at home. She could drive him back to school or to the hospital. But, as he and Lenny had discussed, the total trip back to Sky High would only be two blocks west to the bridge, the bridge itself over the Cedar River, and two blocks further west from the end of the bridge to the Hilliard Arms. Probably no more than a mile, total. Getting back to school was the same, only a trip to the east. Tad used the fob to open the outer door of the Hilliard Arms building.

It was a crummy run-down part of town and this was an old building. There was an even more decrepit building, a dilapidated Laundromat, the Duds 'N Suds, right before you started to cross the bridge heading east. The owner of the Duds 'N Suds had gone bankrupt. Security State Bank had foreclosed. The building still stood near the bridge, shuttered and dark, like so many others in this part of town. This was an area of town that Tad's mother and father often warned him not to linger in after dark. Shantytown was not safe at night. There were no houses at all, until you reached Sally's Hilliard Arms apartment building.

There were several other commercial buildings that had "For Rent" signs in their windows—abandoned taverns, tattoo parlors. There were rats and Mayflies in abundance on the bridge. The pesky insects only came out for a few days each year. When they were out, they were trouble. The slimy mess they created, sometimes a foot deep, had to be shoveled from the bridge. The entire area was dark, depressing and somehow seemed almost depraved.

You had to get closer to Sky High, at least one mile east from the bridge, before you started to see dwellings and buildings that were occupied and looked as though they were thriving (gas stations, gift shops, clothing stores). Otherwise, it was like Oakland: tattoo parlors, crummy facades, an air of desperation and hopelessness. Few people. Fewer thriving shops. Prosperity had eluded Shantytown. And at this time of night on a Saturday night, the entire area, including the bridge itself, was totally deserted.

It can't be much more than a mile back, Tad thought. He had run a mile in six minutes frequently when training for the football season. It's true that the football season had ended back in December with the ill-fated rescheduled indoor UNI game at which Melody was fatally injured, but track was a spring sport. Tad competed in the 100 meter and 400 meter hurdles. He wasn't a sprinter, but he was in the best shape of his life

Running in rented dress shoes might not be the best footgear, he thought. *They might slow me down some, since the shoes are a little big. Still, I should have no trouble making it back to Tad and Janice and Jenny at the gym in*—he glanced at his watch—*fifteen minutes, tops. That is, assuming the marriage certificate and wedding ring box are right where Stevie said they'd be.*

Tad rang the bell one last time before using the fob to the outer door of the building and the key for the apartment door that Stevie had given him. He turned to the left to Unit #103 and unlocked both the regular lock and the deadbolt. Stevie's bedroom was on the second floor. Tad entered the apartment, flipped the light switch that controlled the light at the top of the stairs. He took the stairs two at a time.

Tad understood that Stevie and Janice wanted to tie the knot at the hospital *before* someone called her parents. It would be too late after John and Gina Kramer arrived. Tad knew he was under the gun. He had to make it back before the Kramers showed up.

Who knows how long Janice will be in labor? Mother Nature has a bad habit of playing tricks on people who think they have her all figured out. Janice and Stevie Scranton will be an old married couple before her folks show up at the hospital, Tad thought. *Well, a young married couple, anyway,* he corrected himself.

No one wanted a scene at the hospital, least of all a pregnant woman giving birth. Tad hoped the minister, whoever Jenny managed to get at this hour of night on a Saturday, would hang around. Preach nonviolence and cooperation after the Kramers arrived.

Tad entered Stevie's bedroom. There was the manila envelope on Stevie's desk, just as Stevie had described it. Tad peeked inside. Saw the wedding ring box. It looked huge! He pulled the certificate out just far enough to see that it was the marriage license. *Great!* Tad thought.

He grabbed the manila envelope, tucked it inside his white dinner jacket over his heart, ring box and all, creating a bulky swelling under his white jacket. He turned off the lights. Exited. Began the journey east, towards the Cedar Falls Bridge, running in his fancy too-large rented white patent leather dress shoes.

I hope Miss Sloan and Janice are right about how she'll be in labor longer, because I won't get there until (here Tad checked his watch) nearly ten p.m.

Tad started to run. A leisurely pace he knew he could maintain. He wasn't running full out. His left shoe pinched his foot. It hurt. Still, Tad was covering the ground towards the bridge quickly. The way he had it figured, he'd be one-third of the way there by the time he hit the abandoned Laundromat at the west end of the bridge.

These rented dress shoes fit like oversized clown shoes, he griped to himself, mentally. *Next time, I wear my own shoes. Who knew I'd be running a mile in these clodhoppers?* He glanced down at the uncomfortable, rented, shiny white, too large patent leather dress shoes and continued running east towards the bridge.

Chapter Forty-Seven:
May 7, 2005, Saturday

Jesup, Iowa

"Can I leave a few hours early, George? I've got some personal stuff to attend to. Has to do with school."

Michael Clay—known as Mike Parker in Jesup— was asking his boss at the Kalafut Diner in Jesup to let him off work early. Pogo continued the fiction he began when he started on the job: he wanted to attend UNI to become a teacher.

"I think will be okay, Mike. Is slow night," George answered.

The diner normally closed at eight, but the period after the dinner hour slowed down considerably. You might get a trucker stopping in for a piece of pie, to break up the monotony of his drive, but most of the local diners would be in and out by 7:30 p.m. at the latest.

It was a small town. Either customers went home on a weeknight, to rest up for work in the morning at Deere or Rath packing plant in Waterloo, or, if it was a weekend night, people headed for the big city.

The big city might mean Waterloo/Cedar Falls. Some of the locals even called Independence, a town of barely 5,000 people twenty miles to the east, "the big I." Michael Clay always smiled when he heard anyone term a town that small as "big" anything. But he understood.

Iowa had no really big cities. Des Moines was only half a million people. The Quad Cities had shrunk to around 315,000. Half of those people lived in Illinois. Cedar Rapids, long challenging Davenport as second-largest city in the state, had only 100,000 residents.

Michael Clay was used to Chicago-style crowds. Millions. Three million or more. The small town life of Iowa amused him. It also made him grateful that he was now a man totally changed in appearance. He could disappear *anywhere* now. He wouldn't necessarily have to flee to Mexico, as he had once planned on doing, nor would he have to stay in Poopyville (as he privately called Jesup).

The Michael Clay (Mike Parker) of today could walk into any town anywhere and never be recognized as the overweight, sloppy, hirsute killer who had escaped custody twice after being found guilty of multiple counts of first degree murder. Pogo now weighed one hundred and seventy pounds. He could bench press his own weight.

Always a big man, he was still tall, but every ounce of body fat had disappeared and been replaced with rippled hard-as-rock muscles. The unkempt, dirty brown hair that hung in his unremarkable blue eyes had been shaved off completely. His contact lenses changed his eye color from blue to brown. Anything but blue. Michael Clay had always hated his blue eyes. The blue hue was so ordinary.

It would be one thing if I had Paul Newman blue eyes, but I got my mother's eyes, and she was a tramp. My eyes only look blue if I'm wearing that teal blue color. Or navy blue. My blue eyes just look mean. Mean dirty Navy blue. Like some reject from the military. I like the big brown eyes. Sad puppy eyes. They make me look sympathetic.

Pogo was ready to rock and roll. He knew it was Prom night at Sky High. He had scoped out the area around the school. He hoped to get in close to do a little wet work. Preferably after Tad McGreevy dropped his girlfriend off at home or when Tad was alone.

Pogo had investigated an abandoned Laundromat, foreclosed on by the Security State Bank, which sat near the school at the west end of the bridge. It was easy to gain entry to the old Laundromat through the back door by jimmying the lock. More importantly, the Laundromat was just a stone's throw from the Hilliard Arms.

This was important because Michael Clay figured that Tad and Stevie, best buddies since grade school, would double date. Pogo's thought: *Once Tad drops Stevie off at his home, he'll be alone. If not then, after Tad drops off his date.* Pogo decided he would stay close to his target, no matter what or where. When opportunity presented, he'd be ready to take advantage of the knock.

Opportunity doesn't have to knock more than once for me, thought Pogo. *I was born ready.* He put several knives in a duffel bag. Mike liked working with knives, rather than guns. *It is so much more intimate when you take a mark out up close and personal with a blade,* thought Pogo. He smiled, thinking of the murder of Officer Joseph Hafner the last time he'd set out after Tad McGreevy, when the young officer had pulled him over for speeding.

Pogo got to Waterloo/Cedar Falls shortly before six p.m. He drove to Tad McGreevy's residence. He watched as Tad came out of the house, dressed in an all-white tuxedo with shiny white patent leather shoes. What he hadn't expected to see was a limousine waiting in front of the house. Still, Michael Clay wasn't going to scrub this mission until he was sure it was Mission Impossible.

He followed the limo at a discreet distance as it picked up Stevie Scranton, Janice Kramer, Jenny SanGiovanni, Angie Yancy and Chris Turgasen. When he saw the SanGiovanni girl, he recognized her as the blonde hostage he had tried to take into the attic at her house in the new Harvest Home subdivision, when he had first escaped.

That's the dumb blonde who fainted on me just as I was trying to get her up to the attic. Stupid bitch! Had he been outside, he'd have spat on the ground in disgust.

The very pregnant Janice was picked up from Angie Yancy's house. Angie and Chris, Angie's boyfriend, came out of the house first. Pogo recognized Stevie Scranton opening the house and car doors for Janice, as he trailed behind the first couple. Pogo thought, *Why, you little shit! You've been putting it to her already. You didn't look like you had it in you. She's ready to pop any minute.*

It was eerie how prophetic that statement would turn out to be.

Pogo would follow the limousine for a while. See where that took him. As it turned out, the limo driver drove to the 22.2 acre Beaver Hills Country Club. The occupants of the limo got out. They entered the clubhouse. The limo driver parked and began smoking a cigarette.

Pogo kept his distance and waited out the meal the group was eating inside.

Chapter Forty-Eight:
May 7, 2005, Saturday

9 P.M.

When the ceremonies within the gym began in earnest around eight p.m., Pogo was still watching the driver of the white stretch limo smoke and loaf in the parking lot. He was watching him from across the street, through binoculars. Then, the limo drove off.

Hmmm. Wonder if he went to get a beer. Maybe he needs gas. Maybe he's running an errand. I'll stay put. See what develops. Michael Clay had been sitting in various locations watching this same limo driver smoke for hours now. Pogo was cursing the time it was taking for the dance to be over.

He knew that Proms were often all-night affairs. If this one was, Pogo's hope was that there would be trips back to individual residences to change clothes before the other after-Prom parties began. Most of the tuxedoes were rented.

Nobody wants to pay the freight for a ruined white tuxedo, he thought. *When would you ever use it again?*

About a half hour after the limo driver drove away, at roughly 9:30 p.m., Tad McGreevy emerged and spoke to a skinny cop standing outside. The two of them got into a squad car. Turned on the siren and lights. Pogo crouched lower in his truck as the squad car raced past him.

What the hell? he thought. *What now?*

As the squad car raced for the Cedar Falls Bridge, Pogo slowly followed in his truck. He saw the car drop Tad off at the Hilliard Arms and drive away. In fact, he passed the skinny cop in the black-and-white on the bridge as he tracked the pair.

This is the perfect time to go to the Laundromat. I can see Stevie's condo unit from inside the Laundromat, and my truck and I will be off the street.

Pogo drove his car to the gravel lot behind the abandoned Laundromat. He got out and jimmied the back door to the Laundromat to gain entry. He entered and went up front, near the dirty plate glass windows of the abandoned Duds 'N Suds, passing a wall of twenty empty, silent washing machines. Pogo had his binoculars with him. Through them, he could see Tad McGreevy ring the Hilliard Arms bell twice, and then enter. Lights went on in the hallway and then upstairs. Tad was not inside the house more than ten minutes.

Then, Tad was back outside. There was no squad car. No limo. No transportation. No companion of any kind.

Tad was running towards the Duds 'N Suds. This was Pogo's lucky break. He quickly opened the duffel bag containing his favorite knives. He selected the ones he felt would be most lethal.

When Tad comes running by the abandoned Laundromat, I'll charge out the front door. Stick him like a warthog fleeing through the forest. McGreevy'll never expect an attack from out of nowhere. It's perfect, thought Michael Clay. *I'd like to drive a knife deep into his heart. Like driving a stake through a vampire's heart. I'll stop him forever.*

There was only one problem with Pogo's plan.

Tad wasn't on the north (right) side of the bridge where the Duds 'N Suds was located. He was running on the left side of the bridge, parallel to Pogo's lair, across the street from the Laundromat.

That's okay, Pogo thought. *I can catch him. He won't suspect anyone is after him. I'll run him down.*

This, as much as anything, determined what happened—or didn't happen—next.

Although Pogo had been working out with weights and growing stronger every day, he had not been doing much running. *Running is for sissies*, was what he used to tell his old man, when dear old dad got on him. Occasionally, Pogo would get on the treadmill and set the pace for seven-minute miles. He generally could maintain that pace for only a mile, at most. Pogo was no longer young.

Tad McGreevy had been routinely running six-minute miles in both football and track. Although Pogo was undeniably stronger and armed and also had the element of surprise, Tad was younger, faster and in better all-around shape. But there was an intangible factor. Tad was wearing ill-fitted rented dress shoes, not running shoes.

Who would win this death race to the finish? Would it be a final race for one of them?

Pogo charged out of the door of the abandoned Duds 'N Suds in pursuit of the running boy. When Tad saw a bald guy coming towards him from across the street, running right at him, he didn't recognize the serial killer. It was one hundred pounds and quite a bit of hair ago that Tad had seen Michael Clay "in the flesh." It didn't matter that Tad didn't know who this man was. Tad saw the stranger's aura. He knew instantly that this man, whoever he was, was a killer.

Khaki = Killer!

All his life his parents had warned him about the seamier element found in Shantytown. He knew he was at risk from some derelict if he strayed into this part of the city of 39,000 souls after dark. The fact that Tad didn't immediately recognize Michael Clay didn't mean Tad didn't know a threatening figure when one came at him.

The minute he saw Pogo out of his right side peripheral vision, Tad picked up the pace. His leather dress shoes slapped the Mayfly-covered bridge sidewalk accompanied by the sickening sound of dead insects crunched underfoot. Tad's heart was pounding beneath the manila envelope and the ring box placed over it. His throat was parched. He ran like the devil himself was on his tail.

Because, for all intents and purposes, the devil was.

Chapter Forty-Nine:
May 7, 2005, Saturday

The Race

Tad could not risk turning around to look at the muscled figure chasing him. He could hear his footsteps. He could feel his own breath rattling in his chest. It sounded like the labored breathing of a dying animal. Tad was sweaty and scared.

Pogo was trying to catch the fleeing youngster, but try as he might, he wasn't quite fast enough. Tad was pulling away.

Now might have been a good time to switch to a gun, Pogo thought, as he ran. He was disgusted with himself that he could not manage more speed. *It sucks to get old. Ten years ago, I'd have caught this kid in a block,* he thought, between great gasping gulps of air.

Pogo was running as fast as he could. But the redheaded kid in the white tux was just that much faster. However, Pogo was close and closing. Because Tad did not instantly notice the figure bearing down on him, because his rented shoes were too large, because Pogo had caught Tad off guard, the race was close.

Pogo, reaching out, grabbed at Tad's white rented tuxedo jacket, trailing in the breeze behind the teenager as he ran. Pogo was about to plunge a short, lethal-looking dagger into Tad's chest as Tad, unarmed, struggled in the killer's partial grasp. It was too late to prevent Pogo from taking a swipe at the boy who had plagued him for the past year. The knife slashed through Tad's white tuxedo jacket.

The large red ring box within the manila envelope deflected it. Close to Tad's heart. Pogo lost his grip on the weapon. The knife clattered harmlessly to the bridge pavement.

Just as the khaki killer came within an arm's length of the boy, making his desperate final move towards murder, a shot rang out. Lenny McIntyre had waited patiently for the ambulance to arrive to take Janice Kramer to the hospital. He had escorted the Emergency Medical Technicians into the building and guided them to Janice, in labor in the nurse's office. Then, he went back outside. Got in his squad car. Drove back towards Sally Scranton's Hilliard Arms apartment, planning on picking Tad up on his journey back to Sky High.

It was on the bridge that Lenny's squad car caught up to the young boy, running as though he were being pursued by demons from hell. White against the darkness of the night in his formal tuxedo. Silhouetted by the full moon's light in the crisp spring air. A menacing bald man was chasing Tad with a knife. The skinhead assailant was intent on harming Lenny's young friend.

Lenny shouted, "Halt!"

As soon as he yelled, Lenny wasn't sure it was such a good idea.

Tad might think I mean him! thought Lenny. *That could be a catastrophe!*

Lenny was always a little bit confused about police procedures on his best days, but he was quite sincere about catching bad guys and defending good guys. Lenny was all about helping others.

The skinny, awkward cop took careful aim. He fired at Pogo's legs. Normally, if a policeman is facing a suspect with a gun, he is instructed to shoot to kill. But this suspect had a knife. He was threatening Tad, not Lenny. Lenny McIntyre did not want anything to happen to Tad McGreevy.

The force of Lenny's shot striking Michael Clay in the thigh, spun him to the left. Pogo was next to the bridge's cement railing. In the blink of an eye, he leaped over the railing, plunging into the roiling water of the Cedar River below. The dying mayflies flew into

Clay's mouth, eyes and ears as he fell. Tomorrow, the city would shovel piles of dead insects, a foot deep, from the bridge. Pogo hit the water below and disappeared from sight.

Tad stopped running. Lenny's police squad car fishtailed on the bridge with the screeching sound cars make when driven recklessly. The black-and-white came to rest just in front of Tad, crosswise, blocking the bridge. The red top spun crazily. The siren was on, just like Lenny liked it. Lenny ran to Tad. Both rushed to the bridge railing, tracking the descent of the mysterious bald man. Was he dead? Did he survive the fall?

"Tad, are you okay?"

"Yeah. Sure, Lenny. Thanks." Tad panted after these few words.

Lenny asked a question of Tad. "Who was that guy? Why was he trying to stab you? Is he dead? Do you see him down there?" Both men were still peering over the bridge wall at the water below.

"I don't know who it was, Lenny. But I know his aura was khaki. Khaki equals killer."

Tad gasped for breath, a result of his desperate run and the shock of the attack finally sinking in. He bent over, hands resting on the knees of his white tuxedo pants, body bent forward in exhaustion, panting.

Responding to Lenny's questions, Tad said, "I wasn't going to stop and introduce myself. He obviously meant to harm me. Maybe he thought I had money on me. I *am* pretty dressed up, after all. Earlier, I was driving around in a limo."

Tad smiled at Lenny when he said this last part, but fear made his lips quiver. His throat was parched; he felt sick to his stomach. His whole body was clammy with shock and the sweat of his run. He pushed a lock of hair back from his forehead. His hand was trembling.

Tad sprinted his best speed, a consistent six-minute mile, when he realized that this bald man meant to really hurt him.

Lenny, never the best shot on the force, fortunately did not accidentally shoot Tad. That, in itself, was a miracle.

Tad climbed into Lenny's squad car and said, "Quick! Take me to Janice and Stevie. Fast!"

Chapter Fifty:
May 7, 2005, Saturday

Prom Night

Lenny drove Tad to Sartori Memorial Hospital at 515 College Street. It was not the same hospital where Tad and Charlie were taken after the shoot-out with Pogo at Jenny SanGiovanni's house. For that, Tad was grateful.

Tad had nothing but bad memories of the assault on the SanGiovanni home, Pogo's cold-blooded killing of two fine police officers that day, his wounding of Charlie Chandler, and the threat he posed to Jenny during last year's police standoff. He wondered where Pogo was now.

Will I still see Pogo in my dreams? Is he still out to get me? Tad thought. He shook his head to clear it of such thoughts, blaming them on the mugger on the bridge.

Tad tried to reconcile the attack he had just survived with Pogo's threats against him. The attacker looked nothing like the Michael Clay Tad remembered. Still, the fact that his assailant was an older man sank in when Tad was able to outrun him on the bridge. The guy was in pretty good shape. But he was old.

I'm just lucky I've been out for track this spring, Tad thought. Another extra-curricular activity he had never tried before. Tad thought, to himself, *Age. The great equalizer. It gets us all, eventually. If that guy had been my age, I might be dead now.*

Lenny led the way to the maternity wing, where, right now, Belinda Chandler, Kenny Kellogg and Janet Sloan were the adults present. There was one other woman there, sitting quietly next to Jenny SanGiovanni reading a Bible. It was Sue Ann Raymond, the Methodist minister who had married Melody and Sean Carpenter.

Janet rose and walked towards Tad as he appeared in the waiting area. She asked him, "Shouldn't we be calling Janice's parents?"

Tad smiled and said, "In just a few minutes, Miss Sloan. Where's Stevie?"

Janet Sloan motioned towards the door of the delivery door and arched an eyebrow. "Janice asked for him. She was in a lot of pain and screaming. Stevie seemed to calm her down, so the nurse said to let him in, if Janice wanted him there. But that's why I think we should contact her parents." Miss Sloan looked concerned. As all teachers do, she feared litigation.

"Yes, we will. I'm going to ask the nurse if Stevie can come out here for just a minute. I have something he wanted me to get for him." Tad walked towards a nurse in scrubs who was at the desk near the maternity waiting room area.

"Can you go in there and ask the young man who is holding the pregnant girl's hand to come out here a minute, please? Tell him his best friend has something for him." As he said this to the nurse, Tad pulled the crumpled manila envelope from the inside of his white tuxedo jacket. The envelope looked the worse for wear, as did Tad's ripped white tuxedo jacket, but Tad peeked inside. The contents were all still there, all intact.

Stevie emerged from the delivery room looking frazzled. When he saw Tad, he gave him a big smile. "She's almost crowning, but we need to do this now. Jenny has Sue Ann Raymond in the waiting room. You've got the license. Is the ring here?"

A cry of pain came through the door as it opened to admit a nurse.

"Yeah. I've got the ring and the license. But some nut job attacked me on the bridge. Maybe he knew I had a diamond ring in my pocket and he wanted to steal it. Who knows? If Lenny McIntyre hadn't come back to pick me up, I'd be toast."

"Who was it?" Stevie asked.

"That's a good question," Tad answered. "Who wants to see me dead? Or, who wants to rip off *my* money and *your* diamond ring? I don't know who it was. I don't remember ever seeing the guy before."

"Did he look like…you know…Pogo?" asked Stevie, with trepidation.

"No. That's the weird thing. He looked entirely different, but…" Tad trailed off.

"What happened to him? Did Lenny arrest him?" Stevie asked.

"Actually, when the guy saw he was about to be arrested for assault with a deadly weapon —he had a knife—he jumped over the bridge railing and into the water. Now, I ask you, who jumps twenty feet into the Cedar River over a failed assault? He didn't harm me. He didn't get anything. But he did get away."

"And you have NO idea who it was?" Stevie asked again.

"Well, I know he had a khaki aura. And khaki means killer. I just ran as fast as I've ever run in my life. He tried to catch me. Almost *did* catch me because of these damn shoes. (*Tad lifted one foot, referencing his over-large white rental dress shoes*). Then Lenny showed up and saved the day."

Stevie shook his head from side to side. "Now I owe you for this, too. You saved our lives earlier with the reward money. Now this. How can I ever repay you, Tad?"

"By continuing to be my best friend," Tad answered. " Now let's get this show on the road. You're going to need Sue Ann Raymond, and I think you're going to need at least one witness. Is Janice up for having Jenny come in with us?" Tad asked his hassled friend.

"Sure. I'll just check with her. She might want a minute to get it together. This having a kid is no day at the beach. I can't believe how much she's suffering. It's a miracle that any of us gets born, if it's always like this! They had to do an episiotomy and there's blood running down the inside of her leg. It's just—well, it's pretty grim,"

Stevie said, as he took a deep breath and hustled back inside with the manila folder in his grasp.

In a matter of seconds, Sue Ann, Jenny and Tad entered the delivery room, where a very exhausted Jenny smiled a wan smile.

"Hi, you guys. *OUCH!*" A strong contraction quickly erased her welcoming smile.

"So, are we ready to do this?" Stevie asked.

Janice responded, "I'm MORE than ready. I want this document signed and sealed before my baby is delivered. Let's go." She looked at the bemused Methodist minister that Jenny had hailed to the hospital. Sue Ann had been sound asleep at home in bed. "Short form of the ceremony, Ms. Raymond. We'll do the Catholic bit some other time. No more than five minutes. Then call my folks."

Sue Ann opened the second book she was carrying and began reading the very shortest form of a marriage ceremony, beginning with the words, "Do you, Steven Scranton, take this woman, Janice Kramer, to be your lawfully wedded wife?"

The answers were yes, yes and yes. There was no "You may kiss the bride." The bride was in no mood for kissing anyone.

"I now declare, by the power vested in me by the state of Iowa, that you two are legally man and wife." Sue Ann turned and shook Stevie's hand, as did Tad. She patted Janice's hand, while Jenny leaned in and gave the mother-to-be a brief hug. Papers were signed. There were smiles all around in the crowded delivery room, followed by a loud scream from Janice that caused all the non-essential visitors to quickly exit.

Chapter Fifty-One:
May 7, 2005, Saturday

After the Ceremony

Gina and John Kramer arrived at Sartori Memorial Hospital twenty minutes after Janet Sloan called to tell them their daughter was in labor.

When they entered the delivery room, John Kramer recoiled at the sight of Stevie Scranton holding his daughter's hand. If the minister hadn't been present, John might have taken a swing at Stevie. Instead, he said, gruffly, "What are YOU doing here?"

Janice, who was nearly ready to give birth, looked at her father and said, "Daddy, Stevie and I are together. We are legally married. I love you, Daddy, but I love Stevie, too. And I love my baby. I'm not giving my baby away to Claire or anybody else."

Normally, John Kramer would begin blustering, making noises like, "What do you mean, you're legally married?" but Minister Sue Ann Raymond walked over to the older couple and said, "Can I talk to the two of you outside for a moment?"

The stunned parents left the delivery room—as Jenny and Tad already had—and moved to the outer waiting area.

The minister began, "Janice is eighteen. Stevie is also of age. They have a valid marriage license. Apparently they had been planning on getting married just as soon as Janice was of legal age," Sue Ann explained, holding out the marriage certificate. The inked signatures on the document were barely dry.

"Which was just four days ago!" boomed John Kramer in his deep baritone. Both his daughters and his wife were often intimidated by the deep timbre of John Kramer's voice. He had the kind of voice that radio announcers would kill for, even though he was just the town baker.

"It might have been recent, but I'll bet it seems like only yesterday that you were giving birth to Janice, Mrs. Kramer," said Sue Ann, directing her comments to the calmer of the two parents. "I think you need to re-evaluate what your relationship is going to be with your first grandchild and with your daughter. Janice loves you. But she also loves this young man. They are of age and have made a serious commitment to one another. Give them a chance, why don't you?"

Gina Kramer took her husband's hand and said, "Yes, John. It's too late for ranting at her. She knows what she wants. She wants to be married to Stevie. You really have not given Stevie the benefit of the doubt. Yes, his father committed a terrible crime. But since when do we punish the children for the sins of their fathers? He's trying to help Janice raise her child, and it isn't even biologically *his* child. He's been good *to* our daughter and good *for* our daughter. He's had a rough time of it himself. Give that some consideration. I'm going in to be with Janice now. You can do whatever you think is best, but I don't intend to lose the chance to have a relationship with my first grandchild and my youngest daughter."

Gina returned to the delivery room and took up a position on the other side of Janice's bed, wiping her brow and squeezing her hand when Janice cried out in pain.

John Kramer felt as though he were a tire and someone had just let the air out of him. He sank into one of the waiting room chairs and examined his knuckles for a brief period before getting up and slowly following his wife into the delivery room.

Chapter Fifty-Two:
June 11, 2005, Saturday

Graduation

The party at Charlie and Andrea's was just getting into full swing. Many of the guests had multiple stops to make. It was graduation day for the Class of 2005 and Charlie wanted to honor his young friend Tad McGreevy, who had given him back a purpose in life that, ultimately, led to the woman whom he would marry in just one month, on July 9th.

Tad's entire family was there: his mom, his dad, his sister Sharon. Jenny SanGiovanni's older sister Cynthia and her older brother Frank were present, too.

Stevie Scranton, Sally Scranton, Janice Kramer Scranton and their new baby girl, Neva, had just arrived. John and Gina Kramer were on their way.

Belinda Chandler and her fiancé, Kenny Kellogg, were sipping margaritas (non-alcoholic in Belinda's case) while Belinda chatted with Janice about her darling newborn daughter. The child had a shock of blonde hair, cornflower blue eyes, and a dimple that everyone admired. Janice was obviously in love with the small girl; Stevie even more so.

"What caused you to name her Neva?" asked Belinda. "It's a lovely name."

"Well," said Janice, "we didn't know whether we were having a boy or a girl, but Stevie somehow only thought of *boys'* names. So, we really didn't have a girl's name. We had to decide pretty fast, in the hospital, while everything was happening. They came to me the next day and wanted me to fill out the birth certificate. My dad had a sister, Neva, who died young. Brain aneurysm. I thought it would be nice to remember her. I was going to name her Nevaeh, originally, but Daddy said it sounded like a black girl's name." Janice paused. "I hope that doesn't sound racist. I don't mean it that way. I just mean that it's heaven spelled backwards, but it has Neva in it. So Dad thought just plain Neva, in honor of his sister, would be better—and shorter. My father's been pretty good about changing his perceptions—or misperceptions—of people, so we decided he was right. Just plain Neva will be enough for her to learn to spell when she's three or four, anyway. Stevie actually said, 'Why add two more letters?'" Janice laughed and rolled her eyes. "I had to remind him that she'll have to learn THE ENTIRE ALPHABET at some point."

Janice laughed. Belinda joined in.

Janice continued, "And her middle name is Melody." This information required no explanation.

Stevie was across the room, deep in conversation with Tad. When he heard the group around his baby daughter erupt in laughter, he called over, "Are you making fun of me again, Janice?" His tone of voice was jocular. He was obviously kidding. Stevie added, "You know I'm outnumbered by you women. It's three against one at Mom's house. Not fair!"

Jenny left Tad's side to stroll over to the group around Janice and hold the new baby. Neva Melody Scranton was only five weeks old. When Tad glanced up and saw Jenny holding the newborn child, he stared at the two of them for a very long time with a strange, tender expression in his eyes.

"So, what's next for you and Stevie?" asked Belinda.

"Well, we've been living with Sally. All three of us in one bedroom. Not good. But, thanks to Tad and the reward money, plus Stevie being promoted to full-time at Target on the management track, we have enough saved to get an apartment of our own. It's pretty easy to get credit right now. We might even buy a small house. They have these variable loan things that we're looking at."

"Stay away from those," Kenny Kellogg said, getting into the conversation as he joined the group of women admiring the baby girl. "Those things are gonna' be trouble. If you get one of those variable loan things, you have to be able to flip the house at just the right time or you're screwed. Selling on a timetable isn't easy. Belinda and I were looking at them, but I think we're going to take the old reliable thirty-year fixed thing. I can get us a mortgage at 5.75%. That's about the lowest it's ever been that I can remember."

"You're definitely leaving the Regency Suites, then?" Janice asked Belinda.

"Yeah. My dad and Andrea are getting married next month. Kenny and I are either going to make it a double ceremony with them or wait one month. Kenny wants us to have a really grand honeymoon where we travel somewhere far away—maybe Australia. Maybe China or Japan. So, we have to get married while he's out of school on summer vacation. Dad says it would save all kinds of money if we four just got married at the same time. One fell swoop. Andrea isn't sure, because she thinks I won't like it, but I honestly don't care. I think it's fine," said Belinda. "So be sure to 'save the date' of July 9th, because, if we decide to join them in this fiasco, it will be a big wing ding at the Episcopalian Church on Second Avenue and then a reception at the Holiday Inn in Waterloo. You're all invited, of course," she said, smiling. "I owe Andrea my life. I'm cool with sharing our special day with Andrea and Dad. In fact, I look forward to it" Belinda smiled at Kenny when she said this. Then she hoisted her margarita and said, "Two brides for the price of one! Such a deal!" Everyone laughed.

Janice said. "My sister Claire and my brother-in-law Stephen work at Security State Bank. They have for a really long time. They said this is the lowest they've *ever* seen home mortgages rates. They're talking about trying to refinance their current small house. Or maybe get a larger one. But they said they're not sure if they can swing that *plus* the adoption. They're adopting a baby boy from China, you know. Neva will have a cousin about her own age." Janice smiled. She didn't mention that she and Stevie had given her sister and brother-in-law cash from the reward money to help them adopt their new son.

Just then, Lenny McIntyre entered. Charlie clapped him on the back, almost knocking the slight figure over. Charlie, using a fork and a goblet, tapped on the side of his glass to get the attention of the crowd.

"Attention, Ladies and Germs!" (*Chuckles*). "I wanted to congratulate all of today's graduates. Many of you helped Tad and me work on the missing person cases and I want to congratulate US, because we're three for three. That doesn't happen very often in law enforcement." Charlie looked pleased.

Then Charlie continued, "And I want to personally thank the Cedar Falls Police Department, especially Officers Evelyn Hoeflinger, Rita Cernetisch and Lenny McIntyre. You guys are the best! And Lenny—you really saved the day on Prom night!" The three officers in question raised their glasses and toasted each other. Lenny looked down at his feet. Bashfully. Awkwardly.

"And," Charlie added, "although we don't know who attacked Tad yet, I'm sure Lenny's colleagues on the force will find out. We know he was wounded when he went into the water, so his body may wash up downriver. They'll keep looking till they find him."

One of the younger members of the group found Charlie's stack of old vinyl records. In addition to discovering these relics, the young graduates were interested in hearing vinyl.

Tad said, "I heard on television that vinyl is *THE* best quality. Better than CDs and digital. And," Tad added with a grin, "certainly better than these old 8-tracks Charlie still has. What are you going to do with all these old 8-tracks, Charlie? Nobody makes 8-track players anymore!" Tad was teasing his mentor, but it was true that Charlie had an entire shelf of outdated 8-tracks near his antiquated stereo system. "So, Charlie," said Tad, "what album do you want us to put on from these antiques over here? The Beatles?" Tad held up the *Help* album. "This one?" (Tad held up *Meet the Beatles*).

Charlie ambled to the other side of the room where the young whipper-snappers were making fun of his music and his music machine and said, "Nope. I've got just the one. It's the *Mother, Jugs and Speed* soundtrack album."

"W-H-A-A-T?" Tad said.

"I'm not kidding. The Brothers Johnson are on this. From the movie with Raquel Welch and Dick Butkus."

When the group heard those names, the older folks in the room howled with laughter.

Then Stevie said, "Now you've got me really curious. Why THAT album out of all of these fantastic albums in your wonderful collection?"

Tad's voice was thick with sarcasm.

Charlie winked at Stevie and said, "It's from a movie about Emergency Medical Technicians, like the ones who came to Sky High and saved your bacon when Janice went into labor. So have a little respect." Charlie added: "1976. Bill Cosby. Raquel Welch. Harvey Keitel. Larry Hagman. Bruce Davison. Valerie Curtin. Dick Butkus. Trust me on this: it's a great album! You've got Paul Jabara's version of *Dance*. Peter Frampton's *Show Me the Way*. Billy Preston on *My Soul Is A Witness*. You do know Billy used to tour with the Beatles, don't you? I think they used to call him 'the fifth Beatle.' And who can forget *Get the Funk Outta' My Face?*"

When the older folks in the room heard the name of the All Time Great Chicago football player mentioned as an *actor* in the movie, they continued to chuckle. Murmurs of "Butkus!" could be heard in disbelief. (And ALL had forgotten *Get the Funk Outta' My Face*.)

The recent graduates, most of them born in 1987, knew none of the names in the movie. Now, Charlie had made each of them curious about the soundtrack to this film, which was made more than a decade before they were born.

With that, Charlie's old turntable was pressed into service. The needle landed with that hissing sound that either means a record is about to start playing or a snake is attacking. The group rocked out to the raucus sounds of 1976. Music from a time when Kenny Kellogg was eleven years old and Belinda was just a gleam in her father's eye.

"You know what?" Tad said, as the album continued to play. "Charlie's right. This *IS* a good album. Don't know about the movie, but the album rocks. I guess you *can* trust *some* people, after all."

He grabbed Jenny SanGiovanni and Tad and Jenny began to dance to Steve Marriott's lyric "I need a star in my life."

EPILOGUE

The river was cold. Blood trailed from the wound on his thigh. He was glad that this was fresh water, not salt water.

He gulped a huge breath of air and went under again to avoid being seen.

He let the current take him downriver. Away from the lights of Shantytown. Away from the police. Away from the boy in the white tuxedo. As he inhaled his last big breath of air, he could see the boy's white jacket fluttering in the breeze above him, the thin, pale face of the cop, and the kid peering into the water beneath the bridge.

He floated for a long time, half-conscious, searing pain in his right hip.

Then he saw it. A small boat tied up at a private dock. A motorboat with a small Evinrude motor.

Pogo climbed into the boat. For a long time, he just lay there. Waiting. Gathering his strength.

He found an old towel in the bottom of the boat. Tore strips from it to use as a tourniquet. The rest of the towel he used to staunch the bleeding from Lenny McIntyre's bullet, which had just grazed him.

I don't think I'm hurt too bad, but that was a close call. I've got to get away from the lights. Get back to my car. Get away.

Pogo untied the small boat from its moorings. The motorboat began to drift downriver.

I'll start the motor when I'm further away. I hope it has gas. I'm not gonna' be caught tonight. And I'm not done with that punk kid yet.

FROM THE AUTHOR

(*Warning: Spoilers may be included in this material. It is meant to be read after you finish **KHAKI = KILLER**.)

Khaki = Killer, the third book in *The Color of Evil* series, was 'born" on a Celebrity lines cruise ship (the Celebrity Solstice) on January 12, 2013, when I began writing the plot while we floated off the coasts of Australia and New Zealand. I knew, in my head, what would happen, and had discussed plot points with good friend and fellow author Sharon Mitchell of Canada. Now the task was to get the plot down on paper (which I managed to do by the end of May, approximately four months later—but not without near lockdown in my Writer's Lair in Chicago. I finished right before Printer's Row in Chicago in early June.)

I'm writing this at the end of June (2013), while waiting for the book's final edit from long-time Editor Karen Burgus Schootman and for the cover art from Vincent Chong of the UK. Another reading will take me until at least September, with more correcting.

Many reading the book will say, "Oh, she just wrote about a man keeping two teenaged girls prisoner because of those women in Cleveland."

The answer to that would be a resounding "No." The Cleveland event did not happen until May 9, 2013. That now infamous case refers to 52-year-old Ariel Castro, who kidnapped not one, but three women when they were teenagers: Amanda Berry, Georgina DeJesus and Michelle Knight. The women were kidnapped between 2002 and

2004 and held against their will until Amanda Berry managed to escape with the help of a neighbor, and police were summoned. Some of the captives were held prisoner as long as eleven years, difficult as that is to fathom. Amanda Berry gave birth to a child while in captivity.

But that Cleveland event happened at a point when I was nearly done with the book.

The second "real-life" crime that readers may well think was the inspiration also took place *AFTER* I had begun the book with the plot firmly in mind—although I was not nearly as close to being completely done on January 30, 2013, when Jimmy Lee Dykes boarded a Midland City, Alabama, school bus and demanded a child hostage from bus driver Charles Albert Poland. We were in Sydney, Australia at the time. The bus driver refused to give over any of the twenty-one children in his care and was executed by Dykes, who then took 5-year-old Aspberger Syndrome sufferer Ethan Kirkland prisoner in an underground bunker, described as being "like a tornado shelter." The small town (population 2,300) and the world waited anxiously for six days while authorities tried to negotiate with Dykes. Ultimately, the FBI stormed his underground bunker to successfully rescue the boy.

So, what was the REAL inspiration for one of the main plot lines of *Khaki = Killer*? What really inspired this book, other than answering the question, "What happened to Melody Harris when she fell from atop the human pyramid at the UNI Dome at the end of Book #2, *Red Is for Rage*?

The true inspiration for much of this book was a double homicide that took place in the real-life setting of this series, Cedar Falls, Iowa.

Red Is for Rage (**Book #2 of *The Color of Evil* series**) came out in January of 2013 in E-book format and in July 2013 in paperback. Two little girls in Cedar Falls, Iowa, went missing on July 13, 2012: Lyric Cook-Morrissey, age 10, and Elizabeth Collins, age 8, cousins.

Their skeletal remains were found on December 5, 2012, victims of foul play. By that point, **Red Is for Rage** was complete. The third book in **The Color of Evil** series was still one month from kick-off.

I read with sadness the story of the two small cousins who were bicycling in Evansdale, Iowa, an area I know well, when they disappeared. I watched taped interviews with the parents of one of the girls and read the police record of the other child's parents (drug manufacturing and dealing, etc.). I could not ignore the fact that this fictional setting of my previous two books had now become the scene of an actual double homicide, one of the most notorious in the state's history. And, as **Khaki = Killer** says (true fact), this after being named one of the safest cities in the state and/or nation, right behind Marion, Iowa. It was mind-boggling that this could happen in the Waterloo/Cedar Falls area. Even today, with five full-time investigators working the case, no one has been charged in the double homicide. It was the murders of Lyric Cook-Morrissey and Elizabeth Collins—still unsolved—that inspired the Heather Crompton/Kelly Carter subplot in **Khaki = Killer.**

For my purposes, the book's time frame had to be winter. The first book leaves off at the end of the first semester of the characters' senior year at Sky High High School in Cedar Falls, Iowa, in December. Bicycling in Iowa in winter would not work, but ice-skating would. I also did not want to introduce many additional new characters that readers had not read about previously. In fact, I've placed a CHARACTER appendix for all three of the books, so far, at the end of this one, to help you keep them straight. I discarded the thought of alphabetizing when I realized that Tad, Stevie, Jenny and Janice should be the first four mentioned, as they are the primary teen-aged characters.

Why not make the kidnapped girls be older? Why not have them be cheerleaders with Jenny SanGiovanni, characters with whom readers would already be familiar? Where would the kidnapper take them? I speculated about an underground bunker; the incident in

Alabama had not yet occurred. I will say that when it *DID* occur, while we were in Australia, I was as mesmerized as the rest of the nation, waiting and watching to see what would happen. Afterwards, I watched a "20/20" television special about the police tactics used to rescue young Ethan and, yes, I drew from that, but the underground bunker I envisioned and the reasons why Declan Hunter might resort to such actions were not motivated by the actions of Jimmy Lee Dykes of Midland, Alabama. The techniques for rescuing both young Ethan and Heather and Kelly, however, were aided by coverage of the real-life incident.

My main goal was to have Tad, using his special gift of Tetrachromatic Super Vision help rescue characters in ***Khaki = Killer***. I wanted the girls in MY story to be rescued unharmed, which, unfortunately, did not occur for Lyric and Elizabeth, and I wanted Tad to help rescue these older cheerleaders, who had appeared briefly in the previous books.

There were also numerous sub-plots: What about Melody Harris Carpenter? How would her fall affect her? What about Melody's baby? What about Janice Kramer and her baby? What about Tad and Jenny? What about Pogo, aka Michael Clay? And then there was the kidnapping, referenced above. Plot line by plot line, the story grew more complicated. I began to feel as though I were a juggler with at least six balls in the air at once.

I also tried to tie up a few loose ends (*Belinda Chandler, Charlie Chandler, Andrea SanGiovanni, Kenny Kellogg, Lenny McIntyre, Pogo, et. al.*) in addition to the main stories. Every conflict in the book—and I think you'll agree that there are many—played out as the characters began to talk to one another.

I term this technique "blocking." I have "blocks" of characters (e.g. Tad and Jenny, Janice and Stevie) and the plot happens whenever I sit down to write and the characters begin to talk to each other. They take themselves places I did not know they would go.

When I began the book, I had no idea who would help Tad fight off Pogo in the inevitable, climactic mano-a-mano fight they must have (which, in this book, occurs on a bridge over the Cedar River).

It is no accident that Pogo's ultimate fate has been left "up in the air." The primary protagonists are just about to start college or real life, and Michael Clay is gone, but not forgotten.

Now, on to some answers to factual questions you may have, especially if you live far, far away (United Kingdom, take note; Australia, too) and have no idea where Iowa is, let alone Cedar Falls, Iowa.

Questions:

Q1) Is all the information about Howard Dean's run for the presidential nomination in the Iowa caucuses in 2004 true...the double-miking by the Kerry camp, etc?

A1) Yes. I was there at the ValAir Ballroom in West Des Moines when candidate Dean self-destructed with "the Scream Heard 'Round the World."

Q2) Is the information about various techniques and strategies for the care and feeding of brain dead patients based on fact?

A2) Yes.

Q3) What about the information about being "double-jointed?" Is everything about panic attacks and depression being linked to hypermobility syndrome factual? What about the remarks about American versus Indian hands and the effects of menstruation on one's joints?

A3) Yes, it is all factual information.

Q4) Did parents, in the sixties and before, actually pressure their daughters to give up their babies, if they became pregnant while unwed and in high school? *(This one is more for the Young Adult audience 18-24 that will not be old enough to remember.)*

A4) Yes, they did. Usually, the pregnant girls were "sent away" to a home for unwed mothers. It most certainly is true that society frowned on unwed girls keeping their children until recent times; it is also true that I just saw a pregnant Prom goer with her classmates while dining out, dressed exactly as I describe Janice. Janice's parents, being of an older generation, might, indeed, have pressured Janice to give up her child to her older married childless sister Claire, especially since the Kramers are described as devout Catholics.

Q5) Is the information about marriage licenses in Iowa (waiting periods, fees, etc.) and age at which teenagers, even pregnant unwed females, could marry without parental permission accurate?

A5) It certainly is accurate for today. Whether the law underwent changes between 2005 and 2013 is open to question, but all of the facts about needing to have parental permission if under 18 (even if the girl were pregnant) are true.

Q6) Where or why did you come up with the idea for a girls' club in an Iowa high school to be called Madchens, a German word?

A6) That particular fiction actually occurred in my own high school. And Annabeth Gish (currently appearing in the television show "The Bridge") was the daughter of professors at the University of Northern Iowa in Cedar Falls and attended the University Lab School on which Sky High is based. (It no longer exists).

Q7) Where did the idea of the collapsing staircase at the Winter Formal come from?

A7) The class ahead of mine, for its Prom, chose the theme "Stairway to Heaven" or "Stairway to the Stars" and actually built a staircase exactly the way I have described, with exactly the results mentioned. (Comic relief, I hoped, in the book). No one was seriously injured, although the daughter of my chemistry teacher did break her leg. In today's litigious climate, someone probably would sue the school.

Q8) Is the information about the Olympics in Greece (who won the shooting competition, Stadium name, etc.) accurate?

A8) Yes.

Q9) What about the Mayflies on the bridge?

A9) Absolutely true. Experienced the phenomenon many times, but only for a few brief days. They die in gigantic piles and are shoveled off the bridges.

Q10) What about the hospital name and address? Fact or fiction?

A10) The hospital to which Janice is taken is fact. The hospital to which Tad and Charlie were taken in *THE COLOR OF EVIL* (Book #1) was fiction.

Q11) Is the information about the Terry Schiavo case accurate?

A11) Yes, including the dates on which her feeding tube was removed and the subsequent maneuvering in the courts, her date of death, etc.

Q12) What about the soundtrack from the 1976 film *Mother, Jugs and Speed*? Sounds totally bogus.

A12) Hey! I used to vacuum to that record! It is a good vinyl record. And, yes, Dick Butkus was in the movie. (Now, he has a restaurant in Chicago, where I am writing this, and they retired his number 89 at a frigid Bears football game on December 10, 2013). *(If you're too young to know Dick Butkus' name as player or coach, look him up on Wikipedia.)*

Q13) **Is the Mayor of Cedar Falls really named Jay Crew?**

A13) No. The Mayor of Cedar Falls is actually named Jon Crews. Most other facts about his tenure are fact.

***

If you'd like to know if and/or when Pogo will come back from a watery grave, and what mayhem might ensue as a result, write me at EINNOC10@aol.com. I'd appreciate the feedback. Just write the title of the book in the subject blank. You can also contact me via Facebook or at ConnieCWilson.com or on Twitter at Connie Wilson Author.

On behalf of Tad, Jenny, Stevie, Janice and all the characters in the series, thanks for reading this third book in **THE COLOR OF EVIL** series.

If you haven't done so, check out Book One (**THE COLOR OF EVIL**) and Book Two (**RED IS FOR RAGE).**

THE COLOR OF EVIL SERIES
CAST OF CHARACTERS FOR ALL THREE BOOKS

MAIN TEEN-AGED CHARACTERS (see pictures at www.RedisforRage.com)

1) Tad McGreevy – tall, slim, reddish-brown hair, soft-hearted, loyal friend. Son of **Jim and Jeannie McGreevy**, a housewife and an attorney. Younger brother of **Sharon McGreevy**. Possesses the ability to see "auras" around others that tell him whether the person is good, bad, kind, etc. The power is called **Tetrachromatic Super Vision** and also can cause blinding headaches. The "color of evil," in Tad's world, is khaki. Other colors signify other personality characteristics, such as red indicating a violent temperament. [Yes, there really is a similar ailment in real life.]

2) Stevie Scranton – blonde, geeky, funny, class clown. Best friend of Tad McGreevy. A bit of a social outcast, but sensitive and kind. Son of **Sally and Earl Scranton**, a housewife and a blue collar worker at the Rath Packing Plant. Older sister, **Shannon**, is one year younger than Sharon McGreevy, Tad's sister. Stevie had some problems at birth (born without a fontanelle) and his older sister, Shannon, has staked out the family territory as "the smart one" leaving Stevie with the designation "troublemaker." Shannon has graduated and works for Layne Insurance Agency. Stevie is close to his mother Sally. His father Earl regards him as a bit of a wimp and is not close to him. Both Sharon and Belinda Chandler are entering their junior year of college when the first book opens, while Stevie is entering his junior year and turns 18 in December of that year.

3) Jenny SanGiovanni – cute, blonde cheerleader. Daughter of **Andrea SanGiovanni (Tuttle)** and **Jeff SanGiovanni**. Jeff had the

Budweiser distributorship in the Cedar Falls area, but Jeff and Andrea divorced and Jeff married the ex-wife of local policeman **Tom Tolliver**, **Tammy Tolliver**. Jeff and Tammy have moved to Boulder as the first book opens. Jeff was an NRA gun nut. He had a vast collection of guns under lock and key in his attic. The couple also has two other children: **Cynthia (Jenny's older sister) and Frank (Jenny's older brother).**

4) **Janice Kramer** – dark-haired, busty Italian cheerleader who once dated Jeremy Gustaffsson but eventually ends up with Stevie Scranton (in Book 3). Her father is a baker and her mother is a housewife. They are staunch Catholics. She also has an older sister, Claire Kramer Richardson, who is married to Stephen and works at Security State Bank. Claire and her husband have been unsuccessfully trying to start a family.

(See actual photos of the 4 main characters described above at www.RedIsforRage.com and attached, plus trailer and synopsis and reviews.)

CHEERLEADERS (first 5 listed), in addition to Jenny SanGiovanni, and other teen-aged female characters: These characters come into play in this and future books. [Some appear in pivotal roles in Books 1 through 3]:

*****Melody Harris** (the smallest of the cheerleaders at 4'8", 90+ lbs, and top of the human pyramid). Melody's fate is left hanging at the end of Book #2, RED IS FOR RAGE, following a bad fall from atop a human pyramid cheerleading formation.

*****Angie Yancy** (dates clarinet player **Chris Turgasen**; President of Madchens Girls Auxiliary Club (MAGIC). Cheerleader. Wants to be a hairdresser after graduation.

*****Heather Crompton** (blonde airhead; cause of a knife fight between 2 Hispanic cousins). Daughter of Nora and Chris. From well-to-do family. With Jeremy Gustaffsson when he is killed by Pogo. Cheerleader.

*Kelly Carter (aka, Kelly Jamison) Step-daughter of **Joe Jamison**. Daughter of **Megan Kelly Jamison**. Cheerleader. Kidnapped (along with Heather Crompton) in Book #3, *KHAKI = KILLER*. Brother Jason died of Leukemia.

Belinda Chandler – Born in 1984. Only child of Charlie and Cassie Chandler. Involved with teacher Kenny ("Cereal Man") Kellogg. Kidnapped and held hostage (along with Andrea SanGiovanni) by Pogo in Book One, *The Color of Evil*. Lives near her father in the Regency Suites Apartment complex, after the murder of Cassie, her mother and Charlie's wife.

Shannon Scranton – older sister of Stevie who is entering her junior year of college as Book #1 opens. Attending UNI on a volleyball scholarship that Coach Kellogg helped her secure.

Sharon McGreevy – older sister of Tad McGreevy. She is one year older than Shannon Scranton. Works at Layne's Insurance Agency.

Cynthia SanGiovanni – older sister of Jenny SanGiovanni. Andrea lived with Cynthia, who works for Layne Insurance Agency, for a brief time after her house was bull-dozed in book one.

Claire Kramer Richardson – older, married, childless sister of Janice Kramer to whom Gina and John Kramer want the pregnant unmarried Janice to give up her child. She works at the Security State Bank with her husband, Stephen.

Male High School Characters:

*Jeremy Gustaffsson – blonde, blue-eyed, Nordic-looking, a natural athlete, nearly 19 years old. BMOC and star of football, basketball and track at Sky High High School. Obsessed with Jenny SanGiovanni (in an O.J. Simpson way). Father, **Leroy,** follows the harness races from track to track. Mother physically abused by LeRoy. LeRoy did time in prison for rape. Brothers **Jimmy and Jeff** are 5 and 6 years younger than Jeremy. Jimmy is an 8th grader and Jeff a 7th grader when Jeremy murders Cassie Chandler. (*Jimmy and*

Jeff, too, are not academic stars and have suffered from moving around the country following the ponies.) Has a terrible temper (hence the title) and an O/C streak. Central character in Book one. Killed in Book #2 by Pogo on Lover's Lane in a case of mistaken identity, while parked there with Heather Crompton.

Alex Jimenez – the aggressor in the knife fight at Sky High, Mexican, owner of a "low-rider" car. Alex is the cousin stabbed by Pogo in Book One and Roberto is the cousin who gives chase to Pogo's car in the first book, *The Color of Evil.*

Roberto Jimenez – Alex's cousin. They rescue Belinda Chandler and Andrea SanGiovanni from Pogo in the Heights, the poorer part of town where Andrea SanGiovanni has heavily invested in real estate.

*Sean Carpenter – boyfriend (and, at the end of Book #2, husband) of Melody Harris. Son of Ruth and Paul Carpenter. Older brothers include **Brian, Blake and Kenneth**. Marries Melody Harris at the end of Book #2, *RED IS FOR RAGE*. Father of Adam Sean Carpenter, his son with Melody. Melody dies in Book 3, *Khaki = Killer*, following a fall from atop the human pyramid at the UNI Dome rescheduled Homecoming game. Prominent in Book #3.

Rodney Black – father, **Bob**, who shoots film of the Sky High Eagles' games and is sports photographer for Channel 5, the local NBC affiliate. Rodney has a crude home-made tattoo covering his entire back of a brain being pushed through the ringer of a washing machine. He has a long history of teasing Stevie Scranton.

*Zack Porfino – father owns the local garage where Jeremy works after graduation. One of Jeremy Gustaffson's followers, although he is a year behind Jeremy in school. Comic relief. In all 3 books.

*Stewie Truitt – one of Jeremy's younger followers. Stewie stutters. Comic relief in all 3 books.

Terry Wilkinson – a large boy in Stevie's history class/ homeroom.

Paul Nicholson – Commander of the Cedar Falls Police Force in Book One, but replaced by Captain Larry Mullen by Book Three.

Hank Henderson – fellow football player for the Sky High Eagles who is 6' 3" and part of the wedding party at the marriage of Melody Harris and Sean Carpenter.

Rich Cromwell – plays bass drum in the band. Is present at the shooting by Earl Scranton.

Jimmy and Jeff Gustaffsson- younger brothers of Jeremy Gustaffsson. 7th and 8th graders in Book One (*The Color of Evil*.)

Chris Turgasen – longtime steady boyfriend of Angie Yancy and clarinet player in the school band.

Scott Fluegel – 19-year-old boy who was kidnapped by Daniel Malone at age 8 and held captive for 11 years in Chicago.

Police Officers:

*****Charlie (Charles) Chandler**, husband of Cassie, father of Belinda. Tad's ally in his search for Stevie. Retires at the end of Book #1. Helps organize teams to find both Stevie and the missing girls in Book Three, Heather and Kelly.

Jake Gordon – first responder to the SanGiovanni shooting. KIA.

Larry Mason – first responder to the SanGiovanni shooting. KIA.

*****Evelyn Hoeflinger** – Charlie's much-younger female partner on the force.

*****Rita Cernetisch** – female partner of Tom Tolliver. Olympic caliber sharpshooter.

*****Lenny McIntyre** – Geeky Officer Friendly at Sky High. Helps save Tad's life in Book #3.

Jim Kinkade – officer from the Fort Madison Penitentiary in charge of transporting Michael Clay to the new prison near Cedar Falls. Killed by Pogo during Michael Clay's initial escape.

Deputy Joseph Hafner – highway patrolman who pulls Pogo over on his way to kill Tad at a football game at the UNI dome and is brutally murdered and buried in a field.

Nels Peterson – 50-ish officer who gathers information from the McGreevys and from the parents of the kidnapped Heather Crompton and Kelly Carter/Jamison.

Larry Mullen- Captain of the Cedar Falls Police Department during the search for the missing girls in Book Three, ***Khaki = Killer***.

Paul Nicholson – Former Commander of the Cedar Falls Police Force in Book #1 (***The Color of Evil***). Related to the schoolteacher (English/History), Miss Nicholson.

Joe Clark – fellow detective on the Cedar Falls Police force, with a desk near Rita Cernetisch

FBI Special SWAT team members:

Shawn VanSlyke – Chief of the team sent to rescue Heather and Kelly.

Walter "Wally" Ohlsen – field commander of the four-man team

Ron Oscow – team member who helps rescue Kelly Carter and Heather Crompton from Declan Hunter.

Townsfolk:

Earl Scranton, Mike Murphy, Lloyd Carpenter (brother of **Paul Carpenter** who owns Carpenters' Corners paint and paper). All members of the class of '63 along with Charlie Chandler.

Ike Isham – now in a nursing home, he owns a cabin in Burnham Woods that many students use as a hangout.

Able Yundt – owned the local movie theater, which was converted from an Opera House. He is 80.

George Bates – orderly in the ICU when Tad is brought in.

*Earl Scranton – age 58. Stevie's father, a blue-collar worker at the Rath Packing Plant. Married to **Sally Scranton**. Father to **Shannon and Stevie**. Goes on shooting rampage in Book #2, seeking revenge for mistreatment of son Stevie. Will be shot and killed by Rita Cernetisch at the Homecoming game when he goes on the shooting rampage in Book 2, *Red Is for Rage*.

*Sally Scranton – Stevie's somewhat eccentric mother, wife of Earl and mother of Shannon, Stevie's older sister.

Wanda, Harold and Sandy James – Wanda worked as housekeeper and babysitter for the SanGiovannis. She and Harold, her husband, adopted Sandy, who was tragically killed in a murder/suicide accidental shooting while Sandy, then aged 12, was playing with guns not under lock and key. After accidentally shooting his best friend, **Johnny Mortoriano,** Sandy turned the gun on himself.

Don and Samuel Denkinger: **Samuel Denkinger** is the town coroner. **Don Denkinger** was a major league umpire from Cedar Falls, Iowa. Samuel performs an autopsy on Dr. Abraham Eisenstadt in Book Two.

*Harold and Ruth Harris – parents of Melody Harris, their only child. Of Swedish descent. Prominent in book 3 and at the end of book 2, when their daughter Melody and Sean Carpenter marry.

*Paul and Linda Carpenter – parents of Sean Carpenter (and his older brothers **Brian, Blake**, **and Kenny**.) Prominent in Book 3.

Dr. Klein – head of OB/GYN department at Cedar Falls Memorial Hospital.

Dr. Karachi – neurosurgeon specialist who travels from Iowa City to Cedar Falls to examine Melody.

*Dr. Abraham Eisenstadt – local psychiatrist who treats Tad. Neighbor to Andrea SanGiovanni in Book #2. Abe appears only in books 1 and 2, as he dies of a heart attack in Book 2 and there is a serio-comic attempt to move him from Andrea SanGiovanni's house back to his own garage next door, so the townsfolk won't gossip. Charlie Chandler is called (by Andrea) to help move the body.

Sarah Eisenstadt – Abe's wife, who goes insane and murders their two children, **Rachel and Zoe** at the beginning of Book #2.

Nora Crompton – mother of Heather, wife of Christopher, local developer. Sister to Declan Hunter. More important in Book 3, when Heather is kidnapped and held prisoner (by her own brother, Declan, as it turns out, in an underground bunker.)

Christopher Crompton – Husband of Nora, father of Heather. Owns a construction company with his father-in-law, **Bob Hunter**. Also dabbles in grain futures.

Declan Hunter – local Scoutmaster shot (but only wounded) at the football field by Earl Scranton on Homecoming night. Vietnam veteran suffering from PTSD.

Claire Kramer Richardson – Janice's older childless married sister. She and her husband Stephen work at the Security State Bank.

Stephen Richardson – Claire's husband. He also works at Security State bank.

Gina and John Kramer – Janice's Catholic parents, a baker and a housewife.

Jeannie and Jim McGreevy – Tad's mother and father. Jim is an attorney; Jeannie is a housewife and local socialite.

Clint McClintock – former owner of the SanGiovannis' house in Harvest Home, who had used the lavish home as a meth lab and built a secret underground tunnel to a nearby field. Clint is never seen in either book, but is simply known to have used the house to manufacture meth.

Pogo, aka Michael Clay, aka Mike Parker when hiding out in Jesup, Iowa working at a diner. Serial killer. Part-time clown. Escaped convict.

*Daniel Malone – Kidnapper of Stevie Scranton and another boy. Pedophile. Pizza parlor owner in Chicago, Illinois, but originally from Webster Groves, Missouri. Important in Book #2. Shot and killed by Earl Scranton at Homecoming in *Red Is for Rage.*

Bobby Hurley – former classmate of **Paul Nicholson** (nephew of Miss Nicholson, the teacher and Captain of Cedar Falls Police Department in Book #1) and owner of a heavy equipment franchise that lends the bulldozers and heavy equipment to the police department to knock down the SanGiovannis' house in Book #1, in order to flush out Pogo (Michael Clay). Married to petite blonde **Nicollette.**

George Kalafut – Owner/operator of the Kalafut diner in Jesup, Iowa, where Pogo works under the alias Mike Parker.

Howard Thompson – Daniel Malone's right-hand man in his pizza business in Chicago.

Harold Drake – neighbor of Andrea SanGiovanni on Cherry Wood Lane who walks his dog Lily each day. Harold also claims to have won the Silver Star.

Aunt Ellen – Stevie Scranton's aunt; Sally moves in with her sister Ellen when she leaves Earl.

Sammy Swanson – regular customer at George Kalafut's diner in Jesup, Iowa.

Gary and Sherry Green: Gary runs Green's Funeral Home in Cedar Falls, Iowa. Sherry works at the Cedar Falls Post Office.

Dawn – secretary to Police Chief Larry Mullen

Teachers at Sky High High School (Lab School of the State College of Iowa)

Mrs. Anderson – History/English teacher. Sends Stevie Scranton to the Principal's office for fighting with Rodney Black, after which he disappears.

Miss Nicholson- History/English teacher at Sky High High School and aunt of Paul Nicholson (one-time Police Chief, in Book One).

*Principal Peter Puck – pedophile principal. Possibly homosexual. Short, fat and balding. Good friend and former roommate in Chicago, **David Simpson**, is openly gay. He aids Charlie and Evelyn in locating Stevie Scranton when Stevie is held prisoner by Daniel Malone. Shot and killed at Homecoming by Earl Scranton.

Mr. Ross – teacher who dressed up as Abraham Lincoln and was summarily fired when Dr. Peter Puck also dressed up as Abraham Lincoln for Lincoln's Birthday festivities.

*Kenny Kellogg, aka, "Cereal Man" – chemistry teacher with a fondness for having sex with his underage female students. Ultimately impregnates Belinda Chandler (daughter of Charlie) and proposes marriage to her.

Nurse Hernandez – the school nurse who treats Stevie just before his disappearance in Book #1.

*Coach Theodore (Teddy) Bare – sadistic, lazy gym coach. Prominent in book one.

*Janet Sloan – Women's Phys Ed teacher and cheerleader sponsor who does all the real work in the Physical Education department at Sky High. A graduate of Southern Illinois.

Mr. Randall – School counselor who counsels Jenny SanGiovanni and Stevie Scranton.